The ANCSA Reprisal

A NOVEL

by Benjamin Thomas

This book is a work of fiction. Names, characters, places, and incidents are the product of the author's imagination or are used fictitiously. Any resemblance to actual events, locales, or persons, living or dead, is coincidental (except as noted in the closing acknowledgements).

Copyright © 2013 by Benjamin Thomas.
All rights reserved.

Printed by Village Books in Bellingham WA
Library of Congress Control Number 2014932490
ISBN 9780692016626

First edition.

Dear Dad,

I don't know if you know but I've wanted to write a novel since 1987. I've finally achieved that with "The ANCSA Reprisal."

I don't know if you also know but you've always been my hero and this was my way to pay homage to that and for Grandpa Ish.

One time you did something that as simple as it was, I've never forgotten.

A guy named Jack had stolen my bike - I chased him down and knocked him off but he was ready to knock me around good.

Thankfully you pulled up and your presence, confidence, and voice stopped him in his tracks. That is the dad I've always known.

Tlin̓óo x̱ó x̱ʼé Paul Dýn Anx̱hakk̓eet

In 1867, the United States purchased the land that is now the State of Alaska from the Russian government for $7.2 million, or about two cents per acre. Over a century later, though not really on anyone's radar screen, the negotiation with Russia could have been considered the most successful the United States would ever know.

Why in 1968, the Atlantic Richfield Company (ARCO) discovered crude oil on the North Slope of Alaska. It suddenly became important that when Alaska was purchased, the Native Tribes of Alaska laid claim to millions of acres of land. The dispute had been tied up in courts for nearly a century.

History, like lightning, rarely strikes twice; however, when it does, its force leaves behind monumental change. The historical stroke of luck the United States unknowingly stumbled upon in 1867, in acquiring the State of Alaska, collided with the historical stroke of luck ARCO found in 1968 on Alaska's North Slope.

The connection, glossed over in history books, is easily one of the most monumental things that could have happened to the United States, to the citizens of Russia, and most notably to the Native People of the State of Alaska.

On December 18, 1971, the oil conglomerates of the world gained an avenue to construct a pipeline and access to decades upon decades of oil harvest revenue. The published price-tag: $962.5 million and 40 million acres of trust land to the native people of Alaska, more commonly known as the Alaska Native Claims Settlement Act (ANCSA).

The unpublished and invisible price-tag: Alaska Airlines Flight 1866 on September 4, 1971, went down on a mountain-side just north of Juneau, Alaska, and with it, one hundred and eleven innocent souls.

More than thirty years after the discovery of oil on Alaska's North Slope – on land that at one time belonged to the Country of Russia - on a steep, tree-lined mountainside just north of Juneau, Alaska, the remnants of man's greed lay buried but not dead.

Prologue

Juneau, Alaska
Late Evening - Wednesday May 8, 2002

"911, what is your emergency?" The 911 operator asked authoritatively as the call was connected. Her white-on-green digital display indicated the call was originating from 3699 Hayes Way.

"Ma'am, I think there've been gunshots next door." A man's voice clear, but not quite calm.

"May I have your address, sir?" The 911 operator followed protocol to confirm the address the system had indicated was genuine.

"I'm at 3699 Hayes Way." Fear was evident in his voice.

With the address confirmed, the 911 operator followed ingrained procedure and dispatched multiple police units to the scene. "What is your name, sir?"

"My name is Jared Crabtree." His voice had a hint of a New England accent.

"Jared, do you still hear shooting?"

"No, ma'am, nothing."

"Jared, I am going to stay with you on the line until police officers arrive. Are you at a safe place in your house?"

"I'm upstairs in my bathroom. I can see the house next door from here."

"Can you see anything going on next door?" 911 asked. As she did this, another call from Jared's neighborhood had come into the 911 call center.

Another 911 operator managed the call, its content indicating a shooting had just occurred on Hayes Way.

"Just a bunch of lights coming on..." Jared's answer was indicative of other neighbors reacting to the gunshots.

"Jared, have you seen any movement in the home next door?"

"Nothing...and there are no lights on in the house at all."

"Do you know your neighbor's name?"

"Jon Brady."

"Does he live alone?"

"No, his wife's name is Molly. They don't have any kids." He added.

"Did you hear any fighting before the shots?" The 911 operator tried to determine if the shooting was tied to a domestic dispute.

"No, ma'am."

"Have Jon and Molly fought in the past?" The inquiry continued.

"No, ma'am. Not that I am aware of."

"Has Jon ever shown any signs of violence? Do you know if he owns a gun?"

"No, ma'am, he is a quiet guy."

"How about Molly? Any signs of violence? Does she own a gun?" The inquiry switched the conversation to the other possible subject in the house.

"Ma'am, no to both questions...In fact, I think she's out of town. We had a barbeque over the weekend and she said she was going to Minnesota to see her family." Jared's response painted a picture of a tight-knit neighborhood.

The inquiry returned to the situation next door. "Do you see any movement?"

"Not a thing, there are still no lights at all."

Sirens could be heard now entering the neighborhood, and a police cruiser entered the street from the west.

"The police should be there now. Can you see them?"

"Yes, ma'am, they're here."

"I'll stay with you until you see an officer at your door."

Moments later Jared opened the door to two imposing figures wearing police uniforms emblazoned with the symbol for the city of Juneau, Alaska. "The police are at my door."

"Take care, Jared." The call ended.

The police officers quickly gathered general facts about Jon Brady and the residence next door. They remained at the door as two more Juneau police cruisers and two Alaska State Troopers arrived on the scene.

Just as a multitude of officers exited their vehicles, a figure slowly emerged via the front door of the Brady home.

The man was bleeding profusely, and he was moving at a crawl onto the lawn.

"We have an injured subject," an officer communicated into the microphone on his shoulder collar. "We need EMS here now!" He realized Emergency Medical Services was already dispatched, but seeing the injured man exiting the house heightened that urgency.

There were now eight police officers on scene. Like all police departments, procedure and protocol exists when shootings are involved, or the possibility of domestic violence. The officers began to follow protocol, but for any police officer, when the moment presents itself, instinct simply kicks in.

Officer Jason Montoya sprinted to the man crawling onto the lush, green well-manicured lawn. Montoya's partner, Officer Caleb "Mac" Macintyre, sprinted to the injured man as well. The remaining officers trained their guns on the home, providing cover for Montoya and Macintyre.

The man muttered, "I...I'm FB...FBI."

The man stammered once more, more audibly, "scene...is...sec...secure..." With that, he stopped, out of breath.

Montoya saw the FBI badge on his right hip, clipped to a pair of Levi's blue jeans. The federal shield was all he needed to see. "Get in there, federal agent down!"

Montoya and Macintyre continued to remain huddled over the injured man as the other six officers, using well-honed training, entered the home with weapons drawn.

The continued cadence of "clear" reverberated loudly as the officers moved from room to room. As two officers entered the basement, "We have a subject in the basement" was heard by each other officer loud and clear.

"He's dead," one of the officers stated. It was painfully obvious to the officer as he observed the subject's body lying on the bottom of the stairwell with a small bullet hole in his forehead and two bullet wounds in his chest.

"We have two other subjects, male and female...both unconscious," Officer Michele Mathis stated. The officer looked around the carpeted basement. She saw blood splatters all around the basement, and evidence that a violent confrontation had occurred.

On the lawn, the officers were administering first aid to the bleeding subject. The blare of ambulance sirens was growing closer. The officer's assessment of the subject's injuries was that they were life-threatening. It appeared he had been shot in the chest, and there was a hole the size of a quarter through his left bicep.

"Agent, can you hear me?" Montoya asked the man lying on the ground, and then repeated the question.

"Da...Dan...Dani..." In distress, the injured man muttered a name.

"I need help here!" Montoya yelled. Jared came over and offered what little assistance he could render. As he kneeled down next to the bloody individual, he was taken aback. The only bullet wounds he'd ever seen were those on TV and those on a Sitka Black tail deer his father had taken down with a 22-caliber rifle when he was a teenager. The man's wounds were not nearly as tidy, and Jared found the blood seeping out of the victim's chest quite nauseating.

An emergency response vehicle from a nearby fire station arrived, and EMS personnel within a few moments began to administer first aid. A second EMS team was shortly downstairs in the basement, administering first aid to the man and woman who'd been hit.

No more than twelve minutes after Officer Montoya and his colleagues had arrived on-scene, two men and a woman – all three with severe injuries – were on gurneys and being prepped for transport to a local hospital.

Montoya assisted the EMS team load into the ambulance the injured male who'd crawled onto the lawn. The man muttered something to Montoya as they lifted him onto the gurney.

Montoya squeezed the injured man's hand. "I've got it. Just hang on."

As he watched the ambulances depart with sirens blaring, Officer Montoya pressed the mike on his right shoulder. "We have two federal agents and a civilian en route to Bartlett." It was the regional hospital approximately four miles away.

Two of the Juneau Police Officers in separate vehicles provided an armed escort for the ambulances as they departed the normally quiet neighborhood. Montoya then instructed the remaining officers to secure the crime scene.

Montoya removed a cell phone from his right hip phone holster and dialed the Chief of Police. "Ma'am, we're out on Hayes Way near the airport. We have two FBI agents and a civilian who have been gunned down, they're all in bad shape..." He knew Juneau, Alaska, would soon become the center of the federal universe.

Montoya sprinted down the stairs into the basement. Reaching his right hand into the top of the ball-collection pouch at one end of a pool table, he found a latch, and a manila envelope fell through. The envelope was there just as the injured agent had mustered the strength to say it would be.

Reasonable logic and the bloodbath in the basement told Montoya the envelope he held in his hand was a vital piece of evidence in a federal investigation. Little did he know he'd just played a brief but essential role in unearthing a thirty-year old conspiracy masked as an awful tragedy?

Montoya's training got the best of him. Though the envelope remained closed; the officer's seasoned vision catalogued the words hand-written on the thick manila envelope: "ANCSA – An Untold Truth."

Chapter One

Tulsa, Oklahoma
January 1970

Joshua Knight, a graduate of Michigan State University in the late 1960's, was blessed with a mathematical mind that could see things two, three, four, and five steps ahead. He had intrigued a Honeycutt Petroleum Corporation Executive in a meeting one early autumn afternoon - on the meeting's agenda, expansion of drilling platforms in Canada's Northwest Territory.

The plan on the surface appeared, simple, rational, and of very good business sense. The company's engineers, scientists, and chief financial analysts had all concurred the deal was wise. There were projections of an additional twenty million barrels per year for easily the next 35 to 40 years.

Knight, at the ripe old age of twenty-four and one-half years of age, was the only one to voice caution as the meeting progressed. Boyishly handsome and slight in stature, he was a bit of an intellectual information junkie, consuming facts at rapid rates, reading upwards of two hundred words per minute, and sometimes reading five or six newspapers in one sitting. What set him apart, though, from the atypical book genius consuming information and facts ad nauseam, was the ability to connect the pertinent as well as the obscure across disciplines.

Essentially, working in the business all of one year, Knight recalled a snippet of information buried in a *Washington Post* article a few months earlier. The article indicated that the Canadian government was in the midst of a revamping of its tax structure. There were three paragraphs devoted to an option that was gaining only modest consideration but still had some life with a few of the country's liberal lawmakers. An "environmental impact tax" was on the table for consideration because Canada's natural resources of timber and fish were being depleted at astounding and statistically unacceptable rates. Oil reserves had not been mentioned, but Joshua had filed that article away in some neuron storage compartment in his brain.

Young Knight voiced his concerns at the Canadian Drilling & Expansion meeting, conveying the likelihood that a natural-resources tax could be on the business horizon, and would be imposed on the Honeycutt Petroleum Corporation and its installation of drilling equipment in Canada's Northwest Territories.

Knight's innate ability to retain minute details about diverse levels of information, would save Honeycutt Petroleum Corporation countless millions of dollars, years later.

Over the next four years, Honeycutt Petroleum Corporation installed over a dozen new oil drilling and extraction platforms in the Northwest Territories. In large part, thanks to Joshua's forewarning, the company had negotiated an economically fair deal to pay one-time impact fees on the new drills, and in return Honeycutt Petroleum would be exempt from any future environmental impact taxes for the next twenty-five years. The one-time fees were hundreds of times less than the company would have likely been exposed to when the "Canadian Environmental Impact Tax" took effect.

Myles Honeycutt was hands-on as CEO of Honeycutt Petroleum, placing him in a rather ordinary office chair in the "war room" when Knight raised his concerns about the Canadian environmental taxes.

Myles appreciated the young employee's ability to visualize factors that were easily overlooked and the gumption to speak his mind in a room full of corporate veterans with exhausting egos.

As he watched from afar over the next year, Myles was impressed by Knight's ability to sift through data and poke holes in diverse business transactions. A year had been enough to promote the young business savant and one of his first assignments was a detailed analysis of the negotiation of something that would impact the oil industry for the rest of its history: the Alaska Native Claims Settlement Act (ANCSA).

Unlike its colossal competitors, Honeycutt Petroleum's headquarters initially were not housed in the traditional economic hubs like New York, Houston, or Dallas; rather, the company's original headquarters were housed in a modest five-story office complex in Tulsa, Oklahoma, two miles from the sprawling campus of Oral Roberts University.

In the early 1970's, there were approximately a hundred and fifty staff working on site. The company's corporate headquarters over the years had expanded to four separate locations: Tulsa, New York, Riyadh in Saudi Arabia, and the one that probably had Myles' father rolling over in his grave – Houston, Texas.

Myles' late father, John Jacob Honeycutt, had founded Honeycutt Petroleum many years earlier. Along with a business degree from Oklahoma State University, he had gained a deep-seated dislike, bordering on hatred, for the University of Texas and anything to do with the State of Texas. This trait John Jacob had passed on to his son.

Knight took advantage of the solitary respite to survey Myles' office on an early February 1970 day. It was impossible to overlook the CEO's affection for the Oklahoma State Cowboys. Scores of player photographs were visible all over the office, all players Knight did not recognize. As well, team banners, a photograph of OSU Stadium, and an OSU jersey encased in an oak armoire caught Knight's eye.

On a wall behind Myles Honeycutt's surprisingly modest mahogany desk was a large photograph of his father, John Jacob Honeycutt, standing at the base of a tall black oil well. John Jacob's blond hair was a bit gray but thick, somewhat disheveled in a modest desert wind.

Joshua Knight found himself alone in the CEO's office that confirmed the family's love for all things Oklahoma State. He'd been escorted just a few moments earlier through ordinary wooden double doors by Honeycutt's slightly heavyset but still attractive red-headed secretary. She told him that Myles was running just a few moments late and would be right in.

The survey of the room ceased as the CEO entered the office. Blessed with a Southern accent, a smooth yet masculine gait, and a nearly flawless profile, Myles Honeycutt was the spitting image of his father. He was a very intimidating man to be in the presence of.

Tulsa, Oklahoma

October 1970

There were two sides to Myles Honeycutt. One was the driven at all costs CEO, and the other, a truly down-to-earth boss like his father.

With genuine respect, Myles offered Knight a drink that the young economist politely declined in favor of a glass of water. He did, however accept an offer of a slice of artisan bread. He spread a dollop of butter with a knife and enjoyed the light nourishment.

Honeycutt dropped two ice cubes into a highball glass and poured a generous ration of aged scotch, then swirled the crystal glass lightly in his hands.

There was something oddly ominous and foreboding about being in the man's office. Knight had heard Honeycutt was a man of two distinct personalities - the man who was presently before him, disarmingly charming and congenial; and the man of rumors, a man with the never-ending quest to conquer, the drive to take no prisoners, the hunger to win at all costs, which is why Knight was summoned to an office that may as well have been that of an Oklahoma State Football coach.

After some sports-chit-chat and corporate camaraderie, Honeycutt sent Knight back to his office with an assignment that was the beginning of the end of life as Knight knew it.

Over the next eighteen months, the Alaska Native Claims Settlement Act (ANCSA) became Knight's focal point. Day after day, charts, green-bar worksheets, and memoranda would be found spread over the large crimson conference table that virtually consumed his office.

Ten to twelve hour days were the norm as Knight pored over engineering facts on projected barrels of oil, attorney opinions on potential liability the company would be exposed to, harvesting oil in the highly inhospitable environment of Alaska's frigid North Slope, and mathematical models examining the profitability of Alaska's massive oil reserves.

Chapter Two

Anchorage, Alaska
<u>Early September 1971</u>

Honeycutt Petroleum dealt in annual revenue figures that approached the five-billion dollar mark. With the likelihood that the Alaska oil field would be productive in the next four to five years, the revenue figure had the potential to grow not only exponentially, but gaudily so.

Possibilities of that nature had led to an increasing interest in the negotiation of the land holdings in Alaska. If the land was tied up in court proceedings for the next fifteen to twenty years, Honeycutt Petroleum and its fellow oil companies stood to lose an astronomical amount of revenue and profits.

For all of those reasons, in the fall of 1971, Joshua Knight was sent to Anchorage, Alaska, to further his analysis of the ANCSA negotiation and to react to data at a moment's notice.

On the shag-carpeted floor of his hotel room, Joshua sat cross-legged Indian style and wept. It was only his second night in Anchorage, and the fear of what had just transpired took over his entire being. The moment was sadly, painfully simple. He found himself exhausted late in the evening on the second day of September, reviewing worksheets he'd prepared while back in Tulsa, when a file had arrived via a messenger.

Moments after the file arrived, Myles Honeycutt called Knight. The congenial, collegial first impression that Knight experienced with Myles a little over a year earlier had abruptly disappeared.

On the other end of the line, was the heartless, robotic tone of a man focused solely on winning at all costs. Myles had kept it short and definitely not-so-sweet, indicating that the files that had just been delivered were from one of his own sources.

Knight, reeling after the phone call, wondered what the hell Myles had meant by a source. The file contained photographic images of documents provided by a source intimately tied to the negotiations of ANCSA. The file appeared to answer his question: the details of the file, according to his smell test, were from the Alaska Federation of Natives (AFN).

Quantifying the players in competitive terms, it was the United States versus the Alaska Federation of Natives. Honeycutt Petroleum really didn't care which party got the benefit of the bargain, Honeycutt simply wanted an agreement to occur post-haste.

Knight's core assignment was to review everything he was given and determine if there was anything that could be the proverbial fly in the ointment with the potential to prolong the settlement of the Alaska Native Claims Settlement Act.

Knight, against his moral and ethical judgment, chose to review the formative documents that had been prepared by AFN. Its membership was made up of some of the most powerful and influential leaders of Indian tribes throughout Alaska. For the first ten years of its existence, its focus was on negotiation of the Alaska Native Claims Settlement Act.

The charge given to AFN from its membership was, in principle, rather simple: negotiate a settlement equivalent in value to the land the tribes were relinquishing rights to.

The approach AFN had in place was simple as well. They'd brought in Washington, D.C., insiders with the ability to sift through the Potomac BS and gain notable credibility with the Powers That Be.

And here in the latter parts of the summer of 1971, the negotiation was nearing tentative agreement. The amount of money was acceptable to the United States Government and was nearing acceptance of AFN leadership. However, according to documents from what appeared to be a source inside of AFN, there was one member who was beginning to express the need for caution and less haste.

The rationale for the member's caution was unknown. He had not expressed anything concrete, other than the simple axiom, "If something sounds too good to be true, it probably is."

September 2nd had transitioned to September 3rd, and it was nearing two in the morning, yet the sky was still ominously the hue of dusk. Knight was experiencing fatigue lending itself to clouded judgment and remorse. The disappointment that he had violated an ethical code had moved to fear, with the realization that he'd broken the law when he reviewed the AFN documents.

Confirming the disappointment and fear, one of his initial projection worksheets was gripped in his right hand as he continued to gaze in shame at the files that he now conclusively realized were not meant for dissemination.

And the numbers on the green-bar worksheet in his grip just didn't seem to make sense. Rumors were floating that the U.S. Government was ready to settle were now quantified with a dollar amount. The United States, in partnership with several oil companies, was prepared to proffer a settlement amount to the Indian Tribes of Alaska for nearly one billion dollars.

The worksheet in his hand pretty much painted the near-billion dollar likely offer as definitively one-sided. Knight was silently in agreement with the AFN member; the billion dollars was a great deal of money, but all of the zeroes were meant to create the illusion that the deal was a rich one. Knight's innate ability to connect unrelated facts raised the hairs on his neck, and a chill ran up his spine as he studied the worksheet.

He had sensed it earlier in the day when the folksy approach of Myles Honeycutt had abruptly disappeared. Knight's never-ending need for information, however, sadly had led to a momentary, irreversible lapse in judgment. Somewhere in the recesses of his insomniac fatigue, he sensed his life was in grave danger. It was the number on the worksheet, an unfathomable amount of money that had injected terror into his exhausted mind.

Violating the law the moment he'd begun to review the AFN document, he now felt a moral tug. The name of the dissenting AFN member, Phillip Black, kept bouncing around in his head. Contact with the man should not happen, but in Knight's heart and soul, he knew the contact needed to happen.

From the transcripts he'd read, Black was flying home to the small town of Sitka on Saturday, as a family member had passed on. Maybe on that flight, an opportunity would present itself to convey his concerns to Mr. Black.

His mathematical mind was formulating a plan several steps ahead. He'd already shared his findings with Myles earlier that evening via telephone that the settlement seemed very disingenuous for the financial return the various oil companies would realize. Knight's voice had been reticent as he communicated his finding.

"Did Myles sense his moral dilemma?" Knight surmised from his dealings with the man over the last year that he would indeed sense Knight's trepidation that might become a liability to Myles' end game.

"Would Myles take action to deal with the man who had now become a liability?" Knight knew he would.

"What action would Myles take to deal with the man who had now become a liability?" Knight knew that answer as well.

In a cerebral process, multi-tasking at genius levels and also at the most primal level, with a focus solely on survival, Knight formulated a plan to 1) get the information to the dissenting AFN member, validating the member's concerns as indeed spot-on, and 2) if indeed he found himself caught in the crosshairs of Myles Honeycutt, at least to ensure his demise wasn't a futile one.

On the pages of a yellow legal pad, he generated three separate but equally important documents. One he prepared for Phillip Black, the dissenting AFN member who shared his financial skepticism regarding the one-billion dollar offer. The title read "ANCSA - The Counter Offer."

The second and third documents he sealed in two separate letter-size manila envelopes and grasped them tightly in his hands as he fell asleep.

The next day was going to be long and frightening.

Anchorage, Alaska

<u>The Morning of Saturday - September 4, 1971</u>

A light, cold mist filled the air outside the hotel as Joshua awaited a taxi. He was wearing an Oklahoma State Cowboys baseball cap, a navy-blue windbreaker, and a pair of loose-fitting blue jeans.

The two bags he had with him were a modest-size suitcase and a worn leather briefcase. The contents of the briefcase were all that stood in the way of the tentative agreement of the Alaska Native Claims Settlement Act. Each time he thought about the documents, he knew he was on the cusp of something historically significant, and his hand squeezed the handle that much tighter.

The cold fog was foreboding, a sign of his gray despair. He was certain his life as an oil economist was gone; however, the primal instinct that his life as he knew it was gone forever was even more certain.

A yellow taxi pulled up to the hotel entrance. The driver not more than twenty years old, got out and smiled pleasantly at his newest passenger. "How are you today, sir?"

Joshua couldn't believe someone had called him sir. Had he aged that much in the last twenty-four hours? "I'm well, but please call me Joshua. 'Sir' sort of makes me feel like an old man."

"Sure thing Joshua, are we off to the airport?"

The driver had long hair that gave him a disheveled look, but his skin was smooth, his eyes a handsome dark brown, and his teeth pearly white. He motioned for Joshua to feel free to jump in the cab, as he put his suitcase in the trunk.

As Ronald climbed into the front seat of the cab, he looked over at his passenger. Joshua had chosen the front seat, though most fares preferred the rear-passenger seat.

"I'm Ronald, but most people call me RJ or Ronnie."

"It's nice to meet you, Ronnie. Kind of an ugly morning we're having, isn't it?"

"I've lived here my whole life, kind of used to it by now."

"Is it always like this?"

"We have some sunny days, but this time of year it tends to get this way. Where are you off to this morning?"

Joshua momentarily felt a sense of paranoia, wondering why this guy would care, but he quickly realized that Ronnie was just making idle chit-chat. "I'm heading south to Juneau for a few days for a meeting."

"What do you do?"

The cab was still meandering downtown streets as the conversation progressed. The squeaky swish-swish of the windshield wipers and the clouds that formed a dark, low ceiling accentuated Joshua's lost feeling. He decided this was probably the only opportunity he would have for a long while to have a normal conversation with another human being. The unscheduled, unannounced meeting he was hoping to have with Phillip Black aboard the flight in a few hours would likely be the last he would have before his professional life imploded.

He didn't know what would come next, but somewhere in the recesses of the chessboard he maintained in his mind, he realized that the meeting with Phillip Black would be his last move. He needed an alternate solution.

He looked at Ronnie and noted he had the distinct appearance of a Native Alaskan. Ronnie's ethnic background might be the opening he was looking for.

"Actually Ronnie, I'm an oil economist. Have you been following the negotiations that have been going on with the Alaska Natives and the U.S. Government?"

"I sure have. I hear that there's a lot of money that might come my way." Ronnie's response confirmed Joshua's assumption.

"What tribe are you with?" Joshua now felt safe asking the question.

"Aleut, my family is from the village of Sand Point out in the Aleutians, but we've lived here since I was four or five years old." Sand Point is a small village six or seven hundred miles southwest of Anchorage, near the head of the Aleutian chain of islands.

Ronnie talked about life in Alaska until the control tower and the ascent of a Boeing 707 into the rainy, cloudy sky came into view.

Joshua realized time was running short. Other than Phillip Black, there was no one to whom he could pass along the second of the three documents he'd prepared. Joshua removed one of the three manila envelopes from his briefcase.

The cab was within a mile of the airport. This was the only opportunity Joshua would have.

"Ronnie..." Joshua began to speak, but hesitated. This was going to be strange and awkward, but adamantly necessary. "...This is going to sound very odd, but I'm going to Juneau to disappear. I said I'm working here as an oil economist, but that is only part of the story. I'm here to monitor the negotiations for my company."

Joshua asked Ronnie to circle the terminal a couple of times so he could finish. "My company has - has been spying on the negotiations." He let that thought sink in.

Ronnie didn't say a word, just staring straight ahead as he drove away from the terminal in a southerly direction, avoiding circling the drive.

"I know this because I have seen the documents, and I have them with me."

Joshua put one of the three manila envelopes on the seat between himself and the cab driver.

"This is my insurance policy, Ronnie. Please don't ever open this, but make sure you keep it in a safe place. After the dust settles, I'll come back for this copy."

The cab was quiet for a good fifteen seconds before Ronnie finally spoke.

"I really have no clue what the hell you are talking about, but my parents have raised me to trust my gut. You seem like you're being straight-up with me. Just two questions, how long will be I holding onto this?" Ronnie asked as the index finger of his dark right hand tapped the manila envelope.

"I honestly have no idea."

Joshua's frank reply seemed to satisfy Ronnie. "You said you had two questions." Joshua added.

"Why me?"

"I'm sorry, Ronnie, but there is really no one I can trust right now, and I'm kind of making decisions on the fly." Even as Joshua said it, he gave a nervous laugh. Operating this way was definitely outside of his modus operandi.

Ronnie turned and looked Joshua squarely in the eye as the cab sat outside of the airport terminal. Ronnie's response was well beyond his years, "I've been raised to believe in hard work and honesty. You have my word - your file is safe with me."

Looking at the handsome young driver, Joshua had one last thing to say as the two men began to open their respective doors of the cab.

"Please don't ever tell anyone about the file, not a soul."

"You have my word."

The two exited the vehicle. Ronnie walked to the trunk of the cab and removed the one suitcase while his passenger stood on the curb acting as benign as possible.

As Ronnie handed him the suitcase, Joshua paid the fare. "Ronnie, thank you for the ride and for...well, thank you."

"You're welcome. Take care of yourself, Joshua." Ronnie casually made his way back to the driver's seat.

"You, too." Joshua said as Ronnie closed the door.

Moments later, he entered the terminal and proceeded to the Alaska Airlines check-in counter. Forty-five minutes later, briefcase in hand minus one of the three manila envelopes, Joshua Knight boarded Alaska Airlines Flight 1866.

Chapter Three

Anchorage, Alaska
<u>Saturday - September 4, 1971</u>

The flight crew made its routine safety announcements as the aircraft slowly taxied to the north end of the Anchorage International Airport's north-south runway. Gaining a modicum of comfort, Joshua let his right foot rest on the briefcase nestled safely beneath the seat in front of him. He was aboard the flight with the sole intent to make contact with the Black family as the aircraft flew south out of Anchorage on its four-stop trip to Seattle, Washington.

He knew that Black was bound for Sitka. What he didn't realize until he'd purchased his ticket was that the flight between Anchorage and Sitka had three stops in the tiny villages of Cordova and Yakutat, and in Juneau-Alaska's capital city.

The first leg of the flight to Cordova was only about thirty minutes, but in that short time, for the first time in a very long time and for the last time, he miscalculated.

Seated in row five were a distinguished man and his modestly attractive wife, both of Alaska Native descent. Phillip and Miranda Black were traveling home to Sitka, Alaska, for the funeral of a family member who'd died suddenly.

As one of its lead representatives in the negotiation of the Alaska Native Claims Settlement Act, Black was integral to the Alaska Federation of Natives. Joshua had learned who Black was while reading through the illegally-obtained materials that the courier had delivered at the request of Myles Honeycutt.

Now, less than two days later, he gripped one of the manila envelopes containing the documents he'd prepared as he arose from his seat in row fourteen.

His mind had rehearsed this moment many times over in the last day and a half. But as he moved forward in the aisle toward row five, his hand trembled. Without a doubt, he knew the information he was passing to Phillip Black would likely destroy the Alaska Native Claims Settlement Act (ANCSA), and with it, his mentor and his employer.

"Mr. Black?"

The man's piercing brown eyes looked up at the young Caucasian man who'd stated his name. He paused for a moment before replying.

"And you are?"

"Sir, my name is Joshua Knight, and I work for Honeycutt Petroleum."

The look on Miranda Black's face was one of bewilderment. Why would an employee of an oil company be talking to her husband?

Her husband, on the other hand, didn't let his facial expression betray much.

"How may I help you, Mr. Knight?"

"I will keep this simple. I'm aware of concerns you may have regarding the offer the government has made." He paused and looked around the cabin. It didn't appear that anyone was paying the conversation any undue attention.

Joshua continued, "I have the same concerns." As he finished, he handed Black the envelope. "Sir, I won't be of much use to my employer after this. Hopefully, you'll find this information helpful."

Black seemed to contemplate what to say.

"Mr. Knight, I'm not sure exactly why you've sought me out and this certainly feels strangely covert. Having said that, I am not sure how you became aware that I have concerns, but I will take a look at the information."

"Thank you, sir."

The surreal conversation concluded as Joshua turned and walked back to his seat.

"What in the world was that all about?" Miranda asked.

"I'm not sure myself. I've begun to have concerns that we're rushing into a settlement, but how that young man knew I haven't a clue."

The conversation continued for a few more moments, and then Phillip told his wife he'd defer reading the envelope's contents until they were on the ground in Cordova. He wanted a little rest.

Nine rows back, Joshua sat down and closed his eyes. He'd completed the task he'd set out to do. Now he'd just have to wait. He also realized by the time the information he'd passed was put to use by the Alaska Federation of Natives and should it curtail the ANCSA negotiations, he would need to disappear. The information he'd just passed to Phillip Black, as simple as it was, would be like a grenade tossed into the middle of the ANCSA negotiations.

Half an hour later, as the aircraft sat on the ground in Cordova, Black made his way back to Joshua's seat.

"Mr. Knight. I've had a chance to review the estimates you're providing, and I concur. I had concerns, but I couldn't put numbers to it. Nice work."

Black continued, "I am heading to Sitka for a funeral, but the information you've provided needs to see the light of day. I'm going to head back to Anchorage the day after tomorrow, and I suggest you disappear for a while. I'd suggest you get off in Juneau and lay low for at least a few days." "My wife and I will take the document you've given me to Juneau. Is it alright if we share it with someone I know at the Attorney General's office?"

"Yes, sir. But I'd prefer that my name be kept out of it."

"I will do my best on that." Black's answer was sincere and fatherly.

Joshua felt a modicum of kinship with the man, and he was thankful he'd made the decision to formally pass his concerns to Black. The proposal from the U.S. government in partnership with a cooperative of oil companies was for around one billion dollars. He had provided Black with an idea for a counter-offer that would generate billions upon billions of dollars of deserved levels of revenue for the native tribes for as long oil flowed out of Alaska into the world market.

What he didn't know was that from the moment he'd landed in Alaska, he had been under the watchful eye of an elite contract team of Honeycutt Petroleum. That small team was already two steps ahead of him, putting into works a plan to make him pay for his covert betrayal and in the process put an end to his ill-advised attempt at delaying the Alaska Native Claims Settlement Act.

Aboard Alaska Airlines Flight 1866
<u>Saturday - September 4, 1971</u>

Yakutat, Alaska, is nestled on the Gulf of Alaska, 220 miles southeast of Cordova, or about a 40-minute flight. There are no roads in or out; subsequently, air travel is the most frequented mode of transportation. The tiny village is home to about six hundred people, a mix of Alaska Native and Caucasian ethnicity. Yakutat's economy is driven primarily by commercial fishing and tourism, the rivers thriving with five varieties of salmon and the chance to truly escape into the wild of nature.

A unique distinction the tiny town has held for a very long time is it is the smallest city in the world served by daily commercial airline jet service.

On a clear day, the flight between Cordova and Yakutat will benefit passengers with some of the most visually appealing and rugged scenery on earth. This morning had a modest cloud cover, but jutting above the clouds was Mount St. Elias, 18,008 feet of glacial rock and ice.

Growing up in Michigan, Knight had not laid eyes upon anything that remotely compared to the mountains outside the oval window on the left side of the aircraft. Despite all of the pressure he'd experienced the last few days, the beauty held him transfixed. As the flight progressed over Yakutat Bay, well into its descent into the villages, Knight was captivated by this part of the world that he'd decided was a very well-kept secret.

Yakutat Bay disappeared beneath the Boeing 727's wings and the village filled Knight's eyes. He had never been exposed to such a remote place in all of his life. Black had recommended going on to Juneau, but this town was intriguing.

Ten minutes later, leather briefcase in hand, Knight deplaned down the metallic aft stairwell, set foot on the concrete tarmac, and walked into the terminal building that wasn't much more than a modest-sized home with a baggage claim instead of a living room.

He'd left an "Occupied" card in seat 14A, with full intent to re-board the flight. But with each step toward the small terminal, the intent to return to the aircraft was dissipating.

In a few days he likely would head south to Juneau and get lost for a few months, but as he felt the long days of the last year disappear and the fear he'd experienced the last few days momentarily subside, he realized this might be the ideal place to disappear.

Knight sat in a gray plastic, hardback chair and casually gazed around the terminal. The people were intriguing. A young couple warmly embraced one another, a mother clutched her infant daughter, a group of sports fishermen recalled the last week of excitement, and others seemed content as they waited to board the flight.

Seated to Knight's left was a grandmotherly woman with dark brown skin, peaceful eyes, and a warm smile. Knight returned her smile and said hello.

Her voice was deep but welcoming. "Hello, how are you?"

Knight enjoyed the feeling of speaking to someone without an agenda. "I'm doing well, how about you?"

"Very well, thank you for asking." Her voice was sincere, her English rather formal, obviously not her first language.

"Where are you off to today?"

"I am going to Washington, D.C. to see my grandkids. It is the first time I will be visiting their home. And you, where are you off to?"

"Actually, this is where I'm jumping off. I was supposed to go to Juneau, but I'm intrigued by this little town. Is it your home?"

"It is. I have lived here most of my life."

As Knight listened to the woman, he wondered what it would have been like to grow up in such a place. Yakutat was physically and culturally thousands of miles from the world he'd known for most of his youth in Saginaw, Michigan.

"My name is Joshua." Knight reached out his hand to shake hers.

As her hand embraced his, he noted the petite feel and signs of age in small brown spots.

"It is nice to meet you, Joshua, my name is Wilma."

Just as Knight was set to continue, the flight began to board. As she began to rise from the uncomfortable chair, he gently took her arm and helped her to stand.

"Thank you, Joshua. Take care."

"You do the same, Wilma. Enjoy seeing your grandchildren."

With that, Wilma exited the building and walked gingerly but gracefully toward the aircraft. Knight found it odd that she'd been at the terminal by herself.

Had he known, she simply enjoyed the moment of solitude when she traveled. Her husband, William, had dropped her off an hour earlier, and she'd insisted that he get back to their Lost River fish camp on the Gulf of Alaska to tend to his fishing net.

As Knight watched Wilma stroll across the tarmac, he was strangely at a loss but equally at peace. He had nowhere to go and all the time in the world to get there. In the leather satchel draped over his shoulder, he had fourteen thousand dollars he'd drained from his bank account. Stretching the usefulness of that modest savings in the little town would be essential to Knight's longevity in hiding.

And he was certain that passing information to Phillip Black would require that no one know where he was. Contact with his family would have to be avoided for some time, but he needed to find a way to let them know he was all right.

That would have to wait. More pressing, he'd need to let Honeycutt assume he'd gotten to Juneau, and hopefully the trail Honeycutt would follow wouldn't lead back to Yakutat.

While his mind was capable of operating at genius levels when digesting data and facts, his intuition and sixth sense were not nearly so strong. Joshua had failed to take note of the dark-haired man who had discreetly exited the aircraft moments after he had deplaned and walked almost invisibly through the terminal.

Chapter Four

Yakutat, Alaska

<u>Saturday - September 4, 1971</u>

Outside the terminal, Knight made his way across the gravel parking lot and watched the taxi of the Alaska Airlines aircraft toward the north end of the nearly two-mile long runway.

The smooth roar of the engines as the Boeing powered up its engines toward take off left him feeling safe, yet all alone. He knew not a soul in this town, save Wilma Jameson, whom he'd just met and who was aboard the flight accelerating down the runway.

A minute or two later, seated in 14F on the right side, Wilma Jameson smiled as her brown eyes gazed out to the west.

Though she couldn't see the four cabins nestled at the end of a narrow peninsula that created a crooked bend near the mouth of the Lost River emptying into the endless Gulf of Alaska, she knew her husband William was likely already tending the family net teeming with silver Coho salmon.

As the aircraft gained altitude and the miles passed, the Lost River faded from view, but not the beauty of Southeast Alaska. Her gaze held as winding rivers, thick green forests, and tan-sandy beaches passed beneath the flight proceeding on its southerly course.

As Wilma turned her attention away from the window, a male passenger in the aisle seat nearest her initiated a conversation. "Where are you off to?"

"I am headed to Seattle to meet my son, and then we're flying to Washington, D.C., to see his wife and my grandchildren," Wilma replied proudly.

"How old are they?"

"They are five and three. And where are you going?"

"I'm headed to Juneau. D.C., that's quite a long trip."

"It is. I never have traveled farther than Seattle, and I'm a bit nervous. My son insisted he meet me in Seattle so we could fly together."

"What does he do?"

"He owns a consulting firm of some kind. I'm embarrassed but I'm not sure, exactly. How about you, what do you do?" Wilma asked, spying the wedding ring on his left hand and gazing at the native woman beside him, across the aisle, her eyes peacefully closed.

The man laughed. "I'm a lawyer. Kind of like your son, I'm not sure what I really do." He gave a light-hearted laugh.

The conversation moved along in concert with the flight for another fifteen minutes or so until they passed over a rugged mountain range filled with vast, snowy canyons and steep glacially-christened rock walls. As the mountain ranges continued and the flight initiated its descent into Juneau, the clear skies were rapidly deteriorating into a thick cloud cover.

"It looks like we're losing our sunshine," Wilma stated in a disappointed tone.

The man concurred as the two looked out the window into the dark cloud cover that had suddenly enveloped the aircraft.

A burst of turbulence violently jostled the aircraft, and Wilma's heart fluttered. She had the sensation of ancient Tlingit spirits all around her.

One of the pilots shared information on the flight's progress and apologized for the turbulence they were encountering as the plane continued its descent in the unexpected, though not uncommon stormy weather.

Aboard Alaska Airlines 1866 - Southeast of Yakutat, Alaska

<u>Saturday September 4, 1971</u>

The only way to describe what Wilma saw outside the right side of the aircraft just after twelve o'clock noon on that early September day in 1971, as the aircraft made its descent into Juneau, were clouds thick as clam chowder. The moisture on the window was seemingly a deluge, and even in the heart of the day the sky seemed ominously dark.

In the cockpit, the exchange with the Anchorage Air Route Traffic Control Center was relatively-routine, as the controller instructed the Alaska Airlines Boeing 727-193 to maintain 12,000 feet and to proceed to the Pleasant Intersection, deviating from the original flight plan of continuing its approach at the Howard Intersection. In air traffic vernacular, an intersection is a preordained coordinate on an air controller's grid to monitor an aircraft's progress from one point to another.

The Anchorage Control Center was having difficulty maintaining contact with a Piper Apache aircraft that a few minutes earlier had departed Juneau International Airport and was on a northeasterly heading for Whitehorse in Canada's Yukon Territory. The communication difficulties with the Apache were enough of a concern at the Anchorage Center to momentarily divert the Alaska Airlines flight from its original heading.

They had two separate communications with the Apache, courtesy of the Alaska Air crew, and a few minutes later the aircraft was finally redirected to the Howard Intersection and instructed to pass over the intersection at approximately 9,000 feet and continue on its descent.

At approximately 12:08pm, the crew informed the Anchorage ARTCC that they had passed through 5,500 feet and then 5,400 feet, and were instructed to contact the Juneau control tower, which they did successfully moments later.

The communication between the airline crew and the Control Center was routine; however, what happened over the next minute or two was anything but.

Wilma continued to watch as moisture saturated the window, dark clouds endless and forbidding. She had stepped up the aft stairway of the aircraft an hour or so earlier knowing this might happen. She'd seen it in her dreams the night before. Her heart was pounding, but just like in her dream, a voice was telling her to have no fear.

She'd not shared the dream with her husband, William; she knew he wouldn't have allowed her to leave if he'd known.

Her soft, dark brown hands gripped the armrests tight. Bluish-gray veins protruded, betraying her age; her hands were not quite shaking but not quite steady. Despite her dream, there would be no concealing her fear.

The night before had been a restless one, and she'd been lost in a very intense dream. She'd seen the aircraft in a gentle and graceful descent into a pillow-soft cloudy sky, descending farther and farther with each passing moment.

Then just like that, *boom*!

She awoke, her heart beating fast, filled with fear. It was then the voice spoke to her, telling her, *"Have no fear."* The voice was that of neither a man nor a woman. She heard the voice and no one would ever believe her, or so the proud Tlingit Indian woman thought.

Now, hours later, she stared out the window, and the sky was just as it had been in her dreams. She'd flown enough to know that the aircraft was well into its descent. She held the armrests tighter and tighter. The voice from her dream the night before was there again. She looked around the cabin; no one else heard the voice.

This time it was clear as could be. It was no longer telling her to have no fear. *"It is time,"* was all she heard. She looked out the window as the clouds rushed by.

The phrase *"It is time"* kept dancing around in her mind. Where had she heard that phrase before? As she looked once more out the window, it came back to her.

On that solemn day so many years ago, her grandfather had spoken those three words when they'd laid her grandmother to rest. She was only eleven years old, and while her grandfather watched his granddaughter endure great sorrow, he knew this would be one of those profound moments to learn to harness inner strength.

He held her hand as they left her grandmother's gravesite, her tears still streaming, and he said, "It is time."

The young girl stared down at her grandmother's resting place, and through the cloud of tears said goodbye.

Her grandmother passed long ago, peaceful in her sleep. Quietly she'd gone just as the sun was rising into the pristine Southeast Alaska sky. The mountains reaching seven thousand feet into the clear blue welcomed each ray of sunshine.

Her grandmother had seen the beauty of that sunrise on her last day. Now many years later, as Wilma looked out the window into the black cloud cover the aircraft was mired in, the irony was as thick as the cloud cover. The world outside the oval window was dismal and dark.

Wilma began to cry. Her heart was pounding as what looked like a mountain flashed by. The terrain looked familiar, but where was the water? On several occasions she'd landed in Juneau, and there was always the distinct expanse of open water.

Wilma looked over at the man she'd been having such a nice conversation with just minutes earlier. She could see that he felt what she was feeling. Something wasn't right, something was dreadfully wrong!

The scream of the aircraft engines was unmistakable. The instruments had dreadfully led the flight astray, and the men in the cockpit were futilely begging the aircraft to climb.

Wilma wanted to scream, but there wasn't time. She wanted to cry, but there wasn't time. She wanted to run, but there was nowhere to go. She simply closed her eyes and thought of her son. Her heart ached as time seemed to stand still. She wasn't afraid for herself; she just wanted to see her son once more.

She knew her time had come, and seemingly the sky turned a bright-bright blue. *"It is time."* She was ready, and she felt her grandfather's hand holding hers once again.

"Bobby..." Her soul screamed and then all went dark.

Chapter Five

Seattle, Washington
Saturday - September 4, 1971

Relaxed in a leather chair, the man leaned back and let the energy of the hustle and bustle outside envelop his thoughts. His brown eyes followed the murky-green of the Seattle waterfront outside the Edgewater Hotel room to a large green and white Washington State Ferry that was heading westbound across an almost serene Puget Sound for either Bainbridge Island or Bremerton. Off in the distance, a few sailboats were gently dancing with the light northwesterly wind.

His attention reverted back to a half-inch thick black binder on the hotel bed. While benign in appearance, the information it contained was significant in its analyses of the quagmire called the Vietnam War.

The Senate Intelligence Committee had contracted with his consulting firm to analyze the information it contained. Its contents were the blueprint for a significant troop withdrawal from Vietnam over the next six months. The Senate Intelligence Committee was provided with an advance copy of the Executive Summary outlining the proposed troop withdrawal. Robert was asked to pick apart the executive summary, which provided details about the withdrawal's timeline, troop levels, and security concerns.

He found it interesting to note what information was conspicuously hidden. Information on how many more men were expected to sacrifice their lives, and the lack of a full troop withdrawal, were buried as minutia versus the prominent facts. He made a mental note to ensure the Senator addressed this particular faux pas before the Executive Summary moved its way up Pennsylvania Avenue.

Robert had received his undergraduate degree in History at the University of Washington, and his master's degree in Political Science at Stanford University just five years earlier.

The five years since his graduation had been a success, since he'd opened his own company on the figurative shoestring budget. In that short time, the political consulting firm had gained a reputation for giving direct answers no matter how unpopular. The man took great pride in each engagement the company had accepted. This one, in particular, was met with a healthy enthusiasm.

Robert locked the binder in the hotel room safe and decided he needed to go for a nice long walk. Half an hour later, he was seated at a seafood restaurant enjoying a glass of wine and a fresh-baked slice of sourdough bread.

His latest vantage point of a departing ferry was much different. It was just a few hundred yards away versus the mile and a half from his third floor hotel room. He enjoyed the peacefulness of the afternoon sun as its rays cascaded across the gentle wake of Elliott Bay.

The aroma of baked salmon and baking bread filled the air and tempted more than a few passersby as it had the Robert. He was enjoying the afternoon to himself, the first he'd had in quite a long time. His body was still on Washington, D.C. time, so the glass of wine didn't seem out of place even at 1:55 in the afternoon.

He sipped the robust cabernet. Its taste was a little piquant, just enough to awaken the taste buds and warm the system. He ordered a bowl of steamer clams a few moments later and asked the waitress for a glass of water as well. For some reason he was feeling a little parched and warm.

Then, out of nowhere, Robert heart dropped into a black heaviness. Here he was at the pleasant seafood restaurant on the Seattle waterfront, yet his eyes were filling with tears, and he had not a clue why. The floor beneath him was trembling, and as he looked around the restaurant, he realized he was the only one experiencing the tremor.

He stared out across a blurred Puget Sound and couldn't shake the trepidation he was experiencing. The ferries were still traversing the placid waterway, sailboats were still off in the distance gently dancing with the light northwest wind, yet peace was diminishing with each passing moment.

At thirty-one years of age, he had the frightening feeling he was leaving this earth before his time. He tried to scream, but the words wouldn't come. He tried to summon help, but his arms were nailed to the table. He tried to rise from the chair, but it was as if his legs were not there.

Despite the clear blue Pacific Northwest sky, the day had gone dark and forbidding. He thought he had reached the end of the road. All of the noise in the restaurant suddenly stopped. For a brief moment it was silent. Then it came.

He heard his mother's voice as if she were right there. "Bobby..." and all went black.

Wilma Jameson's final moments lingered in the air, her spirit lost between heaven and earth as Alaska Airlines Flight 1866 struck a jagged mountainside, a few miles north of Juneau, Alaska, on the stormy early September morning in 1971.

With it, one of the three yellow legal-pad handwritten documents, authored by Joshua Knight, was incinerated in Miranda Black's hand.

The chain of events to follow would prevent either of the two remaining documents from seeing the light of day for thirty years.

Chapter Six

Syracuse, New York
Saturday - December 18, 1971

"A toast to $965 million, my friend." The chime of two glasses of champagne delicately clinking to one another followed the words.

Myles Honeycutt arose and strolled across the Berber carpet, its color almost earth-tone, toward the crackling fireplace. The familiar sound of embers popping gave the man a sense of comfort and he enjoyed the peaceful aroma of a red cedar log curled in the intense heat.

The other man in the room, Adam Ross, raised his glass and spoke in a respectful manner, "To the life of Joshua Knight." Across the room, Honeycutt raised his glass as well.

"To Joshua Knight, may he rest in peace..." Honeycutt spoke with a hint of sly sarcasm. "...If he had stayed loyal, he'd be sharing in our triumph."

The two men were speaking of the settlement of the Alaska Native Claims Settlement Act that had been signed into law just hours earlier by President Richard M. Nixon. ANCSA settled the long-standing dispute between Alaska Indian Tribes and the United States Government over who held title to well over 100 million acres of land within the State of Alaska.

The dispute had been ongoing for nearly a hundred years, an obstacle to getting new-found oil on Alaska's North Slope to market. The settlement of $962.50 million conveyed to the Native tribes of Alaska would finally release hundreds of thousands of acres for drilling.

The two men shared the celebratory moment at Honeycutt's "weekend getaway" in upstate New York.

The "getaway" had five bedrooms, an indoor swimming pool, five acres of lush forest, and most importantly a well-stocked wine cellar. Honeycutt offered his guest a cigar. "Cuban, I might add," said with his unmistakable southern drawl as he handed the robust delicacy to the ruggedly handsome Adam Ross.

"Thank you." Ross clipped the cigar and struck a wooden match. The sweet, tangy taste of the cigar was a relaxing escape.

Discussion and celebration of the success continued until Honeycutt's visitor brought a healthy dose of realism to the euphoria that accompanies a victory. "The incident..." Ross paused, "is still under review. We have one more hurdle remaining. The NTSB investigation, should it be favorable, will ensure we've pulled this off."

"Your caution is admirable, my friend, but I assure you the review will be favorable. The winner's circle is all I know." He pointed around the room at over a dozen trophy-size wild animal heads mounted on the expansive walls. There were a couple of moose heads with massive antlers, a black bear displaying a menacing set of sharp white teeth, a mule deer with lifeless black eyes, and several others. With an arrogant smile, Honeycutt spread his arms wide and rotated displaying the room.

His visitor had no response. He knew any further conversation on this subject would be futile, so he changed directions.

"How is your son?" Ross inquired.

"Little Jacob is doing great, he is starting to talk up a storm," Honeycutt responded with unabashed pride. "Handsome little devil, I must say."

His only child Jacob, born a few years earlier, was already the spitting image of his father. His deep blue eyes were complemented by a thick mane of golden-blond hair.

The news of Kelly Honeycutt's pregnancy had changed Myles. He had become more compassionate to his staff, spent more time with his wife, and even single-handedly built an oak crib. The joy that accompanied fatherhood was unmistakable in Myles' voice as the two men continued to converse, the content bounced between family, politics, and the ANCSA settlement. They were careful to never allude to some unseemly steps that had been taken to move ANCSA along.

Honeycutt transitioned the conversation casually. "We shall meet again and discuss the NTSB review, which I contend with great confidence will be a favorable one."

Honeycutt didn't ask his visitor how the operation had been carried out. Unlike in the jungles of Vietnam where the two men had met, Honeycutt had grown accustomed to others doing the dirty work. It had become second nature and much too easy for Honeycutt to simply order the taking of a life. When necessary, he viewed another's life as nothing more than a liability in the never-ending pursuit of another profitable fiscal cycle.

The two men finished their glasses of champagne and admired the burning cedar embers. Honeycutt sensed the slightest edge of remorse in his visitor's demeanor, and decided then and there that the man's weakness was unacceptable.

"Adam, I sense your regrets. We've known each other for a very long time. We have been through a war together, so please don't lose sight of the finish line now that we are so close. Very soon, you will be an unbelievably rich man."

The reluctant smile on the Ross's face was unmistakable. He would need to be watched, and if he wavered, he would be neutralized.

Myles Honeycutt didn't realize Ross had learned very well from his mentor. His instincts from the hurried outset of the operation on September 2, 1971, to bring down Alaska Airlines Flight 1866 two days later, had been sending out warning signals that he'd sold his soul to the devil this time around.

He realized everything they'd done was what he'd deemed necessary, but he also realized the stakes were much higher. From the moment he and Myles had discussed the most viable option to thwart an effort by Joshua Knight to slow down the ANCSA negotiations, he had quietly formulated a contingency plan.

As the conversation wound down, Myles paused, allowing a piercing stare to strike at Ross's core. He wanted no doubt left about his next point.

"Our business, as you are intimately aware, my friend...requires us every once in a while to do things that our consciences may question. Until now, the measures we've taken have been at arm's length. We were both very close to Joshua, but he had become a very dangerous liability."

Honeycutt was referring to the late Joshua Knight, Honeycutt Petroleum Corporation's prized economist, who, along with the AFN's one dissenting member, had perished months earlier.

Vienna, Virginia
<u>The Same Evening, Saturday - December 18, 1971</u>

A few states south, the handsome and dark-haired man warmly gazed across the dinner table at his family. Their presence had become the one reminder that life had some purity to it.

Three months and fourteen days had come and gone since 111 people had perished in the crash of Alaska Airlines Flight 1866. A final determination by the National Transportation Safety Board (NTSB) as to the cause of the aircraft's unfortunate fate was still under investigation; however, all indications were pointing toward weather, human error, or both.

It was only in the last month or so that Robert had been able to get any decent sleep. The previous evening, the Jameson parents had enjoyed their six-year-old son's role as the lead in the play "Hansel and Gretel. After the school play, their daughter Alexis's sweet voice, in the back seat of the family station wagon, had joined in harmony with John Denver. *"Take me home, country roads,"* she chanted each time the chorus came around. The moment had given Robert and Amelia a glimpse of the possibility that life can indeed have some semblance of innocence and beauty.

Now after a fried chicken dinner with mashed potatoes and cream corn, and an episode of "Hawaii Five-O," the two kids were tucked into their cozy beds. Amelia had fallen quickly to sleep, but Robert, after four weeks of respite, was again waging full-on battle with a sleepless night.

The heartache that had been slowly going into recess was back in force, and he hadn't a clue why. Avoiding a frustrating night staring at the ceiling, he opted for the couch and a good book into the early morning.

Something in the air seemed strangely unsettling. The sensation he was experiencing had parallels eerily similar to another time in his life. Somewhere deep in the recesses of his mind and his soul, an out-of-balance feeling crept in- her soul was not yet at rest.

He extracted himself from the comfort of the large davenport, slowly proceeding toward the light switch, where he extinguished the artificial light in favor of the illumination of a brilliant white full moon. As he looked into the starry night, the unsettling feeling grew more and more intense. He'd had moments like this at least a dozen times in his life.

Nothing was able to extinguish the unsettled feeling. The only thing he knew was that another's spirit lingered somewhere in the sky between heaven and earth.

Chapter Seven

Washington, D.C.

Early October, 1972

Ten months later, life for Myles Honeycutt and Adam Ross had returned to a relative sense of normal.

Honeycutt's daily agenda became more mundane as the days moved on. Scheming, corporate espionage, and orchestrating disparate acts of violence were replaced with hours upon hours ensconced in financial reports, labor relations, and running a large oil company.

At home, little Jacob Honeycutt was no longer so little. He sported intense blue eyes that drank in all that life put before him. His mother Kelly couldn't wait for the day he entered kindergarten and she could get a few hours of respite.

Adam Ross continued to loyally operate at Honeycutt's side, following intently and mostly legally, the development and construction of the Alyeska Pipeline.

Robert Jameson had settled back into running a small consulting firm. The firm was small, eight employees but growing. The company specialized in governmental affairs, analyzing proposed legislation or at times influencing legislation.

It was a late Friday afternoon. The man's watch said it was quitting time. He chased the members of his team out the door, and as the office grew quiet, he stared out the window of his office toward the Washington National Monument.

The weather forecast called for snow, but the crisp, clear sky belied the prognosticators. He'd not taken a walk along the National Mall in a very long time, to simply let the world slow down. The clear sky was calling.

Despite the 25-degree temperature, the crowds around the National Monument were surprisingly robust and comfortably enveloping. Less than fifty yards from the magnificent structure, the man craned his neck upward and marveled at the iconic marble-white, needle-nosed building as it reached into the sky. His gaze returned to the horizontal green-grassed mall, and as it did, he felt a hand on his back, followed by a deep and very calm voice.

"Sir, do not turn around and just act normal."

Doing as he was told, the man awaited what the consequences of compliance would be.

"What I have for you, Mr. Jameson, will change your life."

"Who the hell are you?" The man didn't expect an answer at all, let alone an honest one. None was forthcoming.

The red-haired man paused momentarily and moved a bit closer to Robert. He reached his left hand toward Robert's suit-jacket pocket. The clandestine move was followed by short and explicit instruction. "Don't say another word." The communication was barely above a whisper. "The information in your pocket will make everything very clear."

Against every impulse he had, the man returned his gaze skyward to the magnificence of the National Monument, doing his utmost to portray a casual demeanor.

A career as a political consultant lent itself to interesting moments but this was obviously not in that same category. The encounter was clandestine and disconcerting.

His thoughts were racing, but externally he exuded nothing to betray that. He began the fifteen-minute stroll back to his office, each step casual as he struggled to avoid a panicked, nervous look while scanning the faces of people passing.

Back at his office, Robert leaned back in his black leather chair, sipping cold black coffee and staring at the document that had been placed so covertly in his pocket. It was nothing more than a folded white letter-size piece of paper with two separate notes on it.

The first came down to just a few words: "Welcome to the CIA."

The second was his first assignment: "Myles Honeycutt, Rico Sanchez, and Clay Tanis. They're responsible for 1866."

Robert looked closely at the second paragraph. According to the author of the document, these three men were now on a rather unique list; the United States wanted them dead.

Syracuse, New York

<u>Early October, 1972</u>

The Alaska Native Claims Settlement Act had changed the culture and the landscape for a multitude of Indian tribes throughout the State of Alaska. Nearly one billion dollars had been funneled into the economy with a well-formulated plan.

Thirteen Regional Corporations and more than two hundred village corporations were established to manage the newfound wealth bestowed on the Alaska Native people. Those recognized as eligible Native Alaskan Indians received one hundred shares of stock in their village corporations as well as their regional corporations.

The newfound wealth that ANCSA had been bestowed upon Alaska's Indian people brought with it an aura of the unknown and a strange curiosity. Nearly a year after ratification, it was still resonating throughout tiny Alaskan villages and towns. In places like Bethel on the southwestern coast, meetings had been held in town halls to share just what the news meant.

The financial windfall meant different things to different people. Over the years, this would prove highly diverse. Some corporations would wisely establish long-term strategic plans, while some would fall prey to opportunists boasting of fast returns on the corporation's investment. Some would simply make poor business decisions and find themselves nearly bankrupt three decades later.

Myles Honeycutt couldn't care less what would happen to the corporations that had been established as a result of ANCSA. His world had changed the moment President Nixon signed the Alaska Native Claims Settlement Act. Only he knew what drastic measures had been taken to ensure the gaudy dividends that would be bestowed upon his oil company.

His father had started Honeycutt Petroleum Corporation back in the late 1930's, with one well in the dusty flatlands of northwestern Oklahoma. By the late 1950's, Honeycutt Petroleum owned countless wells throughout not only northwestern Texas but all over the globe, and was third in production, behind only Esso (later Exxon) and Texaco at the time.

The company had done it right. It treated its people well, had been almost obsessively conscious of the environmental impact of drilling, and even had the fortitude to begin research into alternative energy sources.

Then on a foggy night in late 1958, twenty-two-year-old Myles Honeycutt, sitting in the backseat of his parents Desoto, watched in horror as his father clutched his chest and convulsed at the wheel.

His mother reached over and desperately tried to grab the steering wheel. The car had spun uncontrollably several times, coming to a stop only after striking a telephone pole. Moments later, the front of the vehicle was crumpled by the falling telephone pole. Myles looked on in horror as death found his family. He stared to the heavens he'd worshipped every day and screamed for God's help.

More than a small measure of death had found its way into Myles Honeycutt's soul that foggy night. He enlisted in the Marine Corps a few days after his parents were buried. By early 1960, he was fighting the Viet Cong thousands of miles from home and immeasurable worlds from the man he had hoped to become. His parents had groomed him to take over the family business, sending him to his father's Alma Mater of Oklahoma State University, where he majored in Business and simultaneously in Engineering.

The foggy night had changed all that.

The death in his eyes was unmistakable. He'd found the killing of the Viet Cong eerily enjoyable, almost therapeutic.

That look was there again as his cold steely blue eyes panned around his "weekend getaway." The eyes of the black bear he'd taken down on Michigan's Upper Peninsula stared down on him. He almost felt the bear's spirit casting a curse on him. He turned away with a slight chill running down his spine and stared out into the upstate New York forest.

The curse of the bear quickly escaped his thoughts. The steely look in his eyes held as thoughts of the downing of Alaska Air 1866 took hold. He'd ordered it without hesitation. "Spoils of war," he told himself. No remorse.

But something still had the slight chill running down his spine.

He heard his wife's voice upstairs, asking when he was coming to bed. He responded, but felt the chill down his spine growing stronger and stronger. It was the chill of death, and he knew it well. He'd felt it so horribly on the foggy night when his parents had left his world.

"Don't move a muscle." The deep voice commanded with an almost familiar accent, one he couldn't quite place. "Move at all and that'll be all she wrote," the voice calmly continued.

Myles complied and stood frozen, his chill replaced by primal fear. The trophy animals on the walls seemed to be staring down at him, cursing the man who'd taken their earthly spirit.

A pistol was pointed squarely at Myles's chest, leaving no doubt who was in charge of the confrontation. Through a black ski mask, the assassin's eyes were hauntingly familiar, but the accent was creating confusion for Myles.

"My family is upstairs, please don't hurt them," Myles pleaded sincerely. Kelly Honeycutt and their son Jacob were the only human beings on the planet that Myles could truly say he loved. Sadly, Kelly had not a clue what her husband's life was truly all about.

"I'm only here for you. Answer all of my questions, and you have my word that I will not harm them." The measured calm in the assassin's deep voice;

sent another chill down Myles's spine. The assassin had promised no harm to his family, but for Myles, the assassin's tone said that all bets were off.

"I'm here for one reason only. You are going to die, Mr. Honeycutt. How that happens depends on what you have to tell me."

"Who the hell are you?" His arms were shaking and his heart was pounding. He was not accustomed to the feeling of relinquished control. He repeated the question after a long silence.

"A nightmare," the assassin said sharply. "Now let's take this slow." He pointed to a door that exited the kitchen onto a deck wrapping fully around the home. Myles walked slowly toward the door and wondered why his security team had not detected the interloper. After they got out the door, he asked the intruder what had happened to his team.

"They should be the least of your worries." The man was fully in control of the situation. Honeycutt's security team was unaware of his presence.

Chaos was swirling in Myles' mind. Life had come full circle for him. He'd taken lives over and over, and now it was painfully obvious that Karma was here to collect its debt.

Myles again repeated his question. "The way I see it, my life is over. I think I have the right to know who you are and why you want to kill me," he stated almost too calmly.

"You have done something atrocious and you deserve to die, but against my better judgment; I'm giving you a chance to make peace with your maker." The deep voice held grave hostility.

"What the hell are you talking about?" Myles's voice was beginning to quiver. The primal fear had settled into his soul. It didn't feel natural to experience what he was feeling, but for the first time since that moment just before his parent's car spun out of control on that foggy night so many years earlier, he ironically felt like the innocent young man he once was.

The masked intruder hadn't noticed the tiny silhouette of four-year-old Jacob Honeycutt watching from the bedroom window on the second floor. He answered Honeycutt's question and a few more. Ten minutes later, the explosion of gunfire echoed throughout the forest, ending the peaceful sleep Kelly had been enjoying and creating for her a lifetime of nightmares.

Young Jacob Honeycutt looked down onto the forest floor in utter horror. He'd watched the entire scene in silent fear. The moment was tormenting in the present and would be etched into his soul forever.

And the masked intruder was on to the next phase of the operation.

Almost like bullet points, a mental checklist stirred in the assassin's mind. The names had been etched there one night several months earlier, and one now had a strike-through its name. Myles Honeycutt had been dealt with. Rico Sanchez and Clay Tanis were next on the list. "One down and two to go..." The assassin chanted internally, walking almost invisibly through the upstate New York forest of alder and birch trees.

The assassin disappeared without a trace, almost if he had never been there.

Chapter Eight

Seattle, Washington

Saturday October 21, 1972

The assassin was seated comfortably in the brown, year-old, two-door Ford Capri, his thoughts squarely focused on finding Clay Tanis and Rico Sanchez. Each had a bullet reserved in name in a clip of the man's Berretta.

A little over nine months earlier, Sanchez and Tanis had become permanent blips on his radar screen.

A seemingly anonymous man, a month's earlier, had slipped a bar napkin into his suit jacket pocket.

On one side, the names, *"Clay Tanis, Rico Sanchez, Myles Honeycutt - Alaska Air 1866.* Their connection to the assassin's life was on the other side of the napkin: *Alaska 1866 was not an accident*.

The National Transportation Safety Board had investigated the crash of Alaska Airlines 1866 on September 4, 1971, and the cause had been determined to be pilot error and faulty navigation equipment. Were it not for the anonymous message, Myles Honeycutt and two of his trusted associates would be getting away with a horrendous murder that bordered on a terrorist act. The message was not only designed to ensure the three men would die for their deeds, but also to bury the truth precipitating the crash of Alaska Airlines 1866.

On the Seattle Waterfront, the man who'd received the message on a napkin instinctively felt the Beretta on his right hip as he pulled the Ford Capri into a rare open parking spot. The vehicle's door returned a slightly irritating mechanical squeal as he pushed it open.

Unseen but heard on the Alaskan Way Viaduct forty-five feet above, vehicles proceeding north and south at well over fifty miles per hour plus rattled the elevated concrete highway and gave the parking lot an energetic, edgy aura. The realization of what was coming next was setting in. It was madness by design, and it was what he'd signed on for. The intelligence business and all of its patriotism and all of its darkness had become his life.

Without any hesitation, the intelligence operative walked casually with masked confidence across the two-way traffic of four-lane Alaskan Way. Each passerby was assessed for threat level and each face was memorized.

Of the twenty or so people passed, none were determined to be a threat, and certainly none appeared to be spotters for his two targets.

With a benign pass of the seafood restaurant that Rico Sanchez and Clay Tanis had settled into, the intelligence operative catalogued the table the two targets had chosen, the number of patrons at other tables, and the novelty store adjacent to the restaurant.

The reconnaissance he'd done the last four days of these two men was virtually flawless. They had no idea they were being watched. The surveillance wasn't constant; it was designed to detect patterns and tendencies that could be capitalized on. One discernible trait had stood out over the last four days of surveillance: the two men had at least two mugs of beer in the late afternoon.

Intelligence operatives, assassins by training but more by instinct can blend into a crowd with ease. A calm, natural demeanor must accompany a well-constructed disguise in order for a cover to work. This operative had mastered the identity of several aliases and corresponding looks. On this October day, wearing a pair of glasses, with hair dyed gray and makeup that aged him at least twenty years, he looked more like a seasoned college professor than an assassin.

He'd been taught his whole life to read people. And not by the United States Government, but by his father. Some people were easier read than others. The assassin had made some inquiries with the National Transportation Safety Board, trying to determine if the NTSB had suspected foul play in the crash of Alaska Airlines 1866. Each inquiry was met with one negative after another. As the investigation was working toward a conclusion, the favored causes were in the realm of human error and mechanical failure. But something nagged at him; someone knew why the plane had gone down.

As he'd begun to plan this op a few weeks earlier, that nagging feeling was there the entire time. A weak sense of confusion had settled in because this one was personal. The information that had led him on this one-week journey of execution seemed all too tidy and almost pre-packaged.

Against his better judgment, he ignored his instinct and let the personal vendetta lead from one bad decision to another.

Seattle, Washington
Saturday October 21, 1972

"Forgive me for not sitting very long. My back is killing me," a man with golden-blond hair stated truthfully.

He arose from a wooden high-back chair positioned next to the window, his nearly six-foot frame lean and imposing, almost a mirror image of his partner's physique. He arched his back, stretching his arms wide. The half-hour seated in the same position had stiffened his 27-year-old back, a back that had been thoroughly abused through three years of linebacker in high school.

"I know the feeling, my friend. My knees kill me every day. I'm hurting every morning," the man of Hispanic background added, empathizing with his partner as he stood to momentarily get the blood flowing as well.

"Your knees are just feeling the pain of the Northwest's foul weather," the blond man stated, referring to the rainy weather Seattle and the Pacific Northwest is known for. Ironically, as he said this, a warm and radiant ray of sunshine lit the south side of the restaurant.

"We must live quietly for a very long time and ensure we are never found." The Hispanic man proposed.

The blond man lifted his glass in toast. "To living a very quiet and very wealthy life..."

"To living a quiet life, my friend..." The Hispanic man returned the toast and then stood again. "Excuse me. The beer is running right through me?" He laughed.

The blond man remained in his seat and gazed around the trendy seafood restaurant, assessing the clientele. The activity was comforting and quietly contagious: a couple gazing lovingly into one another's eyes, the business man in the corner read the Seattle Post-Intelligencer, and two women relaxed with conversation over cups of coffee, on the sunny, and warm September day. The aroma of baked fish and steaming clams were part of the culture and charm of the restaurant. He had a strong affection for the Pacific Northwest and was enjoying the sounds, the smells, and the visual stimulation that gave the restaurant a peaceful ambience. The sky was blue, the breeze warm. For a moment, he almost forgot how dangerous his life was.

He was nursing the cold beer and a bowl of white clam chowder. He stirred a few crackers into the chowder. He listened as seagulls glided gracefully over the deck outside. Each one seemed to have its own voice, and he was wishing he could get a glimpse into their world. It was not something he would admit to anyone, but he nevertheless had moments such as this. Unfortunately, the moment took a horrifying turn.

Just as he turned his head to look out the window at a plump seagull seated on the wood railing that surrounded the outer deck, he noticed the somehow familiar gait of a man entering the restaurant. A moment of professional respect and also a moment of primal fear entered into his being.

The moment was short-lived. He prayed for his soul as the bullet quietly exited the high-caliber pistol muted by a silencer, moving at an extraordinary rate of speed toward his chest. The searing pain was like someone had punched his sternum with a scalding hammer.

Memories of his childhood flooded his clouded eyes: The time his mother and father had bought him his first two-wheel bike, the time his grandmother had comforted him when his little blue parakeet Skipper died, the taste of his mom's apple pie. The first time he'd kissed a girl. A bright light flashed before his eyes for just a fleeting moment, and then all went dark.

The Hispanic man had just exited the restroom and froze in shock at the execution. Making resigned eye contact with the assassin, the man prayed that his life would be spared. The assassin ordered him onto the ground, face down.

His heart was pounding; aware the moment of truth had arrived. The assassin placed the hot end of the short barrel of the Sig-Sauer pistol against his sweaty right temple, searing a circular burn against his head. He knew his fate and he began to pray for his soul. Then all went dark.

The remaining five patrons in the restaurant sat rigid in horror as the assassin walked out.

He felt no remorse whatsoever for the actions he had taken, only a small measure of regret that he'd not taken the time to torture Tanis and Sanchez.

Two hours later, the assassin was seated in First Class and headed home. His wife and children Mark and Alexis would never know of the life he'd chosen six months earlier.

Hatred and a thirst for revenge had taken hold of his soul. He thought back to the Tlingit tales his father had told him about the dark lure of the land otter. Robert Jameson had graduated from government consultant to government intelligence contractor - merely a soft euphemism for a contracted assassin.

What Robert didn't know was that his vendetta had nearly extinguished any living proof that the Alaska Native Claims Settlement Act had been finalized under false pretenses.

Chapter Nine

Seattle, Washington

<u>Saturday June 9, 1973</u>

Eight months later, an innocent scene was unfolding.

The intent gaze of a young boy's chocolate-brown eyes fixed on the tail engine of an Alaska Airlines Boeing 727-100 at gate C-10 of Seattle-Tacoma International Airport brought a smile to his mother as she watched her seven-year-old son. The beauty of the bluish snow-capped mountains of the Olympic Peninsula forty miles away provided a majestic backdrop to the moment.

Summer's start on the calendar was still two weeks away in the Pacific Northwest, yet the temperature early that morning was already 71 degrees, highly unusual for this time of year. The warmth in the air added a comforting element of peace to the morning for the family of three.

Inside the terminal, all was a bustling stream of gate announcements, flights being boarded and deplaned, and the distinct sounds of jet engines rumbling on takeoff.

The boy's mother Amelia, with her smiling hazel-green eyes, and her five-year-old daughter Alexis sat patiently, mom reading a novel and daughter enjoying a coloring book. Young Mark Allan Jameson couldn't allow his gaze to venture from the scene outside, following the ascent of an American Airlines Boeing 707 into the blue Pacific Northwest Sky.

"Mark, what kind of plane was that?" Amelia asked, knowing the answer full well but getting a sense of joy from the boy's precious knowledge of aircraft types and airlines.

"It was a 707, Mom, probably headed for Chicago," The boy answered with an eager smile. His mom knew he was right about the aircraft and very likely right about the destination of the American Airlines flight.

"What about that one?" She continued, pointing at an aircraft taxiing on the tarmac toward the northern end of the runway.

"It's a 747, and that one I know is going to Chicago, that's where United sends most of those." The boy had a tone of matter-of-fact confidence. "Hey, Mom, when are we going to see Dad?"

"He'll be in Yakutat in a few days, too. He can't wait to be there." It began to dawn on her that he was a miniature version of his father, boyishly innocent and yet highly intelligent, and most notably, highly intense.

At just seven years old, he was already driven and had matured well beyond his years. He also had a high level of competitiveness and unusual athleticism, and these conversations at times seemed almost on the level of an adult.

"Alaska Airlines Flight 1861 bound for Ketchikan, Sitka, Juneau, Yakutat, Cordova, and Anchorage is ready for boarding at gate C-10."

The boy's ears perked up as he tugged at his mom's hand. He couldn't wait to get on board, headed for the family's summer home - beautiful Yakutat, Alaska.

<u>Later, Saturday - June 9, 1973</u>

"Ladies and gentlemen, on the left side of the aircraft you can see the beautiful blue of the Pacific Ocean and the northwestern tip of the continental United States, and on the right side you can see the Straits of Juan de Fuca and the Cascade Mountain Range off to the east. We will be traveling at 35,000 feet and we are looking to arrive in Ketchikan in approximately one hour and fifty-five minutes." Captain Les Horton paused. We are looking for a smooth flight this morning, hospitality and we'll have you in Ketchikan where the Alaska skies today are clear as could be and the forecast is for 70-degree temperatures."

Mark Allan Jameson listened and stared out the right side window at Mount Baker in northwestern Washington: He had already decided one day he'd climb that mountain.

"Mark would you like to read your comic book?" mother asked. Despite his grown up nature and personality, he loved to read Archie and Richie Rich comic books, and watch Bugs Bunny and Scooby-Doo on Saturday mornings.

Somewhere over the Queen Charlotte Islands between Vancouver Island and the Alaska Panhandle, the Alaska Airlines 727-100 banked gently to the right, giving it a slightly northern heading toward its first destination, Ketchikan, Alaska.

Mark found himself awestruck at the snow-capped peaks of British Columbia off to the right of the aircraft. This was his fifth trip on this route already in his young life, but the majesty of flying hadn't waned.

Alexis, his sister, had settled early on into one of the aisle seats. Now she asked her mom if she could sit next to the window for a little while, and Mark less than graciously relented. That change of seats, as simple as it seemed would make a big impact on Mark's life.

As he sat reading an Archie Comic, two stewardesses were working the cabin offering sodas to the passengers. Mark asked for a Coca-Cola, his Uncle Andrew's favorite drink. He looked up and was mesmerized by blue eyes and an angelic face.

The aircraft only had 22 passengers aboard, so the work of the flight crew was minimal this fine June morning, allowing them an opportunity to rest their feet.

The two flight attendants sat at the back of the aircraft in the crew seats. Mark turned around, realizing for the first time in his life just how beautiful a woman could be.

Tara Lynn Collins tapped the leg of her fellow stewardess and seatmate, Lisa Danielson. Tara whispered that they had an admirer. Mark was totally mesmerized and didn't turn around for a good fifteen to twenty seconds. When he faced the seatback again, he was blushing. He waited a good minute and then turned around again, and just couldn't stop looking at the most beautiful woman he'd ever seen.

Tara smiled and gracefully motioned with her index finger for Mark to come back and visit them. He blushed even more and asked his mom if it was alright if he could go to the back and "visit with the stewardesses."

The walk to the back of the aircraft was one of those moments Mark would never forget, his first boyhood crush.

Tara asked Mark to sit down between herself and Lisa. He sat as proud as could be. Tara and Lisa asked Mark questions about where he lived, did he play sports, did he like girls, and what he was going to do in Alaska.

Mark was almost euphoric as he answered each of their questions with as much maturity as he could muster. He stared so innocently into Tara's ocean blue eyes that he simply melted. He would never forget those ocean-blue eyes.

Tara's voice was sweet and soft, and Mark listened intently to everything she had to say. Tara joked later to Lisa that she wished her last boyfriend would have been so attentive when they had conversations. Lisa laughed and agreed that she wished her husband would do the same.

Mark spent the next twenty minutes visiting with the two attractive flight attendants, and when he came back to his seat, he would never be quite the same. The smile on his face stretched ear to ear.

Amelia looked at her son and concealed an adoring smile. Her son was definitely just like his father, a hopeless romantic and a flirt.

Young Mark Allan Jameson spent the rest of the flight with a slight blush to his face, even while reading his Archie comic book.

Chapter Ten

Seattle FBI Field Office
<u>Early September 2001</u>

"Special Agent Jameson, welcome to the Seattle Field Office." Assistant Special Agent in Charge Walter "Walt" Branson of the Seattle Field Office of the Federal Bureau of Investigation extended his hand.

"Thank you, sir. And please call me Mark." Mark Jameson gave him a light smile and a firm handshake.

At almost five foot eleven, Mark surrendered a good four to five inches to ASAC Branson's lanky, muscled frame, easily on the plus side of six feet. With a tussled, slightly disheveled look, his dark brown hair was a distinct contrast to Branson's slightly graying blond hair combed carefully from the right to left.

ASAC Branson spent twenty minutes giving Jameson a tour of the Seattle Field Office. There were a few introductions as they passed agents and support personnel.

Finally, ASAC Branson introduced him to his new partner. "SA Jameson, SA Danielle Westford."

"Around here, it's Dani," FBI Special Agent Danielle Westford said.

With shoulder-length wavy brown hair, deep brown eyes, and soft dark skin, SA Danielle "Dani" Westford was a knockout. The .22 caliber Sig Sauer pistol in the leather holster on her right hip only served to accentuate Dani's aura. When she entered a room, a man could not help but pay attention.

After some conversation getting to know one another, Jameson and Westford settled in and to cover her active cases.

Most were routine white-collar frauds, embezzlements, or extortion cases. There was one RICO-Racketeer Influenced and Corrupt Organizations-case that had just come across her desk a week or so earlier. The RICO case was to be Jameson's first case in the Seattle Field Office but no more than a week after he arrived in Seattle, all bets were off.

On September 11, 2001, terrorists forever changed the face of America. The Bureau's focus turned to fighting terror. For Mark Jameson, an anomaly in Anchorage, Alaska, a few months later would be the case that would define the rest of his life.

Seattle FBI Field Office
<u>A Few Days after 9/11</u>

Mark leaned back in his chair and raised both arms over his head with interlocking hands, putting a bit of tension on his biceps.

His brown eyes were weary as he looked at the bold, white-font clock in the bottom right corner of the FBI's Dell laptop. It was 9:44PM, hour fourteen of this very long day.

The last few days had been the most intense he'd ever experienced, and certainly the most he'd ever experienced as an FBI agent.

The first airplane into the World Trade Center seemed out of place and an awful accident, but by the time he'd seen the second airplane collide with the South Tower on NBC, it was horribly apparent the United States was under attack.

Every ounce of his being, as well as those of fellow agents, wanted nothing more than the chance to violate a prisoner's rights with a bullet in the head.

This was the first time he had been at his desk in nearly two days. He'd been on the street with Dani Westford and a couple of federal marshals, tracking down foreign nationals with expired green cards, expired work and student visas, and others, citizens or not, who found themselves now deemed a potential threat to the United States.

There weren't enough resources. Agents were operating on no more than four to five hours of sleep, and it showed on the weary faces around the large, open room of the Seattle Field Office.

Mark's head rested momentarily against the interlocked hands. He closed his eyes and tried to gain even just a thirty-second catnap. He wasn't the only one.

Twenty-eight seconds in, the nap was interrupted by ASAC Branson's presence. Mark's eyes were opening before he felt Branson's tap on his right elbow.

The dark circles under the boss's eyes and the day-old stubble on his chin were evidence of how long the last few days had been for everyone. Branson had even been out on the street knocking on doors, doing some surveillance, and had had a run in or two with some questionable suspects.

Branson had the respect of the field agents around the office and throughout the Bureau for that very part of his character. He'd been a field agent for sixteen years before being bumped up into management so he rolled up his sleeves on a regular basis.

His unwritten motto was, "If I can't pull the trigger myself, I'm going home." Branson had lived up to that motto over the days following 9/11.

"How are you holding up, Mark?"

He didn't bother to adjust his posture. It wasn't disrespect; he was just worn out.

"I'm making it there, boss." Like a starting pitcher who's made it to the middle of the eighth inning with a one-run lead but has just loaded the bases, he honestly thought he had more gas in the tank. Like a good coach, Branson knew better. He was taking Mark off the mound, at least for the night. Mark watched ASAC Branson survey the room, wondering why he was the one sought out. He could tell Branson was taking him off of the mound, at least for the night. Mark watched ASAC Branson survey the room, wondering why he had been sought out. He had only been in the Seattle Field Office for a little over a week and a half. Even with twenty-five agents in the same room, it was so ominously quiet.

Finally the unspoken question was answered. "Mark, I know you've gotta be running on fumes, so I'm sending him you home to get a good night's sleep. Then I need a favor." It was almost heard an apology in Branson's tone. "The Anchorage Field Office..."   Suddenly Mark knew where this conversation was going.

"...is running short on resources."

Mark smiled tiredly at the boss. "A favor, huh?"

"The flight is at 1:30 tomorrow afternoon, go home and get some sleep. I owe you one."

"No you don't, sir. This has been tough on every one of us. But do me a favor, if you find anyone here who needs a little extra-curricular interrogation - save one for me."

"It would be my pleasure." Branson's smile was genuine, but the sorrow for their country and for those directly affected was still there.

"How long am I going to be up there?" Mark asked, wanting an idea of how much to pack for.

"No more than a couple of days. We've done the weapons paperwork, so you're cleared for the morning at SeaTac and you don't need to worry about that." "Now get out of here and get some rest." He was making reference to documentation necessary for any federal agent to bring a weapon aboard a commercial aircraft.

A few housekeeping items were taken care of and Mark headed for the elevator. Forty-five minutes later, his head against one of the soft pillows of a tan sofa, he finally disappeared into a deep sleep.

Tukwila, Washington
Monday September 17, 2001

In the wee early hours of a Monday morning - a few hours after his exhausted meeting with ASAC Branson, Mark's thoughts were wandering all over the place. His Tlingit Indian heritage had given him a sixth sense or some other spiritual touch with the world around him. Sure enough, he'd gone to sleep feeling very strange about something and the dreams were vivid.

His family trekked each summer to the rugged little town of Yakutat, Alaska, for at least five to six weeks. They'd go for fishing, hiking, beachcombing, and nightly games of cards, Aggravation, or pick-up sticks. Despite a job serving as an advisor to a United States' senator, his dad always took two weeks each summer and spent them with the family in the town where he'd been born. The only summer he'd missed the vacation was in 1973.

Mark's dream brought those days back, a time when life was so much simpler. Each June, after school ended, he'd be aboard a Northwest Boeing 707 or a United Airlines Boeing 747 bound for Seattle, and then jumping onto an Alaska Airlines Boeing 727. On that September 2001 morning, his dream harkened back to those days.

His family was on a non-stop flight from Washington, D.C.'s Dulles International Airport to Seattle on a sleek Northwest Orient Airlines Boeing 707. Little Mark's excitement grew as the Pacific Northwest approached. They were just northeast of Washington State's famous Mount Rainier. At 14,410-feet, it is one of the tallest peaks in the continental United States, and for that moment in time, nothing else mattered.

Mark watched as flight attendants worked the cabin and flirted with his dad. His mom didn't seem to mind-she was beautiful, and Dad was simply a harmless flirt. Mark listened to the whisper of the aircraft's engines as endless miles of the Cascade Mountains passed beneath us.

Time wavered in his dream, and Mark heard his dad mention something about the Indians of Washington State, pointing at Mt. Adams to the south, describing what the mountain meant to the Yakima Indian Tribe. There was pride in his voice that he was Indian.

Mark froze. He was Indian!

Just like that he was back on a playground at an elementary school in Vienna, Virginia. Its name he couldn't recall, but the battles in his heart would not go away.

"You look funny, you dumb Indian!" The sixth-grade bully screamed it day after day at recess. Twenty-nine years later, the nightmare was still so real.

Mark fought to wake up, but couldn't.

"Look at the little shit, the Indian's pissed his pants! What a little shit," the bully continued as he shoved Mark to the ground. He fought back the tears on the playground, escaping to somewhere else in his mind. But the escape in his dreams never came. The bully's voice, so harsh and damning, had never gone away.

Mark awoke moments later with the chills and soaked in sweat. Time had a funny way of putting things in perspective.

Barely six or seven years old, he was on a playground suffering unwarranted and likely now criminal abuse from a 12-year-old kid with nothing better to do than make other people suffer.

He could hear the ACLU defending the bully: "Your honor, he was abused as a child, so he was just acting out repressed memories." And he could hear himself in the courtroom replying, "Up yours, Asshole!"

Mark's problem at that moment was that he wanted nothing more than to go back in time to that day and kick the bully's ass: And then maybe water-board an Al-Qaeda member or two.

Chapter Eleven

Tukwila, Washington
Monday - September 17, 2001

Despite his annoying trip down Nightmare Lane, the sleep had been a restful one, and Mark awoke feeling almost fully recharged. The only drawback was that he awoke to Regis and Kelly Ripa at around 9:15, when he had hoped to wake up a couple of hours earlier. He had to admit he had a bit of a crush on Katie Couric.

The Anchorage flight was scheduled for 1:30pm, but living in the Tukwila suburb twelve-miles south of Seattle, he was only fifteen minutes from Sea-Tac International Airport. After a quick three-mile run and a twenty-minute workout of pushups and pull-ups, he jumped in the shower and packed. By 11:15, he was in a cab headed for the airport.

The stroll out to the D concourse that day was one of those moments a person never forgets. Mark arrived at the security check point about twenty-five minutes before the flight was scheduled to board.

The rest he'd gotten and the energy of the run-slash-workout had done wonders for his demeanor; the pride that went with carrying the FBI credentials ran through his entire being as he presented it to one of the personnel at the security checkpoint.

Observing the diligence with which his FBI credentials were scrutinized; America had changed dramatically in the last five days and he knew it would likely never be the same.

He didn't know if the country had gotten complacent or if the assholes from Iraq, Afghanistan, or some other desert shit-hole had just found a chink in the armor. Whatever it was, he hoped that America would keep its guard up, at the diligent level he was experiencing right then.

The appreciative nod from the personnel at the checkpoint sent a chill up and down his spine. This moment was why he'd become an FBI Agent. America, for all of its flaws was the cream of the crop, and he was proud to be a part of the team sworn to defend it.

As a natural reflex, he felt for the Glock-17 in his shoulder holster as he walked down the long narrow D-Concourse corridor. The passengers were behaving differently from past flights. People were looking at each other-and Mark-with a hint of judgment and mistrust. His Native American skin was light brown; his eyes slightly Asian, and his physique in his humble opinion masculine. He realized he'd been caught in that sense of judgment and mistrust.

Inside the plane, he held a smirk in check. An FBI agent getting profiled-maybe he'd be right for an undercover gig after all? He shrugged. He'd always been a terrible poker player, so undercover had never been a consideration.

Chapter Twelve

<u>Present Time</u>

It is hard to adequately pin down what comprises what life is all about. One day your five years old and everything about the world seems so pure. Most, if not all, have been there and for many, want nothing more than to capture that feeling again.

Then boom, it's as if at exponential speed, the progression of life has taken over and you're in our mid-forties and wondering where time has gone. Lately, that is exactly what our protagonist had been experiencing.

He is Mark Allan Jameson and he didn't know if it's the job, the mortgage, the slight thread of salt and pepper he is seeing on the sideburns but whatever it is; he is kind of slowing things down a bit and reflecting on how he'd gone from a wide-eyed five-year old boy to a forty-something FBI Agent.

Which actually is what this little journey is all about; a few decades ago, he was nothing more than a seven-year old kid - who treasured more the moments when he was love struck by a drop dead gorgeous flight attendant.

More importantly, a woman named Wilma Jameson was taken from this earth in 1971 in an airplane crash when he was very young. She was someone he wished he'd had the chance to know, she was his grandmother.

She passed when he was a still a toddler and he never had the opportunity to know her but so many stories leave him with no doubt that she was a very generous, tough, and proud woman.

Then there's Mark's dad - Robert Jameson. Touted at a young age to work directly for Vermont Senator Daniel Billings until 1979 and then who knows what for about eighteen years - then in 1997 he started a career as an author - the last five novels he has penned have made it on to the New York Times Best Seller list - the best of those in his opinion is "The Meeting."

The two have been close most of their lives, even with Mark assigned at various places around the country and most recently, the Seattle FBI Field Office on the west coast and his dad traveling all over the world doing research for his novels.

As for Mark, he's just a guy who happens to have a job he enjoys, a wife he is devoted to, and three children who he cherishes more and more each day.

But back in the waning days of 2001, life and all of its purity and purity's polar opposite found its way into an assignment he was given and by May 2002 - Mark's life would never be the same.

And in spite of himself, at times he can come across as arrogant or cocky; but in the end he is just exaggerating and embellishing a bit, or maybe a bunch like most of guys do.

Chapter Thirteen

Anchorage, Alaska

<u>Late Afternoon - Monday, September 17, 2001</u>

Alaska was where Mark's family hailed from, and yet he'd not been back for at least three years. Seeing the Chugach Mountain Range off in the distance now was cathartic and surreal. From his dad; he had inherited ambition, drive, and a commitment to strive to be the best at anything he does; from his mother, he'd inherited a bit of a philosophical connection to life. Together his parents had given him a deep sense that life needed a perpetual purpose, and moments were not meant to be wasted.

So a little over five hours after he'd passed through the security checkpoint in Seattle, he was unpacked and allowing the beauty of Alaska to take hold.

And his father's drive was right there; he'd finally gotten a clue what his assignment would be in Anchorage. A check of his e-mail indicated that a Special Agent Sandra Gonzalez would be picking him up at the hotel "promptly at six am" for some place called Paxson. She'd been emphatic that it was six AM.

Who the hell hits the road at six-freaking-AM! Mark shook his head.

Lucky man, being sent to a place he'd never heard of - Paxson was it? He definitely needed an Alaska map.

He also desperately wanted a nice refreshing walk, to maybe find a nice steak or seafood restaurant, and then an office supply store.

In his weary haste, he'd forgotten to pack something he found almost as important as his Glock-17: He needed a Day-Timer.

He'd been to Anchorage several times as a kid, but this was his first time in an official capacity with the FBI, and it felt strange to walk out of the hotel with a loaded pistol in his shoulder holster.

The feel of the fresh, pure air was invigorating. The walk along the city streets was almost therapeutic. The last few days after September 11 wouldn't be forgotten, but Mark needed to believe in something, and the smells, the sounds, and the wilderness off in the distance all reminded him that life had a purpose.

The steak was a perfect medium-rare, the asparagus crisp and buttery, and the rice pilaf smooth with a hint of garlic and ground pepper. He didn't often indulge in this type of dinner while on an assignment, since the FBI's per diem is well short of a tab for a high-end meal that would come out of his own pocket, but the last few days called for some true sustenance.

His mind kept returning to the images he'd seen on Tuesday morning as he listened to Matt Lauer and Katie Couric do their best to report on the terrorism, though it was evident they were in shock with the rest of America. The pain of the families, experienced that day, was something he couldn't begin to fathom.

Mark enjoyed the quiet dinner and the ambience of the restaurant. He hadn't bothered to look for its name before entering, but the patron traffic was reliable evidence the establishment wouldn't disappoint. He walked back out into the fresh Alaska air, around eight in the evening as the sun was just dipping below the horizon, leaving behind soft clouds painted a myriad of yellow, orange, and red.

A couple of blocks from the hotel, he zipped into a 24-hour convenience store and bought an Alaska road map, a bag of M&M's, and a Diet Squirt. At a Rite Aid a few blocks away, he found a Day Timer.

He returned to his room to a rerun of Seinfeld on TV, a *USA Today* sitting on the bed, with a front page photograph of the Twin Towers just before they fell. It felt odd to have a professional connection to something that had the entire country in mourning, angry, and deeply frightened.

The net the federal government had spread over the United States for the last week had been incredible, effective, and producing unpublished results. Normally it would have been unbelievably exhausting, but for law enforcement and intelligence personnel at all levels; the adrenaline, commitment, and a deep-seated hatred for terrorists had most refusing to quit.

At the window, Mark breathed in more of the sweet, cool, refreshing Alaska air, and wondered what was waiting for SA Gonzalez and him in Paxson - wherever the heck that was?

Chapter Fourteen

Tyson's Corner, Virginia

<u>Around 10:00am, Tuesday - September 18, 2001</u>

"They're en route." Walking into a spacious office in an all-brick building just a few blocks from the sprawling Tyson's Corner Mall complex, a graying man with green eyes and a deep baritone voice spoke, devoid of any emotion, into a wireless black telephone. "ETA is approximately six hours. Primary contact disengage signal today is 118 GNP."

"Copy that 118 GNP." On the other end of the line, a man in his late fifties acknowledged the information being disseminated thousands of miles away.

"Secondary is on NTK only. After engaging with contacts secondary is to be neutralized," the baritone voice continued, still devoid of any semblance of feeling.

"Copy that number two is NTK, neutralize," the voice answered, nearly as flat as the monotone voice instructing him from the Washington, D.C., suburb thousands of miles away.

Delta Junction, Alaska

<u>Same Day, Tuesday - September 18, 2001</u>

The connection ended, and the man was left alone with his thoughts and instructions from someone he'd never met.

His eyebrows furled together forming a prominent crow's foot as he contemplated the instructions he'd been given. NTK-need to know- meant his fellow operative had not been read-in on the goal of this operation. He himself wasn't sure of the final goal this time. A lifetime spent never doubting the objective of each assignment had disappeared as he had hung up the telephone. Over the years, his instincts had not once betrayed him, and his instincts were screaming something was horribly amiss.

Whatever the assignment's end-game was, he was determined to find it out, but in order to do so he'd need to proceed as instructed step-by-step. It meant another killing.

Anchorage, Alaska
Same Day, Tuesday - September 18, 2001

The cell phone alarm went off at five am, and Mark Jameson turned on the television to an Alaska NBC affiliate. 9/11 still dominated the news reports, the images the same of the airplanes colliding with the towers, but the repetition only served to reinforce his hatred for the monsters who'd attacked them.

He was finding himself thinking a lot about the past. Maybe it was the Alaska air or maybe it was just the fact that he loved his job, but the events of 9/11 and the case he'd been assigned had him taking stock of his life.

It had been a good many years since the fresh faced little kid loved nothing more than airplanes and flirting with gorgeous flight attendants. He would have loved to relive the innocent pleasures of those days. Life wasn't that simple. But he kept wishing he could snap his fingers or say a prayer, and have the benefit of hindsight.

He wasn't sure what he'd choose to do, but high on the list would be to sit in the Portland, Maine, airport on September 11, 2001, and shoot a couple of ugly pieces of shit square in the forehead. Life wasn't always pretty, and he wasn't ashamed at all to admit he would get a lot of satisfaction out of taking out a terrorist or two, or the whole lot of them for that matter. Why he chose Portland, Maine? That was where Al-Qaeda piece of shit Mohammed Atta started his terror operation rolling. He'd boarded a commuter flight bound for Boston from Portland's airport. Mark would love to have royally mucked up his little rendezvous with seventy-two virgins in paradise.

There were days he wondered if he and his colleagues were making a difference at all, what with those nut jobs professing their love to Allah and doing their best to take out unbelievers in the process. Mark had no problem with devotion to a religion, but when that was bastardized and used as rationale for heinous and extreme violence, he wanted to be one of the few who could ensure that the door swings both ways.

He found himself staring blindly out the hotel window, fists clenched. He took a deep breath and let it out. For now, he was on assignment with SA Sandra Gonzalez.

Special Agent Gonzalez' e-mail had indicated she'd be picking him up promptly at six am on Tuesday morning, and when Mark walked out of the elevator at six ten am, he got a very unfriendly gaze from a very beautiful woman.

Mark stopped short, waiting for a chastise much like the time his mom had caught him with a bottle of Bud when he was in the tenth grade. Instead, what he got was a welcome that didn't match the look on Gonzalez's face.

"Agent Jameson, forgive my demeanor. My parents sent me to a Catholic boarding school, so being late meant twenty Hail Mary's and I'm sort of obsessed with being on time."

SA Gonzalez wore a dark pair of sunglasses and a brown pantsuit. Mark could spot a Fed from a mile away, but anyone could have pegged her as an FBI agent or maybe Secret Service.

"No apology necessary, Agent Gonzalez. I guess I'm making a great first impression."

She accepted his apology and briefly explained the object of their drive, promising to provide details on the way. Almost before Mark could respond, she suddenly moved on to the subject that was still at the forefront around the country. "I don't know about you Jameson, but I don't know why we don't just blow Al-Qaeda to Kingdom Come."

"Good, so I'm not the only one feeling we should round up every last piece of Al-Qaeda Shit and blow their brains out - off the record, of course."

Gonzalez nodded, apparently appreciating his brutal honesty. The FBI, rightfully so, was obsessed with living within the confines of the Constitution, and Mark couldn't speak for his colleagues, but 9/11 had almost extinguished his desire to comply with some of those rules.

SA Gonzalez had a less than conspicuous black FBI Chevrolet Suburban parked on the street in front of the hotel. Her own appearance was all Fed, and Mark's attire announced the same: a pair of tan Khakis, a blue dress shirt, a casual blue blazer, and a pair of dark glasses. And, of course the concealed weapon. The pride in their roles was there again, just beneath the surface as they walked out to the Suburban.

"So from what I read, we've got a bit of a drive ahead of us?"

"We do, Agent Jameson. Welcome to federal law enforcement, Alaskan style."

Chapter Fifteen

Paxson, Alaska

<u>Early Morning - Tuesday September 18, 2001</u>

237 miles northeast of Anchorage as the crow flies, in the tiny outpost of Paxson, Agents Gonzalez and Jameson arrived after a six-hour drive. According to an anonymous tip, two individuals had arrived and were staying at the lodge in Paxson after arriving in a Black Toyota Four-Runner, and had been behaving oddly.

They were described as a very attractive dark-skinned woman and a man who looked to be of Middle-Eastern descent.

Gonzalez pulled up to a gray two-story building that housed a café and a few motel rooms, and parked the inconspicuous black four-door SUV among a couple of pickup trucks, two other SUV's, and three motor homes, but no black Four-Runner.

They scanned the parking lot before opening their vehicle doors. Jameson was the first to set foot onto the gravel parking lot. Gonzalez kept her eyes trained on the door to the café as Jameson stepped in front of the SUV. To ensure utmost visibility, Gonzalez told Jameson it would be best if the two wore the dark blue windbreakers with "FBI" stenciled in yellow all over. The two received a curious look immediately from an older gentleman getting into a Ford F-150 pickup truck.

It was nearly 12:00 noon, and the sunshine made the remote mountain hunting and fishing area comfortably warm. The pollution-free air was refreshing as Gonzalez exited the SUV and the two walked toward the café.

The aroma of frying burgers filled air inside the beat-up door. The two agents made a quick assessment of the patrons of the café. No one fit the description of a dangerous individual, but somehow they'd been led to this place. Because the tip was anonymous, they had no contact here. Gonzalez improvised and flashed her badge to a petite waitress with reddish hair standing behind the 1950's style counter.

She made sure that the customers in the restaurant saw the badge and the firearm on her right hip. Mark followed suit and removed his identification as well.

"Miss, I'm Special Agent Gonzalez with the FBI, and this is my partner Special Agent Jameson. We need to ask you a few questions."

"FBI?"

Mark kept his eyes trained on the waitress while Gonzalez turned to assess the parking lot.

He watched as the waitress, her name tag identifying her as Gina, shifted her hazel eyes uncomfortably while Gonzalez scanned the parking lot. He quietly cleared his throat as he observed Gina's reaction.

Gonzalez returned her gaze to the woman. "Gina, yesterday we received a tip that a couple of people had checked into the lodge here in Paxson in a black Toyota Four-Runner, and were behaving in a very peculiar way." She paused for a moment.

Obviously the parking lot was a source of concern for Gina. Gonzalez probed carefully. "Gina, may I get your last name?"

"Shaffer," The waitress answered.

"Gina, have you noticed anything that would seem odd with any of your customers the last few days?" She purposely turned and scanned the customers in the café.

Gina exhibited no visible ticks or nervous behavior that indicated concern for any customer in the café. "No, Agent Gonzalez, not that I can think of." No hint of a misleading answer. "You might check with Brad, who manages the lodge."

"Just one more question, Gina. You seem very concerned about something in the parking lot?"

"It's nothing, ma'am," Gina said, though clearly she was frightened.

"Gina, I've been doing this for a long time, so I hope you don't mind if I ask. Who are you running from?" Gonzalez asked with a degree of compassion but also professional curiosity.

"No one." Gina answered and again the uncomfortable shift of her eyes shifted down and to the left. She was lying.

"Gina?" Gonzalez said her name with a hint of incredulity.

"Agent Gonzalez, please don't." Gina repeated.

"I wish I could." Gonzalez said. "If you ever need anything, please call this number." Gonzalez handed Gina a business card with her contact information on it, and the two agents headed outside.

Paxson, Alaska

<u>Early Morning - Tuesday September 18, 2001</u>

Just as Gonzalez and Jameson returned to the parking lot, a black Toyota Four-Runner pulled in, its occupants an olive-skinned man and an exotically dark-skinned woman. The driver saw the two agents just as he'd put the vehicle in park, and he calmly tried to put the vehicle in reverse, staring at the two federal agents.

Gonzalez immediately identified the vehicle's license plate - 118 GNP, a Federal vehicle. Firmly and calmly she commanded Jameson, "At all costs, do not discharge your firearm, they're federal agents. But proceed as if hostile."

With weapons drawn, Gonzalez and Jameson pointed their pistols at the two individuals.

"Federal agents! Hands where we can see them!" Gonzalez commanded.

Still seated in the vehicle, the woman and man complied.

"Show us your hands, slowly!" Gonzalez yelled authoritatively. "Now!" she added as the two hesitated a little too long.

The two agents had their weapons squarely trained on the two subjects. The fear in the eyes of the subjects could not be mistaken - they knew better than to move.

"Now!" Gonzalez repeated once again.

They slowly showed their hands.

"Driver, out first with your hands in the air!" Gonzalez ordered. The man complied.

Mark Jameson froze in shock. "But you're-"

"Quiet, Jameson!" Gonzalez barked, as the suspect gave what could have almost been a wink.

"But he's-"

"I'll explain later," Gonzalez said quickly. "Now let's follow procedure.

"Ma'am, out of the vehicle with your hands in the air!" "Both of you slowly to the back of the vehicle, keep those hands up!"

Both complied.

"On your knees!" Gonzalez yelled. Her Glock-22 was pointed right at the woman's head. "Now!" she stated to assert total control.

The woman appeared the less confident of the two. Her gaze showed a genuine fright and almost drugged acquiescence. Gonzalez slowly moved toward the woman after the two had knelt on the ground.

She looked at the woman with the gun pointed right at her vacant brown eyes. The satisfaction was evident in Gonzalez's body language. She and Jameson secured the scene and then the suspects, handcuffing them, reading them their Miranda Rights, and giving a full pat-down search. The arrest and safe scene were a compliment to the United States Government and its training and professionalism.

The confrontation had the intended audience of everyone in the café, as well as a vehicle that had pulled into the parking lot and stopped abruptly, the driver eyeing two people in FBI Windbreakers with their weapons drawn.

Gonzalez and Jameson moved both handcuffed suspects to their black SUV, where Gonzalez placed the male subject in the back seat on the driver's side and Jameson placed the female subject in the back seat on the passenger side.

The black Four-Runner presented a problem - it was purported evidence and needed to be impounded. Paxson was not exactly a prime area for AT&T or Verizon cell towers, so cell coverage was nonexistent.

The SUV's satellite phone was connected to a federal Command Center set up in a large room at a Safe House, but the suspect's presence in the vehicle prohibited a forthright conversation.

Gonzalez instructed Jameson to stay with the subjects and ensure they did not speak to one another. She then walked into the café to inform the customers that all was safe.

She asked Gina to direct her to a private telephone. She placed a call directly to her ASAC's cell phone and received some strange instructions.

Moments later, Gonzalez winked at Gina as she walked out. She hoped Gina would stay safe, and made a mental note to check on her periodically.

Gonzalez and Jameson were essentially prepared for anything – a requirement in their profession- but, this encounter in the middle of nowhere with virtually no backup wasn't covered in any seminars at Quantico.

Gonzalez pulled the vehicle and its four occupants out on the Richardson Highway and drove a few minutes to the north, looking for a pullout. Finding one, she pulled the SUV over and directed Jameson to switch to the driver seat.

Jameson shaking his head, said, "Gonzalez, there's something going on her. You need to know-"

Again she cut him off. "No time, I'll fill you in when we're moving."

Her first task was to remove the handcuffs of the two federal operatives who'd somehow ended up playing a part in a ruse that she'd been instructed not to read Agent Jameson in on until after they'd left Paxson. She walked around to the passenger side of the vehicle, opened the rear right-side passenger door, and proceeded to remove the handcuffs.

The male operative removed a syringe and a 25-gauge needle from a small black leather satchel he had in the pocket of his sport jacket. The knowing look in the dark, eyes of the female agent was met with sympathy but a level of "trust me" on the older agent's face. He slowly pierced the rubber barrier of a vial with the needle and extracted a dose of a drug called Versed, its purpose to knock out the patient and create a period of amnesia.

Jameson pulled the vehicle back onto the highway and began a long drive northward.

Versed is not a drug that can be applied simply by a shot to the arm, it must be administered with an IV. The unidentified federal agent obviously had done it before. He handcuffed the woman's arm to the armrest and set the IV. He then inserted the needle into the IV bag and compressed the syringe of Versed. Within fifteen to twenty seconds, the woman was rendered unconscious.

"Don't worry, we just want her out for a while...not dead. It's not Potassium Chloride." The unidentified agent looked at Gonzalez and Jameson, giving them a bemused smile.

Jameson was still shaking his head as he drove, glancing repeatedly in the rear-view mirror. Gonzalez knew something Jameson did not; the man was one of them – U.S. Intelligence. She'd known it the moment she'd seen the license plate, as 118 GNP had been the indicator of the contact she was to make in Paxson. But she'd been told not to read Jameson in.

"Now, before you make me the next pin cushion, are you not the least bit curious who we are?" The man spoke fluent English. "The intelligence business can be quite the twisted maze sometimes, don't you think? It can be very difficult to tell the good guys from the bad...forgive me, the good person from the bad."

"I appreciate the gender-sensitivity training you've gotten somewhere, but if you're anxious to share who you and your colleague are and who you work for, be our guest," Gonzalez answered, motioning to the woman who lay unconscious in the rear right-side passenger seat.

"And keep in mind, we both are pretty good at smelling bullshit from a mile away." Gonzalez gestured toward Jameson at the wheel.

"I have no interest in lying to you..." The man was a little over sixty years old, dark, distinguished and handsome. But the man's most distinct characteristic was his unwavering confidence. It was in his voice and in his oddly familiar dark brown eyes that held a steely focus on Gonzalez's own.

He continued, "I can now explain this charade," he paused for effect. "Agent Gonzalez and Agent Jameson." "How do you know our names?" She asked. In most circles, the identities of FBI agents are not easily attained. "Who are you?"

Beside her, Mark Jameson insanely started laughing. "I have no idea what the hell is going on, Gonzalez, but that's my dad, Robert Jameson."

Chapter Sixteen

Just Outside of Paxson, Alaska
<u>Late Afternoon - Tuesday September 18, 2001</u>

Agent Gonzalez stared at Mark, who was still laughing as he pulled the Suburban off the side of the road. He turned around to face his father in the backseat. "Now would be a good time to fill us in, dad. "It seems you're a bit more than just an author, huh?"

His father had been direct his entire life, so his quick response didn't surprise Mark one iota, but the content sure did. "I'm CIA, Son." His dad took a slight breath and then continued as if they were having Thanksgiving dinner and talking about their golf games. "I've been with the Company since 1972."

The year 1972 caught Mark off-guard. His dad had been a spy since Mark was in the first grade!

"So, you've kept this hidden not only from your family but from me, your son who is an FBI agent?" His tone was annoyed, but with a hint of professional respect. Being in the secretive world of the FBI, he had a healthy understanding of how the intelligence world operated. After all of these years, why now?"

"I'm a part of something we call the Shadow Squad. And 9/11 has me working quite a bit."

"Sir, I've never heard of it." Gonzalez joined the conversation. "Agent Gonzalez, I'm very impressed by how quickly you assessed the situation back there and determined that I am U.S. Intelligence. Very nice work." The man in back offered.

They were still parked on the side of the road, and Mark decided they should keep heading south, as they had five plus hours to get back to Anchorage.

As the Suburban got up to fifty-five, he jumped back in. "The Shadow Squad - sounds a little Hollywood to me."

His dad gave that deep laugh he remembered as a kid, and then he cleared his throat. "That was kind of the whole intent, if for some reason it was ever sniffed out by the media or a snooping Senate Intelligence Committee - the program's name would make it sound…well,, inept and lacking credibility."

"You're right." Mark's honest sarcasm couldn't stay in check.

"Son, the program's name was my idea."

Agent Gonzalez looked at Mark and laughed. "Nice job, partner."

Mark adjusted his sunglasses with his middle finger - giving Gonzalez the bird - and got another laugh out of her. It was then that Mark noticed the tiny mole on her right cheek just to the middle of her nose.

Agent Gonzalez allowed a nearly invisible smile to form in her dark brown eyes as she noted the extra moment Mark had taken looking at her.

Well then, he's got good taste. But sadly, the moment was short-lived; fraternization among FBI agents was highly discouraged.

And when the two had first met seven or eight hours earlier at Mark's hotel, she'd noted the furtive glance he'd given to the buxom blond who'd jogged by when they'd walked onto the street.

And there was the little matter of the Spook in the back seat.

"Sir..." She realized she was showing too much deference to her partner's father - "...let's see, 1972 and the Company. Let me guess, you had some role in Watergate?"

There was absolutely no "tell" on Robert Jameson's face. If he'd played any role in either the cover-up or the uncovering of that infamous period in U.S. History, he wasn't going to disclose that fact in any visible or verbal way.

Gonzalez looked at her FBI partner for any help he might be able to provide - given the man was his father. She sensed Mark taking her cue as he jumped in.

"Dad, we're either in or we're not. Trust us or don't." Mark's tone at the moment was exactly what she'd hoped for - FBI agent first, son second.

Mark was no match for his father: Robert's silence was deafening. For the moment, he was spook first and father second.

The next five minutes were painfully silent as the FBI Suburban moved at a good clip, proceeding south on the Richardson Highway toward Anchorage, each agent oblivious to the infinite and beautiful bounty of mountainous terrain outside the vehicle's dark, tinted windows.

<u>Around Ten PM - Tuesday September 18, 2001</u>

The two FBI agents and their cargo of an intelligence operative and a woman whose identity was yet to be revealed arrived in Anchorage late on the Tuesday one week after 9/11 had occurred.

The drive from Paxson had lasted almost six hours. Robert Jameson revealing his identity and his purpose had broken the ice. He, Special Agent

Gonzalez, and Special Agent Jameson discussed 9/11, why Gonzalez had joined the FBI, and other general intelligence matters.

When the discussion got around to the heavily-sedated woman in the back seat next to Robert, the conversation came to a screeching halt.

The confines of the vehicle were silent for at least fifteen minutes. Gonzalez and Jameson obviously were not meant to be read-in just yet on what they'd just been a part of.

When the conversation finally resumed, the origins of the Shadow Squad, its purpose, and its type of recruits were the core subject.

In the middle of the conversation, Robert received a call on a small Nokia cell phone. Unbeknownst to the two FBI agents, the phone call would take Robert halfway around the world.

North of Anchorage, Alaska

Late Afternoon Thursday September 20, 2001

The rest of the road trip between Paxson and Anchorage was one of those rare, memorable moments life sends a person's way. Listening to his father talk about something as bizarre as the world of espionage and his role in a highly covert organization (complete with highly cliché name) was disconcerting.

The conversation put something into perspective that now made a whole lot of sense. Hindsight, as they say, is twenty-freaking-twenty.

It was in the early 1980's. Life was good, sixteen years old and Mark was lucky enough to have been chosen along with four high school classmates to attend a leadership conference in Washington, D.C.

He met up with a few girls from the state of Florida, and they somehow snuck our way into a Georgetown bar.

They must have had the look of college students, because they had no problem whatsoever being served drink after drink. They closed down the bar around two in the morning and found their way back to our hotel.

For a good number of years, he thought he'd gotten away with Georgetown until a few days after he graduated from college. Graduation day was predictably euphoric, but what his dad shared when they were having a beer at the Up & Up Bar a few days later caught Mark off-guard.

The Up & Up is just a little hole in the wall, but it has great beer on tap, a comfortable busyness to it, and cute bar staff.

Somewhere in the midst of a great conversation, a look that only a father has in his arsenal shot itself across the tiny bar table. To this day, Mark had never forgotten it.

"Son, do you remember the trip you took to Georgetown back in '82?"

Mark replied that of course he did. As soon as he heard the word "Georgetown, "he knew he was in trouble - well, not trouble in the sense obviously that he would be grounded, but in the sense that he hadn't nearly been as sneaky or as cool as he thought he'd been.

Back then, Mark hadn't really thought about how his dad had knowledge of his teenage escapade in Georgetown, but on that day in 2001, riding with dad and Agent Gonzalez - Georgetown made perfect sense.

Who knows what method was used, but his dad undoubtedly had measures in place, when Mark was younger and not nearly wise enough, to monitor his son's goings-on.

Late Afternoon Friday September 21, 2001

Twenty-four hours after Robert Jameson's revelation to the two FBI agents along the Richardson Highway bound for Anchorage, Mark was on his way home to Seattle, Gonzalez was home relaxing with her Golden Retriever Rex, and Robert Jameson and his mysterious guest were aboard a Lear Jet bound for who knows where.

And it would be several months before any of the three federal agents would be in each other's presence again.

Robert Jameson though had already completed the first part of his latest assignment the moment he'd disclosed to Agent Gonzalez and his son, that he was a member of an elite unit known as the Shadow Squad.

Chapter Seventeen

Strangnas, Sweden

<u>Sometime Just After Midnight - Wednesday April 17, 2002</u>

It had been more than thirty years since Robert Jameson lost his mother, and yet in his mind, in his heart, and in his dreams over and over, it was like it was happening all over again.

Robert's life was a dichotomy on so many levels. He was a bestselling author, a man who'd done necessary things for his country, and a good father who'd raised two successful children- Mark and Alexis. All the same, he was a man haunted over and over by the dream he'd just had. The dream returned often.

Not a fan of psychiatrists, counselors, or the clergy, Robert had never chosen to share the visitation of the date his mother passed. Strangely, the recurring dreams never revealed anything more than the pain he felt when his mother's airplane collided with a mountain-side. But the dream brought back tales from his childhood and that place he called home.

Home wasn't the cabin nestled in the dune grass along the river three miles from the mouth of the great Pacific Ocean. Nor was it the three-bedroom, two-story domicile literally etched into the rocky hillside in what the locals call downtown.

For the man, home was the warmth he felt in his blood when he touched the sand or felt a cool northerly breeze invisibly caress his cheeks. And it was riding in the bed of the old green Chevy pickup through the century-old stand of Sitka Spruce trees that sheltered the forest floor from the area's infamous torrential rains that he found soothing and familiar.

His grandfather had told him countless stories describing the mysterious powers of the thick Alaska forest, and he'd listened with rapt attention. There was the tale of the man who insisted he'd seen his wife at the edge of the woods, only to learn she'd passed away hours earlier. He followed her silhouette into the dense forest and was never seen again. A deeper and more mystical legend passed its way down from generation to generation:

A family was beachcombing along the pale yellow sand on a nameless stretch of beach along the massive Pacific Ocean. As they combed the beach for treasures such as a glass float used in the early 1900's on commercial fishing net's or uniquely beautiful pieces of driftwood, they encountered a furry brown land otter with a light prance to its step, sauntering along the beach. Its footprints were not that of a small animal, but much like those a full-grown man or a much larger carnivore. The imprints in the sand, like the impression of bear claws, seemed almost alive. And the hind portion looked like that of a man's heel.

As the footprints neared the edge of the forest, the mother and father instructed their two young children to turn their eyes to the ocean. Legend says to those who follow the footprints to the forest's edge, "Beware, a soul the land otter must take." The legend further goes that those whose eyes follow the path of the land otter beyond the edge of the forest will be lost.

The mother held her children's hands tight as she turned her beautiful, soft brown eyes upon those of her mate. The father's dark eyes said it all - the land otter would not leave without at least one soul.

He turned his eyes on the forest and allowed his gaze to affix itself on the mossy, damp floor carpeted with thousands of pine needles. His heart was beating fast with fear and foreboding as he took knowing steps toward the heavy hanging branches of Sitka Spruce and red cedar trees.

The mother and the two children continued their walk to the safety of the beach's edge. Suddenly, a great wave crashed upon the shore and carried the three to the forest's edge. The water receded, and the footprints were gone.

Mother and children arose and stood at the forest's edge, screaming and pleading for mate and father, but he was gone.

Robert's grandfather had told him the tale when he was a young boy, and he'd never forgotten. For some reason, he'd never shared that tale with his children, and he had the strange feeling that he needed to.

His thoughts were focused upon the tale of the land otter stealing the father's soul. Memory was returning him to rainy night, in his youth, somewhere on the edge of that leafy green, mossy forest, the world where hidden and mysterious power took hold. It seemed so innocent at the time, but years later when he looked back on the moment, he would know the painful truth: the moment was anything but.

He'd been sitting on a sandy beach nestled against a tall alder tree, tossing stones in a myriad of colors aimlessly against driftwood from far-off lands. Though it wasn't a land otter's footprints leading him astray, his soul was caught in a war between the release of forgiveness and the stranglehold of bitterness. Now so many years later, he realized that through his being ran the lure of the Land Otter.

It wasn't anything mystical - he hadn't done a Ghost Dance like those of the Sioux Indian or a War Chant like the Makah of Northwest Washington – but he had come close to placing the harm of evil upon a decent human being. And the person he'd felt such deplorable for was certainly nothing more than an ordinary human being, a school teacher who'd simply scolded him for speaking his native language.

He hadn't cursed her with physical harm, nor had he wished her ill will, but everything in his being felt that unhealthy thirst for revenge. Robert realized somewhere in his spirit that had he released his deep hate into the wind, the teacher would have encountered immeasurable harm.

As a teenager, that first impulse was held in check; however, the dream this time had met its mark. He felt it.

He rose from his hotel bed and walked to the window. Off in the distance, the six wooden appendages of a red windmill spun gently in a light breeze. The day was sunny and bright. Were it not for the chill in the air and the yellowish leaves on the trees, he'd have thought it were the middle of the summer.

Stealing a page from another man's playbook, he broke the dream down into a list.

Why was he having this dream? There was a haunting feeling that another soul needed something here in the living world to be settled?

What would need to be settled? His dream always returned to one moment.

Another was for searching for rest and peace?

Was it because he'd killed, were their souls the ones haunting him?

"Mother, please help me let you go," He whispered into the empty hotel room.

His father's tale fought desperately for attention, but the fight was a lost cause. As the sunlight cascaded across the Swedish sky, he searched the blue and prayed for those haunted souls. He took a deep breath and let the feeling pass but only to be saved for another time. He was in Sweden for one reason - duty called, and at present he had no time for such a distraction.

He'd killed the "who" behind the downing of his mother's plane, but after all of these years he still had no clue as to the "why."

Upstate New York
<u>Evening - Wednesday April 17, 2002</u>

Across the Pacific Ocean in a nameless forest of pines and spruce in Upstate New York, the third generation Chief Executive Officer (CEO) of Honeycutt Petroleum Corporation encountered a haunting blast of wind as he sat on his dark wooden deck.

Unlike the haunted man, Jacob Honeycutt lived his life rarely thinking of the past. Most would feel regret, remorse, or maybe even a true sense of guilt for what they'd done in life, but not Jacob. Each day was simply moving on to the next financial conquest. But very much like the haunted man, the souls who'd perished on Alaska Airlines 1866 thirty years earlier were searching him out, begging for release for the sins of his father, Myles Honeycutt.

A strange, cold, ghastly feeling took hold of him. Powers and forces stronger than him, were orchestrating the unveiling of the truth behind Honeycutt

Petroleum's gaudy wealth. Unknown to him, Jacobs' haunted feelings were in concert with Karma and its pursuit of redemption for his father's sins - in play several thousand miles away.

Anchorage, Alaska

<u>Wednesday April 24, 2002</u>

"This is Miranda Mathis. As you can see behind me, the Anchorage Fire Department is battling a major fire. We're out near the Dimond Mall. At this time, we're not aware if there were any people inside the structure when it caught fire ,or if there are people still inside." The perky strawberry blond reporter provided her report for the Anchorage ABC affiliate.

It was around seven in the evening, and two battalions of the Anchorage Fire Department had responded to the fire at a small office complex about six miles south of downtown Anchorage. Two hours later, with the fire out and investigators on-scene, the ABC affiliate pulled Miranda off the story and sent her home for the evening. Little did they know that the fire department would unearth a story much bigger than a building ablaze.

<u>Three Days Later</u>

"This is Miranda Mathis. We're back at the scene of a fire we covered a few days ago. As you can see behind me, what used to be an office complex is now charred rubble. The fire, however, is not the story here."

She paused for a moment as the camera zoomed in on the building that resembled a fire pit.

"There is yellow police tape surrounding the entire building. According to the Anchorage Police Department, skeletal remains were found in the building, and information we've received from the medical examiner's office indicates the cause of death is not tied to the fire."

The camera panned back out to provide a full profile view of the attractive reporter with the building as a backdrop.

"No other information is being released at this time by Anchorage Police or the Medical Examiner, but we'll be following this story as it continues."

<u>Four Thousand Miles Away, Same Day</u>

The haunted feelings Jacob had encountered at his Upstate New York home hadn't escaped his being even as he'd flown in the Honeycutt Petroleum Gulf Stream IV the next morning from Syracuse to Houston, Texas.

But seated at the original mahogany desk his father Myles and his grandfather John Jacob had used when they served as CEO, Jacob was all business, reading through a quarterly financial report one of his accounting staff had provided.

Honeycutt Petroleum Corporation at the time was number two in the world behind Exxon in terms of gross revenues, net profits, and crude oil production. It wasn't a fluke that the company had become so successful. Jacob didn't have an off-switch, and most who encountered him, either in his personal or his professional life, would describe him as competitive, go-for-broke, and intense. Very few would consider themselves to be a part of his inner circle, but the man in his late fifties entering the office was probably his most trusted associate.

"Adam, what's up?" Jacob asked the man with graying blond hair, who despite his age looked military-fit, with broad shoulders, a chiseled profile, and a perpetual natural light tan.

Normally, Adam Ross would not show up on the CEO's 45th-floor office unannounced. Ross worked five floors below his boss's top-floor suite in the Honeycutt Petroleum Tower in downtown Houston, Texas.

But this was different. A fire a few days earlier in Anchorage, Alaska, had gotten his attention.

He and Jacob's father, thirty years earlier, had leased three offices in complex in an area of Anchorage that was just beginning to grow. Now the area was metropolitan; the area had become home to the Dimond Shopping Mall and a host of residential neighborhoods and mini malls.

"We've got a very big problem."

Jacob looked at his Chief of Security. He was taken aback; Ross had an ashen-white look on his face. "Adam, you look like you've seen a ghost." As cliché as it sounded, it was apropos. "What's wrong?"

"Joshua Knight..."

Jacob swallowed hard, his Adam's Apple almost choking the next breath. The name was one of the few that could provoke fear. He didn't say a word as Ross continued.

"They've found his remains."

Jacob was speechless for a few moments. He'd never guessed this would ever happen. Finally he cleared his throat.

"Have they identified him yet?"

"No, but they will. We need to prepare for that possibility."

"You and my father were very cautious. I don't see how they can ID him." Despite his initial fear, Jacob masked his concern with a sense of false confidence that the authorities would not be able to identify Joshua Knight's remains.

Another ten minutes, and the conversation concluded with a directive to Ross to keep him fully informed as events transpired in Alaska.

Alone again, Jacob leaned back in his chair and stared out across the Gulf of Mexico. It had been thirty years. As far as he knew, there were only two men living who knew what had truly happened - and both had just been in this 45th floor office.

Only Ross knew there was another man, Phillip Black, who had been a purported pawn and perished with his wife aboard Alaska Airlines 1866.

What Jacob's father, along with Ross and a man named Rico Sanchez, had orchestrated was an incredible fraud against the United States and the Natives of Alaska. It all started back in 1970, when Myles Honeycutt had first encountered a young man named Joshua Knight.

Jacob had a sneaking suspicion that once they ID the remains as those of Joshua Knight, Honeycutt Petroleum's days might be numbered and any means necessary, should be taken to prevent that.

Chapter Eighteen

Cabo San Lucas, Mexico
<u>Early Evening - Friday May 3, 2002</u>

Between a day-long fishing trip, a scuba excursion, and a couple of rounds of golf - the last five days had been well-earned and thoroughly enjoyed downtime for the operative. Deeply tanned and mildly relaxed, wearing khakis and a white Bermuda Shirt, he strolled into Sammy Hagar's Cabo Wabo and ordered a Corona, prepared to continue the downtime enjoyment.

It didn't last.

The vibration of his cell phone brought it all to an end. There was no asking how the vacation was going, no apology for the interruption, nada.

"Anchorage, Alaska. Ronald Johns." The voice said nothing more. Instructions that only stated a name were simple - the subject was to be killed.

The operative finished the Corona and ordered another. The downtime, as usual, was never long enough. He had no idea who Ronald Johns was, but something felt strange for the second time in less than a year. And for the second time in a year, instinct was engaged.

Chapter Nineteen

Seattle, Washington
<u>Late Morning - Saturday May 4, 2002</u>

It had been more than eight months since Mark Jameson's surreal ride from Paxson, Alaska, to Anchorage with his father and Agent Sandra Gonzalez. He hadn't seen her again in that entire span of time. The Seattle office was surprisingly quiet, the antithesis of the organized, yet frenetic pace that previously had a stranglehold on their FBI team months earlier, after the 9/11 attacks.

ASAC Branson approached Mark's desk, clearly with an unwelcome assignment. Mark knew his boss well enough by now to know that Branson honestly regretted some of his orders. The men and women under his command were some of the best law enforcement personnel on the planet, which he openly acknowledged, also admitting that there were times when the expectations - both in terms of workload and dedication to their vocation and country - were almost unrealistic.

Mark was going to Alaska again, the next day, a direct request from FBI Director Terrell Archer. Either Mark was in the Director's crosshairs, or there was something about Mark no one was talking about.

The assignment had nothing to do with the 9/11 events. It seemed a few weeks earlier, they'd found the skeletal remains of a guy named Joshua Knight in a building that had burned down.

Mark was sure the boss wondered what he was doing in the office on a Saturday. He'd been out of the town most of the previous week, so he stretched the truth a bit and indicated he was doing research on a case. He really had no reason to be in the office on a Saturday morning; the weather was terrific, the sky was a deep blue, and the mercury on the thermometer was predicted to top out at seventy-eight. But the "Shadow Squad" once more had piqued his interest. It had been several months since Mark and Agent Gonzalez had been clued in by his father that the organization existed.

The last seven months had had plenty going on - 9/11, some RICO cases, some white-collar stuff, and even a bank robbery or two had kept him busy. But today he'd woken up early and decided to go to the office and engage in a little research project. It was the most futile he'd ever encountered.

A few calls to some contacts with the CIA and a Navy Seal buddy produced nada. All Google turned up was something about a TV show back in the 1950's featuring a guy who'd started his own crime-fighting agency.

Maybe Mark's dad was just full of B.S., but he knew better. There was no doubt the Shadow Squad existed, but their mission, whatever it might be, was a well-kept secret.

Seattle, Washington

Early Afternoon - Saturday May 4, 2002

Mark had had the dream again - the one with the bully beating the shit out of him on the Vienna, Virginia, playground, so he'd awoken feeling very strange, like there was something odd on the horizon. For whatever reason, he'd always had a sixth sense, of premonition; he couldn't describe what was going to happen, but could sense something in the air the way animals can sense an impending earthquake.

His mother had told him on more than one occasion that when he was three, he stood at the door of his grandparent's cabin on the Lost River in Yakutat for ten minutes, waiting for his grandfather to come back from the fishing nets. His dad had noticed and asked how long he'd been at the door, and his mom told him that despite her persistent requests, Mark wouldn't budge.

His dad headed back down to the fishing nets about a quarter of a mile from the cabin and found his grandfather William with a messy wound to his forehead.

Soon they were back in the cabin, Mark's mom and my grandmother taking care of a deep gash in his forehead. He'd fallen after a minor version of a rogue wave – approximately eight feet – had struck his sixteen-foot skiff while he was tending to his net at the convergence of the Lost River and the Gulf of Alaska.

Mark could still see them dressing the wound with cotton swabs and soap from a white basin. His grandpa's 63-year-old face showed the telltale signs of a life spent working in the elements-sun, rain, sleet, and snow. But, man, he was a handsome guy, like Mark's father. Robert had confided, many years later over shared beers that he wondered if his half-Caucasian, half-Tlingit son had inherited the special Tlingit connection with nature.

Mark couldn't imagine a higher compliment than to be told he'd inherited his grandfather's gift. He'd loved that man more than anyone in the world, and even now as he recalled those early days, he was tearing up missing him.

Mark's thoughts of the past were interrupted when SA Dani Westford walked up to his desk.

"Hey there, what are you doing here? I figured you'd be out golfing," Dani teased. "You're either concentrating on something important or you're constipated."

"Hi, Dani. Until an hour ago I was just catching up on some paperwork, but now I'm getting ready for a trip to Anchorage. I'm heading out in the morning." He glanced at the computer screen, hoping it didn't reveal anything about what he was looking into. "And I'll ask you the same thing. It's a beautiful Saturday, so what are you doing here? Hiding out from all your admirers?" Dani's dark brown eyes, jet black hair, and nice build, with her brains and drive would make her a catch for the right guy.

She shrugged, "How's your love life?"

They hadn't talked in a couple of weeks, since she'd just gotten back from a two-week assignment on the East Coast.

Was she flirting? "It's pretty slow right now," Mark said with sad honesty. "…how about you?"

"Just a couple of dates, but definitely nothing to write home about."

"So how come we've never hooked up?" Mark asked jokingly. Well, not totally, but he and Dani, despite their close protective relationship, were more like brother and sister.

"You've never asked." Dani had a smirk on her face. That kind of attraction for them both just wasn't there.

"So, you want a ride to the airport?" She asked.

"I'd love one. We haven't talked in a while." Mark answered with a smile and added, "So what are you working on that has you here on a Saturday?"

"I have to meet with Nancy Gault early Monday morning on a RICO case she's trying to plead out, so I'll be back here tomorrow." Dani was referring to the Assistant United States Attorney.

Dani and Mark had been assigned several cases together, but lately she'd been assigned quite a bit to suspected or potential domestic-terrorism cases, while Mark had stayed with white-collar. But Dani still had a few cases on the desks of various Assistant U.S. Attorneys.

Mark had just caught the Joshua Knight case and hadn't a clue why. Murder usually isn't in the FBI's repertoire unless the decedent is a federal employee or on federal land, but Mark was just a worker-bee, so he was doing as he was told.

Mark looked at his watch-2:05pm. He needed to go home and pack for the four-day trip to Anchorage, Alaska, but he had something more imperative on his mind.

Time enough to pack and get in a good run. Within fifteen minutes, he was heading southbound on Interstate Five in his Jetta with the sunroof wide open.

He turned on his CD player, he hit slot three, and waited for Pete Townsend's "Let My Love Open the Door" to come to life. Despite a job that demanded a high degree of professionalism and decorum, he thoroughly enjoyed jumping into his car and singing along to songs of the 80's, 90's, and early 2000's. There was a nice peace that went along with songs like "Something

Happened on the Way to Heaven" by Phil Collins, "Walk This Way" by Aerosmith, and Bon Jovi's "Livin' on a Prayer." While the life of an FBI Agent could be highly diverse, challenging, and some might say fascinating, a day in the life of an FBI Agent was much like those of anyone else – it was a job with headaches, the long days when he found himself irritated with the boss, and the never-ending to-do list. Music was his solace away from the office, along with golf and rock climbing.

As Mark drove south past Boeing Field, the music helped, but even on a beautiful, warm Saturday afternoon the bully pummeling him in his dream had him on edge.

He pulled into the garage of his Tukwila condo, and with his laptop and briefcase in hand he scaled the stairs two steps at a time to the fifth floor. Ten or fifteen minutes later, he was on South Center Parkway jogging and getting admiring glances from a few female drivers as well a male driver or two. At least he hoped the female glances the female glances were admiring. A pair of Iron Mans dimmed the bright late afternoon sun as he jogged along, listening to Chicago, No Doubt, The Police, and Bob Seger along the way. He found a boost of adrenaline and a second wind with Chicago's "Stay the Night." Out in the open air, he felt full of life and was thankful to God for what he'd been given. Little did he know that for the first time in his career, his life was in danger.

Chapter Twenty

Tukwila, Washington

<u>Mid Afternoon - Saturday May 4, 2002</u>

The day kept getting better and better.

Mark's cell phone vibrated, and despite a deep-seated desire, he couldn't ignore the damn thing. The caller ID read "Anonymous."

"Hello." Despite the fact that he had just stopped mid-run, his breath was calm within seconds.

On the other end of the line was a voice he did not recognize - a very sultry female voice.

"SA Jameson, my name is Lindsay Drummond. I am like you, a federal employee. Someone has decided that they want me to keep tabs on you." The woman's voice was serene but at the same time highly authoritative as she gave the SA acronym for Special Agent. "May I call you Mark?"

"For the time being, you can call me Agent Jameson." He answered. He was shocked, intrigued, and perturbed. "Ms. Drummond, how did you get my number?"

"We have a common denominator, Agent Jameson. You're working the Joshua Knight case, and it is on our radar screen as well." Her voice was determined and feminine at the same time. And she didn't answer the question.

"Who?" Mark played dumb; his family sometimes teased that he did that very well. "I don't recognize that name."

"Agent Jameson, please don't insult my intelligence. We both know that you are investigating the murder of Joshua Knight."

"Ms. Drummond, what is the point of this little chat?" Mark asked; annoyed but intrigued.

"I'm sure you've heard the term intelligence chatter?" She paused to let the strange question sink in. Intelligence chatter was a media-driven phrase, defining information agencies such as the Central Intelligence Agency, the National Security Agency, and a host of other three-letter acronym agencies gather intercepting telephone calls, e-mails, and the like.

"The name Joshua Knight has been popping up. And now, so has the name Jameson..." After a pause had Mark's rapt attention, she continued, "...and we're not sure why." She'd sounded so confident until that last little comment.

"You're not giving me a warm fuzzy feeling at all. How about we start over?" Mark interjected.

A hint of a laugh on the other end of the line. "That's why we're keeping tabs on you," she said calmly.

Mark had not a clue what else to say but keeping his mouth shut had never been his strength, so what followed was the first moronic thing that came to mind. "No offense, but you sound more like mall security...So, again I'm not getting a warm, fuzzy feeling with you keeping tabs on me. I think I'm fine all by myself."

"You're not getting rid of me with some junior high jabs, Agent Jameson. We'll be in touch. By the way, don't let it go to your head, but you're a good-looking guy."

Taken aback by that last one, Mark scanned the surroundings to determine if someone was watching him. He was now more than intrigued and found it almost comical-this woman who says she's a Fed was hitting on him - *Our federal dollars at work.*

Saturday May 4, 2002

After Mark got home, he wolfed down a McDonald's double cheeseburger, no onions, a large fry, an Alaskan Amber, and a huge chocolate chip cookie. He wasn't planning to work for Chippendales.

He melted into a papa san chair and threw an authentic leather NAIA College football toward his ten-foot ceiling, thinking hard about the conversation with Lindsay Drummond.

What did she mean that his name had been popping up on the intelligence grid?

He decided he needed a distraction and plugged in the movie "Contact" as he popped some buttery popcorn.

Seattle, Washington
Sunday May 5, 2002

Mark seemed to be caught up in something that might or might not be a threat to national security. Dani dropped him off at SeaTac around 8:15 on Sunday morning. His flight was departing from a gate at the end of the D Concourse and it was a good long walk from the ticket counters to the security area and then out to the concourse. He stopped at a Starbuck's for a 16-ounce Green Tea and a chocolate chip muffin, then scoped out a comfortable locale at the flight gate to people watch. Well, it wasn't just to people watch- he was an FBI agent. At the Academy and day-to-day on the job, they provided in-depth training on assessing and gaining acute awareness of surroundings.

Like most gate areas, it was relatively easy to gain a vantage point to observe the passengers. It had simply become a force of habit. Mark purposely waited until the aircraft was completely boarded before he began to make his way toward the gray-walled jet-way.

Waiting provided the opportunity to assess the majority of the passengers who'd boarded the flight, and since he was a red-blooded heterosexual male, the lovely ladies of Washington State had his undivided attention as they walked by. A truly stunning woman arrived just as the gate agent made the last call for all to board.

The woman was mid-to-late 30's, with sandy-blond hair, soft white skin, and ocean-blue eyes. She was wearing an ivory blouse that was doing its best to disguise a very curvaceous torso and dark slacks that accentuated her full hips and athletic legs. She was disarmingly beautiful. It wasn't just her gorgeous eyes or her alluring figure; there was something about the way she carried herself that had Mark's rapt attention.

She boarded ahead of him and sat down in seat 1A in First Class. Mark smiled as he walked by, but she didn't seem to notice. He was seated in coach right behind First Class, seat 6F. Amazing how something as simple as a number can define our place in life.

Over Southeast Alaska

<u>Sunday May 5, 2002</u>

The day before, ASAC Branson had not only told Mark he was heading to Alaska, but had provided some very detailed background information that he'd set aside until now. Taking advantage of the legroom and the conspicuously empty seats in 6E and 6D, he was ready to fully engage in the reason he was headed back to Alaska.

Joshua Knight.

Opening the Day-Timer to a blank letter-size page, he captured a few key facts from Branson's document.

The first entries were rather simple, but so began one of the biggest federal cases ever, though strangely enough, it had never made *Time Magazine*, the *Wall Street Journal*, or the *Washington Post* - not even a two-paragraph blurb.

<u>Sunday May 5, 2002</u>

- ✓ *May 5, 2002 - SA Jameson assigned via request from ASAC Branson to a case in Anchorage, Alaska.*
- ✓ *Subject: Skeletal remains found in a burned-out building near Diamond Shopping Mall. Remains are those of a man named Joshua Knight.*
- ✓ *Federal jurisdiction rationale: According to NTSB database, Joshua Knight perished aboard Alaska Airlines Flight 1866 in September 1971.*
- ✓ *SA Jameson Note: Need to disclose personal connection to this case - see bullet #3 (my grandmother was also aboard that flight).*

The National Transportation Safety Board was responsible for the investigation of his grandmother's downed aircraft and had listed Joshua Knight as one of the passengers who'd perished aboard the flight.

It was the last two entries that had the hairs on his neck at full attention - did Branson know this when he'd sent Mark to Alaska, or was this just an awful coincidence?

Seated in 6F, Mark finally put aside his notes and watched as the landscape of Alaska came to life. The Boeing 737-400 had just passed 15,325 foot Mount Fairweather, a snowy-white peak nestled in one of the narrowest geographical locales in the state. If one were to look at a map of this part of Alaska, one could see that just thirty miles of United States territory separates the country of Canada from the great expanse of the Pacific Ocean.

Just a few minutes ahead, at 35,000-feet Mark's flight would be passing over his summer stomping grounds of Yakutat, Alaska. He'd requested a window seat on the right side of the aircraft, specifically to enjoy the view he'd known since he was a kid. The coast of Western Canada and Southeast Alaska, with the mountains and the Pacific Ocean, provided a peace he couldn't adequately describe.

His portable CD player was playing Larry Greene's "Through the Fire" from the "Top Gun" soundtrack, and he felt a little amped up. The majestic scenery he was soaking in and the exchange with the mysterious Lindsay the day before also helped set his mood.

The tan-colored sandy beaches below held his rapt attention as the flight cruised over Alaska's coastline at approximately 480 miles per hour. He was a little embarrassed to admit that even at nearly 37-years old he was still captivated by flying.

His attention was suddenly diverted as the stunning woman from seat 1A sat down in vacant seat 6D, the aisle seat nearest him. His heart was beating like a rocker's drum.

He pressed the "stop" button on the CD player and removed his headphones, laying them on his lap.

"Hello, Mark." The woman smiled. "Lindsay Drummond." She extended her hand, and as Mark took it he felt the slightest electricity of an emotional connection.

She looked at his hands; they were in a reactionary posture. "Please relax, because I promise you we are on the same team."

Mark's hand posture did not relax, but not because he felt threatened. He'd never seen anyone so beautiful. His voice box had shut down. He'd already felt something the night before on the telephone, an attraction that he couldn't describe, and now seeing her in person, she was intoxicating.

"This is not exactly subtle surveillance." He finally managed, trying for cool.

"I'm nothing if not direct," she said smiling. "We still don't have specifics on why your name is on the grid." She seemed to have a sincerely apologetic look in her clear blue eyes.

"No offense, but I'm not holding my breath." Mark reciprocated her directness.

She paused. "I'm not authorized to be anything more than an intermediary. Call it quasi-surveillance at this point, Agent Jameson. My main job is to keep tabs on you."

The aroma of her perfume was lulling Mark to let down his guard. Despite her buttoned-up outfit, everything about her was sensuous.

Mark braced himself. "Can you at least tell me who in our government wants to keep tabs on me?"

The awkward silence answered the question.

"That's alright, Ms. Drummond. Probably not a fair question."

"Please call me Lindsay."

"Lindsay it is. I shouldn't put you on the spot...at least not yet...but I can't resist. My guess is you're a spook...either Puzzle Palace or The Company," he said quietly, ensuring the two passengers in the seats behind them did not hear. "If I'm right, you owe me dinner sometime." He couldn't help flirting with her.

He'd referred to the National Security Agency, also known as "The Fort" or the "Puzzle Palace," which ran operations overseas, but the rules had changed somewhat after 9/11. And the Central Intelligence Agency, known in certain circles as "The Company," definitely had parameters not to operate inside our own borders. Sometimes agents tended to forget those parameters.

"Need to know." Lindsay's teasing voice laid a hint. The CIA loved the term "need to know."

Mark turned and stared out the window. The 737-400 was just passing over Yakutat, and the day was crystal clear. He was torn: Lindsay or Yakutat from 35,000 feet?

Tara Lynn Collins, the blue-eyed drop-dead gorgeous flight attendant he'd met when he was just a kid had set the bar very high for every woman he'd met since. Now Tara Lynn Collins had just become the runner-up in life's beauty pageant.

Lindsay won his undivided attention. He would have liked to say it was the angle that she worked in the intelligence business, but that wasn't close. She clearly knew her effect on Mark. There was a smile in her ocean-blue, almost turquoise, eyes that was saying thank you. So the tough, direct exterior had a bit of vulnerability?

Since they couldn't discuss federal business, they moved to small talk. He was hoping she wasn't professionally lying, but she indicated she'd never been to Anchorage. She asked a variety of questions about Alaska, and Mark was happy to describe the attractions of the landscape and the people.

After they'd taken a verbal journey of the 49th state, he wanted to know some key facts about this gorgeous woman.

He chose to follow her lead in directness and asked if she was seeing anyone. Her answer gave his heart hope.

Lindsay arose and said that they'd be in touch. As she returned to her seat, he rose from his seat to stretch. He knew he needed to slow things down.

"Mark, take it one play at a time, and the game'll take care of itself." Coach Cashman back in high school had barked at every practice. Mark was his starting tailback, pushed day in and day out. The constant reinforcement had seemed so annoying at the time, but now seemed so germane. He made a mental note to thank Coach Cashman if he ever saw him again.

Chapter Twenty-One

Somewhere over the Gulf of Alaska
<u>Sunday May 5, 2002</u>

From the left side of the aircraft, the vast expanse of the Gulf of Alaska looked endless. The faint impression of white caps could be seen, evidence of strong winds at work below. Those same strong winds were at work at 37,000 feet as Lindsay Drummond watched her glass of Merlot lightly shift on the tray table. Moments earlier, the cockpit crew had announced some moderate turbulence ahead.

Lindsay removed the glass of Merlot from the tray table and enjoyed a modest taste. She allowed herself to feel something she hadn't experienced in a long time, if ever.

During the few minutes yesterday on the cell phone with Mark, she'd felt the connection, and now after a professional and then personal conversation with him she'd felt it again. She saw it in his eyes as well.

She knew it wasn't wise to lower her shields for the last nine years of her life as a CIA operative, most of those black ops, she'd seen and done things that were almost unspeakable. She'd killed men and women who were a direct threat to the national security of the United States, she'd tortured terrorists without remorse, and once she'd killed a man out of pure and unadulterated hate.

It was that one time that haunted her when she closed her eyes. It was haunting her now.

Late September 2001

The CIA's Directorate of Intelligence Counterintelligence Center Analysis Group-CIC/AG-had intercepted an encrypted e-mail that indicated a known Al-Qaeda subject was scheduled to meet with an unidentified man in the town of Strangnas, Sweden. Nothing in the e-mail would have caused the average citizen concern, but one of the CIA supercomputers had caught a trigger combination. The city name of "Strangnas," the phrase "Meeting at the Hotel Rogge September 23, 2001," and "September 11, 2001 Assessment" were flagged by the CIA Supercomputer.

A data analyst wrote down some notes on a legal pad, conducted some relatively easy research, and found that no conventions were scheduled for the Djaknegarden Room for September 23rd. Other analysts followed the trail of the e-mail to its origin in Al-Basrah, Iraq. She pushed it up the chain.

Two days later an Eyes Only assessment was sitting on the desk of the CIA Deputy Director of Operations. The e-mail had led to the surveillance of Abu Sanjay Aziz, an operative of an Al-Qaeda cell who had tortured CIA undercover operative Juan Morales. Morales had been known as Abdul Auyob Rashid, and for nearly two years had been one of Aziz's trusted agents.

Unfortunately, just a few nights before 9/11, Aziz put each of his men through a game he called "the Tell." Aziz loved to play poker and decided he would spice up the game a bit. The object of the game was simple. You get a card, you read the card, and Aziz observes. You lie, you die: you speak the truth, you live.

Juan's first card read, "I am a servant of Allah." He passed the first test.

Three hands later, Juan's card read, "I am a servant of a foreign nation." He didn't pass the test. His tell was a miniscule clench of his jaw as silently read the card in his mind. Two days later, he was dead. Eight bullet holes in his body: two to his knees, two to his shoulders, two to his hands, one to his chest, and one in the head.

<u>September 23, 2001</u>

The ruse was right out of the movies, and Lindsey almost laughed at the irony. Her job in reality was not nearly as sexy and exotic as it was portrayed in a role played by Emmanuelle Beart in the first "Mission Impossible," although she knew she would look damn good in a black teddy.

She fit the profile of a beautiful Swedish damsel in distress. That ruse had needed no more than a minute; three of the four men had too easily exited their Mercedes to assess the woman's flat tire. Three perfectly placed shots in a span of four to five seconds decimated 75 percent of the man's security detail.

The woman took a shot at the driver's side window, and removed a smoke grenade from her purse, and threw it into the vehicle. With the Sedan filling rapidly with hydrochloric acid, the man and the last member of his security detail were left with no choice but to exit the vehicle or be scalded alive. The woman was waiting as the two exited the vehicle on the passenger side.

She plugged the security man, and then her pistol was pointed directly at the subject's head.

"Please don't. I'll do any" The subject's plea was interrupted by a bullet to his knee. He screamed, but no one would hear him. They were on a desolate stretch of highway just twenty miles west of Stockholm and halfway to the man's destination of Strangnas, Sweden.

The woman was here to avenge the death of a close friend and fellow intelligence officer and to find out what role the man had played in 9/11.

The man was whimpering and writhing in pain, but the blond showed no remorse or compassion. She replaced a magazine in the Sig Sauer .22 automatic pistol with a silencer and pointed it directly at his other knee, pulling the trigger once more.

His scream this time was a wine-glass-breaking pitch primal fear. Each breath was a hyper-ventilating exercise in futility. Life as the man knew it was coming to an end. Now he just wished the woman would just get it over with.

"Fu...fuck you...you...you bitch," he gasped between breaths. "Just...just finish this."

"Aziz, you killed my partner in cold blood, and I know you had something to do with 9/11. My partner, he had eight bullet wounds in him. Do you remember those, you shit?" The woman shot his right hand. Her heart was beating at a normal rate of 65 beats per minutes; she'd prepared for this moment for the last ten days, and the scene was well orchestrated.

As the man named Abu Sanjay Aziz screamed, she diverted her attention to the four other men on the ground. She had shot them once each in the head. She was not surprised whatsoever by the arrogance of this man and his security detail, and how easy it had been to take out all four so simply. A helpless woman is cliché but effective.

Fifteen minutes earlier and ten miles south, two agents had hidden in the woods awaiting the arrival of Aziz's four-door Mercedes Sedan. They'd radioed ahead to the woman that Aziz was ten to twelve minutes out. The area had no homes or businesses for miles in either direction and had been chosen two days earlier.

Needless to say, she was following the method he'd used in Juan's execution and repeating the technique on Aziz, but over a few minutes versus two days. Her next shot was to his left hand. The man was experiencing more than just pain now; he was nauseated and began vomiting and his eyes were losing some of their lucidity. The woman didn't care about the excruciating pain she was inflicting.

"You little piece of shit. My partner deserved some dignity." The woman snorted, her anger escalating.

She shot him in the right shoulder. He was convulsing but still lucid enough to feel and recognize what was happening.

The woman stood over his slumped body and looked directly into his dark eyes. "Why did you kill my partner? Tell me, and I'll finish you now. Don't tell me, and I shoot you some more and leave you here to bleed to death. Tell me, you little cockroach." Her heart rate was hovering at a tick around 75 beats per minute.

She tapped her feet impatiently. She turned to start walking away, then pointed her pistol at the head of one of the dead security detail and fired. She dragged the man's body over to Aziz. The man's grisly, disfigured face was its own form of torture, and Aziz vomited again. He tried to close his eyes, but she placed her hand over his right eyelid and pulled it open. "Not a pretty sight is it?"

"I'm waiting, Aziz," she chided.

He was defiant. She shot the dead man again. This time the top of his head was nearly gone. Aziz looked at the grisly mess in utter horror.

"Give me an answer now."

Aziz continued to be defiant, foolishly so. The woman removed a knife from an ankle holster. She held it within a half-inch of his right eye. The fright was more than evident in his facial expression. He'd had enough.

"He...he tried to stop Mohammed..." Aziz said crying, referring to Mohammed Atta, one of the perpetrators/monsters behind 9/11. "Plea...please fin...finish me." He pleaded, a whimpering, whipped dog.

"What are you talking about?" The woman asked.

"He...knew about our plan." The man mumbled and pleaded for her to finish him again.

"What else do you have planned?" She commanded this time. The knife was again within a half-inch of his right eye.

"Nothing else, I swear." The man repeated.

The woman shot him in the left shoulder. A curdling scream was reduced to whimpering. He was bleeding profusely.

"What else is there, Aziz?!" She commanded again.

"Nothing..." He answered, whispering.

"Nothing I swear?" She repeated to the dying man.

"Please finish..."

She stepped back and shot him square between the eyes. Aziz saw the flash of light, and then all went black.

Chapter Twenty-Two

Just Outside of Anchorage, Alaska

<u>Sunday May 5, 2002</u>

Emerging from her trip down that haunted memory lane, Lindsay gripped her glass of wine and realized her hand was shaking. She stared out the window as the aircraft passed Kayak Island and began its northwesterly turn toward Anchorage, Alaska.

She did not deviate from her gaze out the window as she blinked away tears that were defying her order to remain strong. Ironically, those tears were the most visible sign of real strength she'd shown in a very long time.

It was then and there that she decided her life needed a semblance of meaning. She was amazed at the way fate worked; something had put her in Mark Jameson's life for a myriad of reasons.

<u>Sunday May 5, 2002</u>

Five rows behind Lindsay, Mark's thoughts were on the gut feelings from the dream of the morning before. He'd had a premonition the day would be strange in some way. When he received the cell phone call from Lindsay that afternoon on his run, he realized his premonition was spot on.

"Damn!" He muttered as outside the window the snow-capped peaks and pristine forests of the Chugiak Mountains passed beneath the aircraft, now below 15,000 feet and descending into the Anchorage area. *"What the hell is going on?"* His thoughts raced with the chaotic events.

Nothing can ever prepare a person for those unexpected, life-altering moments. There's the sad sudden loss of a family member or the happy exhilaration of a newborn joining the family. And then there's the unbelievable moment when you meet that one person who just takes your breath away. That had just happened to Mark.

The flight had now descended below 10,000 feet, and the graceful approach continued as the grinding return of flaps extending on the aircraft's steel wings and adjustment of engine thrust enveloped the cabin. Normally that moment got Mark's adrenaline flowing, even though he'd heard it countless times, but between Yakutat and Anchorage that day he morphed from a man still clinging to his days as a wide-eyed five-year-old into 37-year-old man who'd met a most amazing woman.

He watched out the right-side window as the Boeing 737-400 descended onto the tarmac at Ted Steven's International Airport from a northerly heading. To the west was Mount Redoubt, an active volcano that on occasion disrupted air traffic in the Anchorage area. Today was not one of those days, though Mark felt as if life had just steered him into a cloud of confusion.

Ten minutes later, he was walking toward the baggage claim past a stuffed 10-foot Kodiak bear and an 11-foot polar bear that greeted passengers at the Alaska Airlines concourse.

A few steps later he passed a trendy bar. *"Only in Alaska…"* he thought.

He looked around the terminal for any sign of Lindsay, but she was gone. He'd watched her deplane ahead of him, and she'd made no effort to look behind her. Mark was pretty good at tailing people, but Lindsay was a pro.

Anchorage, Alaska

<u>Sunday May 5, 2002</u>

Mark sat in the back seat of a clean and comfortable cab downtown Anchorage, enjoying the crisp, warm, clean air.

The cab driver looked to be maybe mid-fifties, a dark-skinned man with pearly white teeth and an infectious smile. "How are you today, sir?"

"I'm doing very well. I love coming to Alaska, but it's been awhile." How's your day been so far?" Mark's senses were on high alert, and at the moment he didn't trust anyone, not even a cab driver.

"Can't complain. It's 70 degrees, and I'm going to get in eighteen holes as soon as the day's done, so all is good." The identification on the dashboard indicated his name was Ronald Johns.

"Ronald, that sounds perfect. What's your handicap?"

"The name's Ronnie, and it's my three-wood and my putter." Ronnie gave a hearty laugh.

"Mine's the driver and the guy holding the driver." Mark responded, and they both laughed.

"What brings you to Anchorage?" Ronnie asked.

"Business, though I'm hoping to enjoy the sights some," he answered sincerely.

He stared out the window as the cab passed Delaney Park located just south of the skyline that constitutes downtown Anchorage. He saw a couple of young women running, a man jogging with a fluffy black and white Alaskan Husky, and I saw a few couples strolling. Somehow the moment brought extreme clarity to his entire being. He was in Alaska as an FBI agent but somewhere deep down he felt something else as his gaze absorbed the Chugiak Mountain Range off in the distance.

It felt like he'd been tossed back thirty years or more, the snowy peaks and clear blue Central-Alaska sky reaching deep into his soul. He didn't understand what was happening, but his heart ached in a way he'd never experienced before. He closed his eyes, hoping to blink the feeling away.

"Grandson..." His grandfather's voice resonated inside seemed to take over Ronnie's cab. "I'm waiting for you..."

Mark blinked, and the voice was gone. Ronnie was still driving the cab north on Minnesota Drive, watching the two women jogging. Whatever Mark had just experienced, the rest of the world ran on, oblivious.

Anchorage, Alaska

<u>Sunday May 5, 2002</u>

Ronnie the Cabby dropped Mark off at the lobby entrance to the Westmark Anchorage Hotel, reminding him to see Laura at the Great Alaska Bush Company, a well- known strip club. Was he pulling Mark's chain?

The lack of pollution welcomed him, the air was pure as he breathed it in, his lungs realizing a strange sense of déjà vu. He'd known this feeling every summer as a young boy.

The Chugach Mountains and the blue hue the forest cast across the horizon was something he let his being each time he returned. The soothing massage of the Alaskan breeze was taking him back a good twenty years to when life seemed so much simpler.

But today, all had turned surreal, almost upside down. The Glock-17 in its right shoulder holster felt oddly foreign. The exhilaration was snuffed out as his cell phone vibrated, outside the entry to the Westmark.

It read anonymous again and his heart jumped, sure it was Lindsay.

"Agent Jameson..." The voice came across and quickly he realized it wasn't Lindsay.

The accent was distinct; male, Alaska Native, confident - "...the case you are working is going to open up some very old wounds. I am truly sorry for that but unfortunately fate has caught you in a very tangled web." The voice paused.

"Who the fuck is this?" Mark angrily but quietly asked. Looking around, it was a bit of relief to see no one was within in earshot.

"Come now, Mr. Jameson, you know that is not how this works." The man oddly enough, respectfully chastised the FBI agent. "It all leads back to Joshua Knight." The man stated.

"Who are you?" He asked oddly, with an equally respectful tone.

"The man who started all this, I want to finish this but on my terms." The Alaskan's voice paused; Mark could hear the man breathing lightly on the other end of the line and heard a baseball game in the background – the guy's television must have been on.

"Started what?" Mark continued the conversation.

"Start with Joshua Knight, Agent Jameson and the rest of the pieces will fall into place."

"Up Yours Asshole!" His mind screamed but he bit his tongue. It seemed silly but the guy was sending Mark on a hidden-treasure hunt when he had the answer right there but that wasn't how the asshole wanted to play.

"Joshua Knight's a ghost my friend, care to give me a hint why he's the key to whatever it is you started?" It was a stretch but Mark thought he might give it the old college try.

He decided to give a major hint. "What he knew is what brought down your grandmother's airplane." The answer came with a minor inflection, whatever it – it was personal to this guy and having this very strange conversation had made it very personal to Mark.

He took a moment to absorb the caller's comment. He thought it quite a coincidence that the skeletal remains that had been found had come the FBI's way was from the very date that his grandmother's plane had gone down outside of Juneau; the Alaskan and his call only fueled the feeling that coincidence was anything but.

Mark was going to say something else but the line went dead.

His ears were flush red. He could feel it. The primal instinct of hatred was instantaneous; that feeling of adrenaline running through every ounce of his being took hold. That feeling you get when you watch a movie and you just want so bad to see the villain taken down, that was exactly what Mark was feeling. The only problem was he had no idea who the villain was but he knew he was going to put a bullet in the piece of shit's head.

During the conversation, the caller ID indicated another anonymous call was trying to get through but obviously Mark needed to ignore it. He could still feel his ears still boiling red with anger. If it weren't for the message icon on his phone, he wasn't sure he wouldn't have gotten focus back quite so quickly.

Thankfully Lindsay had left the message. The message was short and sweet but simply hearing her voice calmed him down.

"Hello Mark, it was nice to meet you face to face. We've got more to talk about, when you get settled in – please give me a call." He hung up the cell phone after saving Lindsay's message. It told Mark it would be saved for fourteen days.

His heart was pounding like crazy. Do you ever have one of those moments where your frustration just bottles up without release? Well, that's how Mark felt. He wanted to beat the living daylights out of a faceless piece of – well you get the picture.

Mark stood on the street watching as a few vehicles drove by. In Seattle, the vehicles of choice were BMW, Honda, Volkswagen, and Lexus. Here in Anchorage SUV's, sturdy pickups, and family sedans easily outnumbered high-performance automobiles.

After the strange cell phone communication, having a few moments to relax was obviously not viable.

His eyes scanned the street and was not sure why, whoever the guy was on the call a few moments earlier certainly wasn't going to be that easy to find. He put on his sunglasses and continued scanning the street more to cover his eyes that probably looked a bit pissed.

Eight years in the FBI and nothing had ever come close to what Mark had experienced in the last two hours.

Chapter Twenty-Three

Anchorage, Alaska

<u>Sunday May 5, 2002</u>

So now you know Mark has met Lindsay face to face, had a very pleasant conversation with some schmuck with a Native-Alaskan accent, and learned that whatever had caused Joshua Knight's disappearance was tied to the airplane crash that took his grandmother.

At this point, he had no clue what he was in the middle of but it was becoming clear it was about much more than just an investigation into a thirty-year old disappearance of an oil company economist and the deaths of a few of his colleagues.

But the Native-Alaskan had confirmed it was related to the case Joshua Knight case that had come the FBI's way.

Thirty years ago, Alaska Airlines flight 1866 went down just west of Juneau. The National Transportation Safety Board (NTSB) had determined that it was faulty navigation system operation and pilot error; with all that had just transpired in the last few days, that seemed highly unlikely.

Then the telephone call; remember that dream Mark had with the sixth grade bully pushing him around in elementary school, well that feeling was back but he didn't want to just kick someone's ass but he had to find the piece of shit first.

And slower than he would like to admit, the FBI intuition had returned in full force. He wanted to know what would have possessed someone to bring down flight 1866 in Alaska. Was it terrorism, revenge, or something else?

Mark's job requires consummate professionalism and judgment at all times meant to save lives but at that moment, all he wanted was to have his trusty Glock-17 pistol in his hand when someone else shot first.

The bible says "to love thy enemies" – the only time loved his enemies was when they were dead.

To borrow a line from Larry the Cable Guy – "Lord I apologize."

As Mark walked into the lobby he was doing his best to keep nerves in check. Everything now seemed strange as he checked into the hotel.

"Sir, this envelope was left for you." A polite young clerk, his nametag read "Josh", said as he handed Mark a brown manila envelope.

After the officious steps taken to check in, he was in an eighth-floor room overlooking the widespread Anchorage area to the south and somewhat to the east. A sporadic razor thin cloud cover softened an azure-tinted sky adorned with warm rays of sunshine.

Anchorage, a metropolitan area home to well over 250,000 citizens, is a very beautiful city.

Picturesque views and the peace of nature can be found almost anywhere. Mountain ranges, wildlife, or a quiet hike in the foothills can be just as easily found as a museum, a zoo, a vibrant bar, or a great restaurant.

A pint of Mac & Jack's at a sports bar sounded perfect just then but unfortunately he needed to open the manila envelope. And wouldn't you know it; it seems this was the real deal. There was a picture of him running along Strander Boulevard in Tukwila.

Attached was a yellow post-it note and in beautiful, flowing handwriting... *"Just so you know I'm good at my job..."*

"Lindsay" was initialed beneath the handwriting – she was showing off.

Sunday May 5, 2002

He caught a glimpse in the mirror as he placed a travel size bottle of Peppermint Listerine behind the toothpaste and toothbrush. He hadn't shaved that morning and noticed the hint of a five o'clock shadow. He rubbed his chin and felt that familiar scruffy feeling.

Mark walked out of the bathroom and walked to the window of the eighth floor hotel room. He looked at the sunny sky, at the activity on the street below, and at the various buildings adjacent to the hotel. He wasn't looking for anything in particular, just passing time.

A decision to relax a bit took a good fifteen minutes to come to. He sat on the queen size bed and watched a little ESPN.

Okay he watched a little of the Food Network.

Lying on the tan-colored comforter that draped the bed was the picture of him running the day before. The item stole any relaxing attention to Giada De Laurentiis seasoning a flank steak would have given him.

He still hadn't figured out what federal agency Lindsay worked; however, she could have worked for mall security for all he cared. Just so she kept him from getting shot.

Chapter Twenty-Four

Anchorage, Alaska

<u>Sunday May 5, 2002</u>

At nearly four o'clock, Mark's cell rang again.

He was expecting it to be the jerk with the Native-Alaskan accent, but it was Lindsay.

That Tlingit didn't work very reliably, he had to admit. He'd guessed wrong twice about who was calling. And worse, he didn't have any inkling that he'd been watched and even photographed the day before on his run. His ancestors had to be damn proud.

"Hello Mark." Lindsay paused for effect. "Did you get my message?"

"I did…both of them." He didn't let on about the call from the Asshole.

"Mark…" Lindsay said his name ominously.

The silence sizzled between them. This was more than just an assignment. She knew it and she knew he knew it.

And she was a very good spook, Fed, or whatever she was, because what came next Mark didn't expected.

"Mark, we know about your last call."

"You've got my phone tapped! Isn't that a violation of my civil rights?" Mark let his annoyance into his voice.

Lindsay didn't even bite, but kept on point. "Do you have any idea what the caller meant by this all being tied to Joshua Knight?"

Her question frightened Mark a bit. She apparently had no clue what the guy with the Native Alaskan accent was talking about.

Again, there was an awkward silence. He wanted to just get this over with. He wasn't sure what life suddenly had in store, but he was either going to die defending himself or finish whatever this was all about.

"I have no idea, he said." I'm going for a run. After I get back, let's touch base."

"That sounds like a plan, unless you'd like some company?" Lindsay paused.

He was thinking about how unbelievable she'd look in a jogging outfit and was more than tempted to say yes, but wanted some time to think.

"Some company, but I think I'd be a bit distracted, to tell you the truth." He tried to lighten it up, but she didn't bite.

Briskly, Lindsay gave him her cell number and told Mark to call after he got back from his run.

Before he hung up, he had to say it: "Lindsay, under different circumstances I can't think of anything I'd rather do than spend time with you."

There was a moment of silence that frightened him a bit.

He wanted her to know he wasn't one of those guys who would take for granted just what a privilege it is to be in the company of a lovely woman. He wasn't quite ready to start writing her poetry, but he was definitely sensing a burgeoning attraction.

When he heard her sweet voice respond, he knew the sensation was real for both.

"Thanks, Mark," she answered in a surprisingly shy manner. The silence after they'd hung up was awkward and excruciating lonely.

Anchorage, Alaska
<u>Sunday May 5, 2002</u>

In the 68-degree, sunny Alaska afternoon, Mark's run was rhythmic and full of purpose; unlike most runs, his focus was on what he'd learned over the last few hours rather than the endorphin rush.

As he approached the intersection of 15th and O Street, his cell phone rang. It read "Anonymous" again. He was tired of guessing who it might be.

FBI Agent Sandra Gonzalez' voice sounded strange and out of place, though she was actually the one person he was expecting on this assignment.

Unfortunately, the urgency in her voice took away any relief.

"Mark, do you have your firearm with you?"

"Sure do." It was in a military holster he used when he ran.

"Take it out, now!" Sandra commanded.

He stopped and panned the entire area in his line of sight. He saw the source of the urgency in Sandra's voice, cursing himself for not noticing it earlier, or sensing Sandra's surveillance.

Some Tlingit – actually, some FBI agent, too. He had no doubt that he was the pride of his ancestors and his instructors at Quantico.

He was within twenty feet of a yellow cab parked on a curb on 15th Avenue just fifteen or twenty yards from N. Street. A man sat still in the driver's seat. As Mark got closer, it appeared the man was waiting for something, and in his right looked to be holding an envelope.

Mark pulled the Glock-17 from his holster as he approached the vehicle; all of his senses on high alert. He began to raise his voice, finger poised to fire. He was about ten yards away, and ducked down in a crouched stance.

"FBI - Put your hands where I can see them!" He commanded firmly.

The man was not moving. There was a photo in the man's right hand. The left hand slowly moved off of the steering wheel.

"Slow, Mother Fucker, or you're dead!" Mark snapped with the gun pointed squarely at the man's head.

It was Ronnie the Cabby from earlier in the day.

As much as Mark liked the guy, he kept the pistol pointed squarely at his head. "What the hell is going on?" he barked.

"Joshua Knight is what is going on. Now that you're here in Alaska, I'm in danger," Ronnie stated.

"Fuck you! What the hell are you talking about?" Mark yelled.

"Get in the fucking cab and I'll tell you!" Ronnie the Cabby shot back.

The Glock was begging to be fired. Well, Mark was begging to fire the Glock. Semantics... Regardless, Ronnie the Cabby was in serious jeopardy of joining his ancestors at any moment.

"Out of the cab!" Mark ordered. "Now!"

"I don't think so," Ronnie calmly replied.

It can be extremely frustrating when only one party is yelling in an argument. At that moment, that was exactly how Mark felt. Even more, he hated it when his demands are ignored. "Now!" He yelled again.

"Get in the fucking cab!" Ronnie finally had had enough, and yelled at Mark with true gusto. He had that effect on certain people.

This was nothing more than a standoff in the middle of Anchorage. And Mark was getting tired of Ronnie's use of the F-Bomb; it just didn't sound right when he said it

Just as Ronnie started to open his door, two black Chevrolet Suburban SUVs turned east off of O Street at high rates of speed and boxed in the cab. Mark hoped it was the good guys.

Anchorage, Alaska
<u>Sunday May 5, 2002</u>

"FBI, hands where we can see them!" FBI Agent Sandra Gonzalez was the first out of one of the two SUVs and had her Beretta pistol pointed squarely at Ronnie the Cabby's head.

At least five or six agents jumped out of the SUVs, weapons drawn. Two of the agents had rifles, and the others had pistols pointed directly at Ronnie.

"Fuck you!" Ronnie said and refused to obey their order. All of the agents were behind the hoods of the FBI vehicles, except of course for Mark.

At the FBI Academy, he'd spent a lot of time at a mock-town commonly known as Hogan's Alley, preparing for a wide variety of less than friendly encounters. Its acres came complete with stores, banks, and other amenities that you'd find in a small town. On one of the training exercises, a fellow trainee and Mark were exposed to a situation eerily similar to the one he was now in the middle of.

It was a mock carjacking on a sunny afternoon. Two suspects were holding a woman at gunpoint in the middle of a quiet city street. The assignment: secure the situation until backup arrives.

They didn't succeed on the first attempt, as the hostage situation went south in a hurry, and instead of securing the situation they ended up in a flurry of bullets (paintball, that is). The only one left standing was Mark's partner.

Thankfully, this real-life encounter didn't result in a flurry of bullets, and Mark hadn't had to wait more than twenty seconds or so for backup to arrive, seeing how Ronnie the Cabby was probably just moments from Mark blowing him to kingdom come.

Now everyone had their weapons trained on the cab driver as SA Gonzalez yelled for Mark to slowly move backwards, the remaining agents would cover him.

He was still kneeling in a crouched position when something on Ronnie's forehead caught his attention.

A red dot formed in the middle of his forehead. A sniper's laser had the poor guy painted.

"Ronnie, duck!" He yelled, but it was too late.

A trickle of blood oozed like a slow-moving red stream, through creases on his forehead downward to a crow's foot. His eyes were still open, but the stare was vacant. Ronnie had been executed right in front of a team of FBI agents – right in front of Mark.

It took just a millisecond for the initial shock of the sniper's bullet to dissipate.

The agents instinctively ducked and turned, index fingers on their weapons' triggers, and their eyes trained in the assumed direction of the origin of the bullet that had sent Ronnie the Cabby to join his ancestors.

"Mark, take cover!" The air had grown ominously silent after Ronnie had been snuffed out. SA Gonzalez' voice broke that silence and broke Mark's trance.

He'd been exposed to corpses at Quantico, but that didn't prepare him for the first time. Seeing the startled fear in Ronnie the Cabby's eyes just as life escaped him was a memory he would never be able to fully chase away.

He was still in the crouched position when SA Gonzalez and two other agents grabbed him and dragged him for the cover of an FBI SUV.

Within fifteen minutes, the block was saturated with law enforcement vehicles. The Anchorage Police Department, Alaska State Troopers, and federal agents had the scene secure, yellow crime-scene tape creating a wide perimeter.

Ronnie's body had been left as it was in the cab, but to ensure that the image of his slumped body didn't end up on the eleven o'clock news, a dark tarp had been draped over the yellow cab. As they had been trained, they also made sure that license plates and the cab number on the roof of Ronnie's vehicle were covered with crime-scene tape.

The execution of Ronnie the Cabby had occurred in the city limits, giving the Anchorage Police Department jurisdiction on-scene. Mark, SA Gonzalez, and the other five agents who'd been on the scene when Ronnie was taken out were asked to surrender weapons. In addition, they'd all been separated for their own protection (legal that is).

After more than two hours of interviews on-scene and at the Anchorage Police Department, their weapons were finally returned after it was determined they weren't Ronnie's shooter.

Mark was very impressed with the professionalism and crime-scene management the Anchorage detectives exhibited throughout that evening.

At around nine, Mark finally met with SA Gonzalez. He had a lot of questions.

Chapter Twenty-Five

Washington, D.C.

<u>Sunday May 5, 2002</u>

"Johns, Ronald, confirmed." The operative's voice bordered on robotic as he spoke. A few hours earlier, he'd conducted the operation as instructed and eliminated Ronald Johns as a threat.

The op couldn't have worked out any better. Not only was Ronald Johns eliminated in a very public place, but the FBI had been on-scene lending a bit of mysterious drama to the scene.

"Op executed with precision - well done. Remain in Anchorage, await further communication." The faceless voice on the other end of the line for the first time ever displayed a slight hint of appreciation.

"Hold in Anchorage, copy."

The Operative hit "end" on his cell phone and realized a moment of well-deserved self-satisfaction, momentarily allowing a smile to take hold. For the first time in a very long time, he took stock of what his life had been about and realized just how good he'd become.

There were operations that no one would ever know about. He'd orchestrated some very notorious "accidents" and some highly visible "executions" - most with the intent to alter history, but this one was in a league all by itself.

Any instinctual trepidation he'd had days earlier had dissipated, as he'd squared up the laser on Ronald Johns's forehead while he sat in his cab, and he realized his handler knew exactly what he was doing.

Most operatives are not read-in to the end-game of an operation, the intent to maintain compartmentalization and minimize the risk of exposure. But his handler had read him in on the why of this, and he was the how. There were a few things the handler didn't loop back his way, and he knew it, but so be it.

And now he had the night off. A filet of halibut and a glass of Merlot sounded like the perfect way to wind down and let time pass.

Four time zones to the east, the handler made a telephone call that would move FBI agents Sandra Gonzalez and Mark Jameson around like pawns on a chess board.

Chapter Twenty-Six

Anchorage, Alaska

<u>Sunday May 5, 2002</u>

Leaving the headquarters of the Anchorage Police Department, Sandra and Mark got into an FBI SUV and headed east on East Tudor Road with no apparent destination in mind. The sky still had the look of early dusk, and it was nearly 9:00pm. Alaska's continuous daylight was comforting not to be heading into darkness. A minute or so later, they turned north along the well-lit and well-traveled Boniface Parkway. Alaska and its oil revenues gave the dividend of well-maintained state roads.

Strangely enough, the headquarters for the Anchorage Police Department were located about five miles from downtown Anchorage. This was Sandra's town, so Mark surrendered and let her be the tour guide, but he definitely had questions that she was going to answer.

As they passed a white Ford Explorer with two large Alaskan Huskies in the back, and a wife and husband smiling and chatting about their day, he couldn't help but wonder what a life like that would be like.

Wake up in the morning, walk the dogs, go to the local coffee drive-thru, go to the office, come home, walk the dogs, and maybe two or three times a week make love.

He wasn't mocking that life, just wondering if it might ever come his way.

Sandra caught him staring and smiled. "Pretty dogs, aren't they?" Her voice had a soft, almost harmonic tone to it that suited her dark coloring. Her mother was of Hispanic descent, and she had a Caucasian father in the Air Force.

She'd followed in her father's footsteps and graduated in 1991 from the Air Force Academy in Colorado Springs, Colorado. She'd spent two years flying airplanes, when the FBI recruited her. After stints in Puerto Rico, Charlotte, and San Diego, as the new millennium approached she was assigned to the Anchorage Field Office.

"So what the hell were you doing following me?" Mark's tone wasn't nearly as harsh as the words.

"Mark, we received a tip that you've somehow pissed off someone powerful. It seems they want you dead." Sandra didn't say where the tip had come from, but he guessed it was Lindsay Drummond – aka CIA or NSA or Spook.

"Until a few hours ago, I wouldn't have believed you. And whoever wants me dead must know what Joshua Knight is all about, don't you think?" He answered, assuming by now that Sandra and the rest of law enforcement in this town now knew that Joshua Knight at one time had been a pain in someone's ass – at least according to newly-deceased Ronnie the Cabby.

"The dead Cabby's excited utterance has the attention of everybody, any idea why he would have a connection to Joshua Knight?" Sandra was all FBI as they talked; it was familiar territory for both of them and helped move the SUV north along Boniface at a relaxed pace.

They discussed the case for a bit, mostly conjecture about what the connection could be. Mark didn't share anything yet about his conversation with Lindsay, the telephone call from the guy with the Alaska Native accent, or anything else. It felt awkward keeping information from a fellow agent, but until he knew what he didn't know, they would stick to facts they did know.

"I need a bite to eat." Sandra interjected.

Mark idly noted a red-and-white Cessna 402 landing from the east, approaching Anchorage's Merrill Field near the highway. Merrill Field was an airport for private and small aircraft a few miles east of downtown Anchorage. "I agree. What you in the mood for?"

"There's a Red Robin not too far from here, is a burger alright with you?" "Perfect." Mark loved their Banzai Burgers with a couple of avocados.

Sandra asked for a somewhat private spot, and winked to the young hostess, so they were seated in a corner booth away from the evening crowds. It wasn't a date, not that Sandra wouldn't be a great date, but 1) she was a fellow fed, 2) she could kick his ass in a fight, and 3) Lindsay.

He hadn't called Lindsay yet, no- he'd be smarter than this but he was sure that by the time he'd walked into Red Robin she knew what had happened.

Back to Ronnie the Cabby and his connection to Joshua Knight:

"We've got to figure out what the connection is between the dead cab driver and Joshua Knight." Sandra took the initiative. "The cabbie wanted to pass something our way, and obviously what he had to say would have some traction. Someone's feathers have been ruffled over a guy who has been dead since the early 70's?"

Sandra pulled out a dossier that provided a pretty good outline of the deceased economist. "It's not been easy finding information on Knight. His personnel file at Honeycutt Petroleum was full of commendations, memorandums...nothing to suggest he was going off of the deep end. Transcripts from interviews police had with colleagues back then indicate that he had just been sent to Alaska to monitor the progress of the negotiations of the Alaska Native Claims Settlement Act – ANCSA."

Mark was trying to figure out where the FBI had gotten its information.

"I've gotta ask, how'd we get his personnel file so fast, and why?"

"The FBI helped with the NTSB investigation of the airplane that he was supposed to have been on. They actually got a little bit more that might pique your interest."

Her next summary didn't disappoint. "One of the interviewees indicated Knight and Myles Honeycutt had become very close. Just in case you don't know who he is, Myles Honeycutt was CEO of Honeycutt Petroleum back in the 70's and had promoted Knight to an executive position rather rapidly. Knight's promotion memorandum cites his ability to connect obscure facts into day-to-day business decisions as a primary factor."

After the waitress had come by and taken their order, Mark excused himself to make a call.

On the third ring, Lindsay answered her cell phone. It was nice to hear her serene, sultry, yet strong voice on the other side.

She didn't leave any doubt that she knew what had happened. "Hi, Mark. I assume that was you and some of your fellow agents I saw in blue windbreakers on the breaking news a while ago..." It wasn't a question. "...and I've gotta tell you...I'm glad you're alright."

A couple walked by as he held the phone to his ear, and they smiled as he held the door open for them. The guy had the decency to say thank you; one of

Mark's biggest pet peeves was the lack of respect people show when someone does something polite like hold open a door or let a car merge into a lane.

He felt kind of strange, like he'd stood Lindsay up on a date. Though "*I'm sorry, I was in a shootout*" was probably one of the best excuses a guy could have for being late.

"For the record, I was the one in shorts and a gray Seahawks Tee-shirt." He couldn't resist making light of his role.

"Oh, that was you." Lindsay played along flirtatiously. Mark couldn't wait to see her, hopefully later that evening.

They set a date...er...a meeting for eleven or so at the Solstice Bar & Grill in the Westmark Hotel where he was staying.

Then he got back to Sandra and the thirty-year old case that they'd just involuntarily taken off of the evidence shelf.

Anchorage, Alaska
Sunday May 5, 2002

Sandra dropped Mark off at the entrance to the Westmark around 10:15. He had a good forty-five minutes to get upstairs and change into a pair of jeans and a relaxing polo.

Replaying the encounter in his mind with the recently departed Ronnie the Cabby, he kept hearing his excited utterance – "*Joshua Knight is what is going on. Now that you're here in Alaska, I'm in danger.*"

Was Ronnie talking about the Native guy who'd called when Mark got to his hotel? Why hadn't Ronnie simply abducted him when he got in his cab at the airport? And finally, why hadn't he heard from the Native-accented schmuck after what had gone down a few hours earlier?

Mark had his laptop turned on and was prepared to create an elaborate Excel document, outlining detailed facts on what they knew to this point. But he remembered something his dad had told him when he was in college. "Son, if you want to absorb something you're studying, you don't type it and you don't read it, write it with your own hands until your mind captures each word."

It was 10:35pm, and he had a few more minutes before the liaison with Lindsay, so he took his dad's advice and sat down on the queen-size bed, grabbing his letter-size Day-Timer. It was nothing official and not subject to discovery in the cases he was working, just a good place to write down random thoughts on an investigation.

It already held notes he'd jotted down on the flight, not long before he'd met Lindsay.

<u>Sunday May 5, 2002 - Written aboard Alaska Airlines Flight 81</u>
- ✓ *May 5, 2002 - SA Jameson assigned via request from ASAC Branson to a case in Anchorage, Alaska.*
- ✓ *Subject: Skeletal remains found in a burned-out building near Dimond Shopping Mall. Remains are those of a man named Joshua Knight.*
- ✓ *Federal jurisdiction rationale: According to NTSB database - Joshua Knight perished aboard Alaska Airlines Flight 1866 in September 1971.*

- ✓ *SA Jameson Note: Need to disclose personal connection to this case - see bullet #3 (my grandmother was also aboard that flight)*

Thanks to Sandra Gonzalez, there was definitely new material:

<u>Sunday May 5, 2002 - Written at Hotel Captain Cook</u>
- ✓ *Joshua Knight – working on ANCSA analysis for Honeycutt Petroleum – mentored by Myles Honeycutt – CEO*
- ✓ *Myles Honeycutt, died 1972 – apparent suicide but no note???*
- ✓ *Clay Tanis, murdered 1972 – six witnesses all noted assassin was graying man with glasses. Assistant Security Chief for Honeycutt Petroleum*
- ✓ *Rico Sanchez, murdered 1972 - Alaska Bush Pilot – more research needed. Murdered along with Clay Tanis. Not sure where to start?*
- ✓ *Native Alaskan-accented caller ("on his terms") – what the hell???*
- ✓ *And me – why I am a threat to somebody? Connect the dots.*
- ✓ *Ronny the Cabby – who the hell was he and why was he shot?*
- ✓ *And find out what ANCSA is all about?*

It was a good start, hopefully enough to open the floodgates. But first there was Lindsay.

Chapter Twenty-Seven

Anchorage, Alaska
Sunday May 6, 2002

Mark got to the bar at 10:55, a few minutes ahead of Lindsay, and camped out in a corner booth, with a good view when she walked into the room.

Lindsay looked incredible, and every part of Mark's being wanted to tell her so, but this was supposed to be a meeting between two federal agents. The jury was still out on Lindsay's actual occupation, though Mark couldn't help thinking she'd be a great Victoria's Secret Model.

When she sat down, Mark kept his mouth shut and let her start the conversation. The fact that it was taking a moment for her to say something spoke volumes.

He had nervous feeling running through him as he watched her. There was a lit candle on the table, and the flame shimmering in her blue eyes was somehow heartwarming, peaceful.

She caught Mark staring, but her eyes had an appreciative twinkle. A line from "Top Gun" ran through his head: "This was going to be complicated."

Their little meeting didn't get farther. Just as she settled into a chair at the table, Mark's cell phone rang and so did hers.

"Mark, we have a lead on who might have taken out the cab driver. You and I are headed for Nenana." It was Agent Gonzalez.

Before he responded, he looked over at Lindsay, who was on the phone as well. He whispered, "Nenana?"

Lindsay shook her head in the negative; Mark was being sent somewhere in the middle of nowhere again.

After we finished our cell phone conversations, Mark asked Lindsay who had called her.

"My boss." That was all he was going to get out of her.

"Don't forget, Ms. Drummond, you owe me dinner someday if I find out you're CIA."

"Now I'm Ms. Drummond...What happened to Lindsay?"

"It just came out, sorry..."

"No one's called me that before." Her smile as she answered was overwhelming. As their gazes held, it seemed this connection somewhere down the road might be so much more.

Then she gave herself a little shake of the head. "...Nenana, where the hell is that?"

Chapter Twenty-Eight

Suburban Washington, D.C. - Tyson's Corner, Virginia
Sunday May 6, 2002

S & S Fitness Adventures The painted-white sign on the plate-glass window for the last twelve years had served its purpose.

The office was typical. Four desks, four staff members, an always-brewing coffee pot, a small printer/copier, and photographs adorning the wall.

Like most small businesses, S & S Fitness Adventures had two private offices. One was what most would expect shelves filled with binders, a couple of four-drawer file cabinets, piles of paper on a grey-Formica credenza, and miscellaneous items tacked up above a PC and monitor.

The other office had the same look, with one exception: the walls were reinforced and sound-suppressed, the computer was rarely used, and there were six cameras invisibly installed throughout.

And there was a white board the office's occupant had insisted on being installed.

His insistence on the white board was to visualize the major aspects of an intelligence operation. S & S Fitness Adventures operated legitimately, catering to high-end clients searching for private mountain-climbing excursions, SCUBA-diving trips, and other exotic adrenaline-induced activities.

The company's mission was perfect. The staff members were contracted adrenaline junkies who, unbeknownst to their clients, were also private contractors-for-hire in the intelligence business - S & S's other more vital niche.

In fact, no client had ever been to the S & S office. All of the business was handled via telephone, e-mail, and other electronic means.

The company's clientele provided a perfect cover for one of S & S's operatives, who occupied the sound-proof room and worked primarily in seclusion.

From the small office in the Washington, D.C., suburb, some significant but publicly unknown operations had been orchestrated.

From the downing of an aircraft in Libya, to the kidnapping of a Cali Cartel mistress, to the orchestrated resignation of a United States Senator days before his planned announcement to run for President of the United States, his small team of eleven rather ordinary operatives had done things that had altered history.

And now the Shadow Squad had the dubious assignment to right wrongs it had been a part of thirty years earlier. A wrong the man with the white board had started thirty years earlier when he'd killed Clay Tanis, Rico Sanchez, and Myles Honeycutt.

Chapter Twenty-Nine

On the Parks Highway, Between Anchorage & Nenana, Alaska
<u>Late Sunday May 6, 2002 and early Monday May 7, 2002</u>

Nenana, Alaska, is about an hour's drive south of Fairbanks on Alaska's Parks Highway, and from Anchorage it is a good four and a half hours' drive north.

Sandra had called around eleven pm, electing to drive up from Anchorage rather than fly to Fairbanks first thing Monday morning.

Sandra had been home for just ten minutes when the Anchorage ASAC - Assistant Special Agent in Charge - had called to let her know that an anonymous tip had been phoned in. For some unknown, odd reason, the Nenana depot of the Alaska State Troopers had received a tip that initially hadn't made sense. A couple of hours later, the tip had some traction. The call was definitely not typical for the small outpost in the rural interior of Alaska. It was only a few words: "The Anchorage Cab Driver is the target."

Seeing how Mark was the last person Ronnie had any interaction with, ASAC Coulter had assigned the Nenana tip to two very qualified agents, in Mark's humble opinion. So he and SA Gonzalez had a road trip at around one in the morning in the early stretches of May. They'd be getting to Nenana sometime right around sunrise.

They headed north in an FBI Sedan with music and their conversation to fill the three hundred-five mile drive. The first hour or so the discussion was light, discussing their love lives – or the lack thereof - what they thought of the Bush Presidency so far, vacations, and the like. As they started up the Parks

Highway between Wasilla and Nenana, the conversation moved to the Joshua Knight Case.

"I'm still trying to figure out what connection the cab driver would have had with Joshua Knight that would have him taken out on a city street in broad daylight." Sandra posed the question of the hour.

A phrase Mark had seen on a bumper sticker somewhere had always seemed a good philosophy:

Keep It Simple Stupid - KISS. As far as he was concerned, there was no time like the present.

"You know, a girlfriend in college had this little thing she'd like to do whenever we'd drive from Bellingham to Seattle for a concert or something. She'd ask me a question like 'What's your favorite movie?' and she'd want me to say the first thing that came to mind. Mind if we apply that to our case?" Mark didn't wait for her answer.

"What's your gut reaction?"

Sandra paused for only a second. "Well, the FBI is involved because of Joshua Knight. So let's find out who he was."

"What about you?" Sandra asked him.

"I say we find the guy who took out Ronnie the Cabby."

Sandra paused again, but Mark could sense the wheel's turning. "Funny, you chose to start in the present, and I chose to start well into the past." She added, "So are you glass half-empty or half-full?"

"I've never been a big fan of that phrase. But if you're asking, am I a pessimist or an optimist, I'd definitely say I'm an optimist, How about you?" He returned the question.

"So you probably don't like the phrase, six of one, half dozen of another?" She shot a question with a question.

"Even worse than half-empty half-full, and you didn't answer my question."

The wheels were turning again for a moment and then she answered the question. "At least we have that in common. I'm an optimist."

The banter went on for another minute or so and then the conversation hit an FBI nerve - and a personal one. Sandra made an observation that at the time seemed rather immaterial but was actually the impetus to connect dot after dot.

"Humor me for just a bit, okay?" Sandra paused for a second, grabbed her bottled water, and consumed a healthy volume. "The past is pretty simple. Knight was supposed to have died in an airplane crash, but instead, his remains are found in a building that burns down just a few months ago. Quite a coincidence that either way he was a dead man, don't you think?"

Silence - until that moment - Mark hadn't believed that the coincidence was anything more than a strange, sick, and twisted alignment of the stars.

Sandra looked at over at Mark.

"Are you alright?"

"Sandra, my grandmother died on the plane that Knight was supposed to have been on. If you're right, then my grandmother's death probably wasn't an accident."

Sandra startled, looked over to see a surprisingly vengeful look in Mark's deep brown eyes.

"What are you talking about?"

"Wilma Jameson. Just look on the flight manifest, okay?" His voice was strained.

SA Gonzalez was wondering just who was this guy seated next to her in the FBI Suburban. *His dad's a spook, he's a damn good FBI agent and now it seems his deceased grandmother has a connection to a guy who supposedly died in an airplane crash but his remains are found eight hundred miles away in a burned-out office complex....*

She didn't say it, but she had the strange feeling that Mark Jameson was more than just an FBI agent. Something disturbing was going on.

Outside of Syracuse, New York

<u>Monday May 6, 2002</u>

A lean white cat walked across the spotless granite counter, its tiny paws delicately negotiating the narrow edge near the stainless steel sink. Against the shimmering reflection of the u-shaped faucet, the feline rubbed first its soft pink nose on the right and then left, satisfying an odd primal need to feel the firm caress of an inanimate object. On to its next conquest, the cat gently scaled down the cherry cabinet doors beneath the stainless two-basin sink. With the familiar sound of a soft landing on pink pads, it quietly and gracefully walked along the gray slate tile.

Each evening around dinner time, the ritual repeated itself. That is, when the cat's master was around.

Jacob Honeycutt spread his lean, fit frame on a dark leather sofa, watching his white cat saunter across the kitchen floor.

"Jasmine, come here, baby." Honeycutt said, watering down his deep voice to a gentle whisper. The white feline was one of a choice few who knew this side of the man.

Jasmine had joined Honeycutt's life as a kitten five years earlier. From the moment she'd entered the plush four-thousand square foot dwelling, the townhouse had become her playground. Essentially there was no area that was off-limits, even if Jacob were entertaining a lady-friend.

Jasmine jumped up on the man's chest and rubbed her nose against his. Jacob stroked the cat's soft fur, and almost instantaneously Jasmine was happily purring.

The man marveled at the dichotomy that was his life. He pondered his existence at moments such as this. Jasmine reminded him that somewhere inside resided a decent human-being.

Somewhere, he'd lost what all humans are born with, that youthful genuine innocence. He knew exactly when he'd taken that definitive step from an innocent boy and a decent young man to a conniving, manipulative, and lethal human being.

A cool late October 16, 1972 evening was horribly marked in his tortured mind. In a deep slumber, he awoke to the frightened sound in his father's voice. Myles Honeycutt had a gun pointed at him by a man in a black ski mask.

He listened as his father confessed to a horrible thing. Even at four years old, he understood. The confession he heard was devastating: his father was an evil man. Myles Honeycutt's wavering voice had confessed that he'd ordered the downing of an airplane carrying the mother of the person wearing the mask.

Moments later, the gunfire delivered a silent scream deep inside little Jacob Honeycutt's psyche. He'd never voiced it.

Not so for Kelly Honeycutt. As her young son sat in his room frozen in fright, she ran down the wooden steps of the luxury getaway "cottage" the family held in Upstate New York.

She searched the home, screaming for Jacob's father, Myles. As she finally circled the home outside, Kelly saw the silhouette of a body lying on the deck.

A pool of blood stained the expensive wooden planks. She knelt to turn him over. What came next, she spent the next eighteen years in intensive therapy trying to expel, to no avail.

His intense blue eyes were lifeless as they seemingly stared toward the starry sky. But the bullet entry on the right side of his skull and the exit above his left eyebrow had left Kelly Honeycutt with a life-long void and a visual memory that would never fully go away.

On October 16, 1992, exactly twenty years later, Kelly Honeycutt succeeded in expunging the vision; sadly, her "success" broke Jacob's twenty-three year-old heart. She ended those awful memories not with a pistol but with a prescription bottle of sleeping pills and two glasses of an expensive Australian wine.

Those two deaths twenty years apart had destroyed any goodness in the life of Jacob Honeycutt. As a young boy, he had tried to work through the death of his father, but when his mother was gone, everything that had given him any sense of a moral compass was virtually cremated with her.

While he was in college, he'd learned his on-again, off-again girlfriend had stepped out a few times with a very good friend from his fraternity.

He wanted the fraternity brother to live a life ruined. The steps he took were simple. A copy of an English syllabus and the first test hidden beneath his frat brother's mattress, coupled with a tip to the English Department, served to get the "friend" called before the school's Dean of Students. The frat-brother vehemently proclaimed his innocence over and over as the Dean contemplated his fate. Jacob sat by his side, feigning with an Oscar-caliber performance a belief in his denials.

The frat brother survived the review by the Dean, but his academic career was forever tarnished. The stigma that he was a cheat stuck, and by his junior year he dropped out of school.

Jacob repeatedly justified to himself the vengeance he'd taken on his frat-brother. The guy had violated guy-code and slept with Jacob's girlfriend. A few years working to restore his reputation seemed appropriate retribution.

The feeling that he had that kind of power was overwhelming for Jacob, and as he met opposition in business, love, and life, he relished in the high he felt when retribution came to pass. Little did he know that retribution's door swings both ways.

Gently, Jacob nudged Jasmine off of his chest. The vibrating cell phone demanded his attention.

He answered, staring at the caller ID. He'd been awaiting this call for the last two days, and his heart rate jumped a few beats as the phone number appeared. He was working with a new contact, and he'd acquired the man's services through an intermediary, one he'd never met face to face.

As the son of Oil Magnate Myles Honeycutt and now an oil CEO in his own right, Jacob had acquired his father's thirst for power at all costs. Like his father, he'd cultivated contacts all over the world. Most were legitimate, but a chosen few navigated in the shadows. One of those contacts was a Saudi intelligence operative he knew only as KP. Jacob had no clue whether that was the man's real name, but it really didn't matter. He knew when he had an assignment on foreign soil that KP was the one to call; he'd leave a message with a waitress at the Long Island Martini Bar in Westchester, New York, that he needed to find his old friend KP.

What he did know was that KP very effective. He never knew how or when, but he'd pass a name to the waitress and the job would be done.

Eight lives, eight deaths Jacob was accountable for. The first had stung somewhere in his psyche, the second a little less, and by the eighth taking a life was simply the removal of an obstacle. Each had their justification. Just like the frat-brother who had slept with his girlfriend.

Now Jacob listened with heightened concentration as the man spoke. The words were purposely benign, but the message was clear; the chess pieces were moving into place.

The conversation became the rationale for a road trip. His personal white Gulfstream G-V was wheels-up at around 8:00pm Eastern Standard Time, the destination Anchorage's Merrill Field.

Aboard the aircraft, Jacob stirred ice cubes in a glass and sipped on Diet Coke. He was doing his best to keep his nerves in check, but knowing that the first part of his operation appeared to have been a success couldn't be contained.

Four other men, all dressed in well-tailored dark blue suits, occupied the aircraft's pure-white cabin. Jacob had asked for a little privacy after they'd departed Syracuse. He sat near the aft wall in a beige leather chair, staring at the Tuesday edition of the *Anchorage Daily News*.

On the way to the airport, his cell phone had rung again; it was the sultry voice of a female operative. Telling him that a newspaper article would be awaiting him at the Syracuse Airport. The caller said he would truly enjoy it.

Now Jacob sat at the aft of his $25 million aircraft reading a story entitled "Cab Driver Dies in FBI Standoff."

The article summarized the events that had transpired on Sunday afternoon just south of downtown Anchorage. An arrogant, winner's-circle smile - very similar to his father's - crossed Jacob's face as he read. The article indicated that an FBI agent appeared to have been a target as well. The agent's name was not mentioned, but Jacob knew it was Mark Jameson.

According to the article, the Anchorage Police Department indicated that in the midst of the standoff, a shot from an as-yet undetermined location estimated to be a block away had taken down a cab driver. Because the cab driver's next of kin had not been located, his name was being withheld.

Jacob knew who the cab driver really was, and smiled at the thought. "One down, three to go." And the last three were very personal.

Chapter Thirty

Outside of Nenana, Alaska

<u>Monday May 7, 2002</u>

Agent Gonzalez deftly maneuvered the FBI Suburban around a moose that had ambled its way onto the Parks Highway. Thankfully it was a few hours before dawn, so the moose would avoid the heavy summer traffic headed toward Denali National Park.

Mount McKinley, aka Denali, is a peak in the Alaska Range and the highest mountain in North America. At 20,320 feet, it attracts visitors from all over the world; some come by cruise lines, some by rail, and a good number by RV or personal vehicle. A few even jump aboard small single-engine Cessna aircraft and experience Alaska in a once-in-a-lifetime way, landing on a strip of glacial ice.

Gonzalez and Mark passed the Park with little to no fanfare. This trip was in the quiet of the night and their assignment took understandable precedent.

While the trip didn't lend itself to any sightseeing, it provided the two FBI agents with the opportunity to form some conjecture around the long-ago death of Joshua Knight and the hours-old assassination of Ronald Johns, aka Ronny the Cabby.

The two agents had discussed the crash of the airplane that Knight had purportedly been on, and how he could have his name on the flight manifest, while his remains would be found 800-miles away and, more importantly, so many years later.

It was Gonzalez who made the keen observation that would eventually put the FBI on the right path.

"Doesn't it seem strange that I'm focused on Knight, and you're focused on the dead cab driver? Looking at our notes, we've got Myles Honeycutt and a couple of Honeycutt Petroleum personnel getting taken out. Other than the cab driver, the other names we've got on the radar screen died back in the 1970's. And the common denominator is Honeycutt Petroleum Corporation."

"Are we thinking that someone had an axe to grind with these guys, or something more sinister?"

"I'm not sure, but take a look at the situation. No offense, but you're in the mix somewhere too. Your grandmother dies on the plane that Knight was supposed to have been on. Then right in front of you, a cab driver tells you this is about Joshua Knight, and he's snuffed out."

Mark nodded at Sandra. "Honestly, I'd already been thinking about that - what an awful coincidence."

"In my experienced opinion, I think you've been assigned because there is a connection there somewhere."

"And here I thought that maybe the Bureau just thought you and I are the cream of the crop."

That one drew a soft snicker. "Aha, I'm sure that's it."

But Mark took what she had to say to heart. She was right.

He didn't want to come across as arrogant but everything about this case so far felt very much like it revolved around him. His grandmother's name on the manifest with Joshua Knight, and Ronny the Cabby being taken out in front of him, were strong indicators, but what Sandra hadn't mentioned was the fact that they had been partnered up months earlier, when they'd mysteriously encountered his father and tales of the Shadow Squad.

Mark's gut told him that somehow he and Sandra had been surreptitiously pulled into a Shadow Squad Op. If so, there was a good possibility that Lindsay Drummond was a member of that team.

Sandra noted her partner's silence. "Care to share?"

"We've been focused on Knight, our cabby, and Honeycutt Petroleum in the mix. But remember the conversation we had with my father not long after 9/11 - something about the Shadow Squad?"

"Of course I remember that conversation, it's exactly why I think you're a piece of this puzzle."

"Does that mean my father knows what we're looking into or that maybe in some odd way they're all connected? In some strange confluence you and I have the luck to be at the connection?"

Sandra allowed a smile as she looked over at Mark.

"Funny enough, I've had a gut feeling about this case. Ever since I got a call that you were in danger. Look how that turned out."

"So, where does that leave us now?"

"You said it earlier - we need to find the common denominator. Something has guys from the 70's connected with our dead cab driver and somehow you're in the midst of it."

Mark's brown eyes had a deep, intense quality that Gonzalez found very attractive. But again, the Bureau thing got in the way. And she remembered the way Mark had been distracted, months earlier, by the buxom blond jogging the streets of Anchorage.

As soon as Sandra said it, the term *common denominator* rattled around in Mark's mind that was begging for some rest. He'd been on the go for almost twenty-four hours, but the comment had his mind in hyper-drive. "Remember what I'd said earlier, about keep it simple stupid?"

She nodded.

"Well, whatever this was all about was something material to the 1970's, just like you said." He paused for a moment to ensure she was engaged with the train of thought. "Let's PDF our Day-timer notes to my partner in Seattle and let her do some research. You and I need some rest soon - well, at least I do."

"I agree. I honestly feel like we're being sent on a wild-goose chase to Nenana. I'm not sure how fruitful this trip is going to be."

"No shit" was at the tip of his tongue but he kept it in check. He was mostly frustrated because this trip had disrupted his time with Lindsay. "Well, let's check into the motel for a nap after we get the PDF to Seattle."

"Sounds like a plan to me."

They decided to drop discussing the case for now. It could wait until they had more information.

Nenana, Alaska

<u>Monday May 7, 2002</u>

At around six am, they finally pulled into Nenana, the first order of business to contact Mike Lynch, in charge of the Nenana Post of the Alaska State Troopers. After a brief phone conversation with him, Sandra relayed to Mark.

That someone had telephoned the Alaska State Troopers Headquarters in Fairbanks to report the shooting of the cab driver in Anchorage.

Mark was thinking to himself, *Whoop-de-freaking-do*, until she continued, "According to Trooper Lynch, the caller had overheard a man with a native accent mention the Cabbie's name when he was on a café's pay phone.

"Native accent...?" Mark asked but couldn't elaborate. Sandra had no clue about the friendly call he'd gotten when Ronny the Cabby had dropped him at the Westmark about fifteen hours earlier.

"The Fairbanks Troopers traced the anonymous tip to a pay phone in Nenana. You know the drill. We'll question folks who were in the vicinity of the pay phone when the call was made, check with the local restaurants. If we get lucky, we'll get to interrogate somebody and really have some fun. And in case we're deposed, I didn't say that."

Mark loved her answer. The FBI handbook doesn't call for waterboarding, but he'd recently become a fan.

Lynch had encouraged them to check into the hotel and get some shut-eye; there would be no one at the café where the pay phone was located for at least another two hours. He got no argument. Mark was a bit surprised they'd be able to check into a hotel so early, but it was Alaska.

They were booked at The Roughwoods Inn just a stone's throw from the Parks Highway Bridge with a birds-eye view of the picturesque convergence of the Tanana and Nenana Rivers. The seven rooms were actually very comfortable as well as utilitarian- nice clean beds, a kitchen, cozy couches, and a TV.

As they pulled into the motel's parking lot, the two agents both did the same thing. Their gazes passed over the other three vehicles in the lot, looking at each license plate, each interior, at the perimeter of each vehicle for any sign of a threat. None appeared to exist.

Ten minutes later, they'd checked in and agreed to share a room –they were hopefully only there for the day, and Mark had no problem crashing on the couch.

Just as they were ready to crash, Mark realized he hadn't sent the PDF to Dani back in Seattle.

"Hey, Sandra, before we crash do you think we can send Dani the PDF?"

"How about we jusd sent an e-mail?"

That made sense, probably there wouldn't be a Kinko's out here in the middle of Alaska anyhow.

"We'll send it after we get a little sleep if that's alright?" Sandra plopped herself down on the single queen-size bed.

Chapter Thirty-One

Nenana, Alaska

<u>Monday May 7, 2002</u>

The road trip in the middle of the night had taken its toll – much more than Mark realized as they drove throughout the night. The conversation with Special Agent Gonzalez and the image of Ronny the Cabby with a sniper's shot taking him out had him on edge.

On top of it all, they were in the middle of nowhere in Nenana, Alaska. It was a pleasant, quaint little town, but he hated to admit he was homesick for Seattle, I-5, and bumper to bumper traffic. Not to mention the fact that this little town wasn't his first choice, or even in the top five of where he wanted to be just then. Worse, the lack of his usual Monday morning run was causing his body a feeling of withdrawal. But all he wanted was the feeling of a pillow and a comforter on the spacious couch.

Funny enough, the mental and physical exhaustion had him experiencing a feeling that he had not known for a long while. It was more than just sleep deprivation he had the oddest sensation of simply being in the here and now.

Finally succumbing to exhaustion he closed his eyes. A dream of late was repeating itself. As he slept on the top of the plush comforter, the dream took hold.

He dropped a mocha he'd just purchased, and FBI Agent Mike Hollis and he were sprinting for a bank that was being robbed as they'd learned from a frantic woman running from it. He'd been on a couple of raids as a rookie FBI agent in Denver, and this shouldn't have been different, but it was. No backup, no breach plan, no SWAT, just Agent Hollis and him.

Hollis calmed the female down who'd come running out of the bank. "Ma'am, how many are in there?"

"Just one...a young kid...he's...he's really nervous. He was stuttering the whole time."

"Ma'am, does he have a weapon?"

"Yes, sir, he does." She described the pistol the assailant was holding. "It sounds like a Sig-Sauer," Hollis said, looking at Mark.

The two agents sprinted the last seventy-five yards or so and pinned their backs against a brick wall out of sight of the assailant.

"Mark, this is for real. You ready?" Hollis said, looking at his younger partner.

Mark didn't have time to answer. The robber came walking out of the bank, just a kid.

"FBI, drop the bags and don't move a muscle!" He was back in Denver in the mid-90's facing a guy who'd just robbed the Bank of America.

Young brown eyes were looking at him with defiance, but there was fear there, too. He had a Sig-Sauer pistol in his right hand, pointed right at Mark.

"Drop the gun!" Mark commanded once again.

"Fuck you!" He yelled.

"Drop the gun now!" Mark commanded again.

He saw the twitch in his eyes. The bank robber was out of it, probably high on either coke or meth. It was all in slow motion as he watched the robber's right index finger start to compress on the trigger.

Mark's adrenaline was rising, but the mind was in control. His commands for the robber to drop the gun were to no avail.

Mark pulled the trigger and watched as the bullet obliterated a young life. He was on the ground, his face down in a pool of blood.

"Suspect down! I need help now!" Mark shouted over and over. The scene was chaos as sirens blared and agents moved about.

He stood there staring at the kid's lifeless body. The robber couldn't have been more than 23 years old. "He wouldn't drop the gun," Mark told SA Mike Hollis, repeating it time and again.

"Mark, you did your job, you had no choice." Hollis gripped Mark's shoulder, attempting to shake the shock from his system.

"But he wouldn't drop the gun," Mark said, resigned to what he had just done.

Hollis left for a moment and Mark kneeled, fighting for words. He saw the pool of blood and started to cry.

"Mark, Mark...it's alright," Hollis said, gripping his partner's shoulder.

"Mark, Mark..." Sandra had a grip on his shoulder. He had been sleeping for two hours, and it was almost eight forty-five.

He was soaked in sweat, and it took a moment to return to May 2002. So much for being in the here and now. In reality, he didn't shoot that kid, and he'd thanked God every day since that the kid dropped his gun, but this dream had him wondering how he would deal with it if he ever had to take a subject down that way.

"You alright?" Sandra asked.

"Yeah," he said unconvincingly.

"Why don't you jump in the shower? We don't have a wireless connection here, so I'll pay a courtesy visit to Lynch and let him know we'll do a follow-up at the cafe late this afternoon. I'll also e-mail your day-timer page to Dani from his office."

Mark didn't answer, still caught in the dream.

She seemed to sense it. "You want to talk about it?" Sandra asked sincerely.

Over the last eighteen hours, the two had developed a pretty strong bond, and Mark wasn't so uptight that he wouldn't let his emotions show. The dream was a hybrid of a first showdown where he had almost fired the weapon, and the day before with Ronny the Cabby taking one in the head right in front of him. "The Cabby getting plugged right in front of me, I can't get that shot to his head, the startled fear in his eyes, out of my mind..." He swallowed. "It messed me up a bit."

"Until yesterday, I'd never seen someone die in front of me either. Best thing to do is get the incident out, front and center."

Sandra was right. Mark remembered a session at Quantico focused on Critical Incident Stress Management. In the best of circumstances, when a traumatic situation is encountered, a well-trained counseling team is dispatched; however, the immediacy necessary at the law-enforcement level to clear any of the FBI agents at the scene of Ronny the Cabby's death took precedent. Then there was the call to get the FBI north to Nenana.

Sandra was playing the FBI CISM playbook as best as she could. They talked out what Mark had seen, how it made him feel, and what he could have done differently. Finally, she said what his high school baseball coach would when he'd booted a grounder at shortstop: "Shake it off..." though she added the FBI jargon he'd grown accustomed to and relied upon: "...and let's get back in the saddle."

Mark took her advice, thanked her for the pep rally, and headed for the shower. She said she'd be back in a bit with a couple mochas. The next hour or so would turn out to be even stranger than the last eighteen-the fun was just beginning.

Nenana, Alaska
<u>Monday May 7, 2002</u>

SA Gonzalez drove to the Nenana Trooper's Office after she'd called him. She'd told him she needed to make a few copies, and he offered the Canon Copier/Printer at his office.

Trooper Lynch was a monster of a man. Born and raised in Minneapolis, Minnesota, he'd quickly grown accustomed to the frigid cold of Interior Alaska from late October to mid-March. During the spring, the weather was often better than what he'd experienced in Minnesota. There was little humidity, the sun was in the sky from around six in the morning until eight or nine, and as the days passed, each day got a bit longer until late June.

Agent Gonzalez guessed Lynch was six foot three and weighed around two hundred thirty pounds. His light African American skin was smooth, but his eyes showed the hint of stress that accompanies a very tough job in a tough environment.

As he shook Sandra's hand, she could feel the calluses on his palms. He was an outdoorsman. A notable scar across his right arm showed he'd been injured, probably shot, at some point in his career.

"Line of duty?" She asked.

"Pulled over a stolen car; kid got two shots off before my partner took him out. The kid got off one lucky shot," Lynch answered.

"How'd you end up in Alaska?"

"I've been a Trooper my whole life, had five years in when I got hit. As you can imagine, it frightened my family. Well, without boring you with all of the details, my wife did her research and found that Alaska might be a safer place to be a cop and a great place to raise two kids," Lynch said with an infectious smile. "So here I am in a town of less than 500 people. My kids love it here, and my wife just can't get enough of PTA meetings and carting the kids to ball games."

"So how about you?"

"Actually, I hated it at first, but the people and place, it grows on you. There are days I miss the hustle that went with being in a city of a couple million, but there are more days when I'm glad I live in a town where I know almost every person's name."

His enthusiasm for a nice family life was refreshing for Sandra. She hoped one day she'd experience that.

The conversation continued for a few more minutes, and then Lynch helped her connect the FBI Laptop to the office Local Area Network so that she'd get access to e-mail. Lynch led her to the station's printer/copier/scanner and assisted her in scanning a page from Agent Jameson's Day-timer.

Chapter Thirty-Two

Nenana, Alaska

<u>Monday May 6, 2002</u>

Sandra was right. Mark felt much better after a shower and a shave. It felt good to wash away, even if only figuratively, the last day away from his physical being.

The motel bathroom was small, and it was difficult to move around. It dawned on Mark while he was shaving that the motel had been well stocked with supplies. Sometimes he knew he was not the brightest apple in the tree, and this was definitely one of those moments.

Sandra wasn't going to be back for at least another hour, but still he had to mutter an obvious question. "What kind of motel is this?" He asked the empty room as he walked out into the bedroom in nothing but a pair of boxers.

"It's sort of what we call a Safe House," a woman's voice answered.

Surprises of one kind or another had come around corner after corner lately, but just then was probably the biggest.

"Lindsay?" Mark finally managed. He had serious doubt that he would remember his own name at that moment. Blonds were his weakness, and Lindsay's sandy-blond hair and her eyes like the blue waters of the Caribbean were intoxicating. "Nice," Lindsay said as her gaze ventured slowly up and down his torso.

What's was nice to know is that I have some effect on women, Mark thought. Maybe not always a good one, but in this instance he could tell it was mutual attraction. Being admired was a nice feeling. Mark was not planning to work for Chippendale's, but he did his utmost, almost obsessively so, to take good care of himself.

"Thanks," he said, embarrassed. Mind and heart were wrestling with one another. Why she was here was high on his list of questions, but right then, just as important, he was so happy to see this gorgeous, intriguing woman. Unfortunately, telling her that would have to wait.

"So what the hell is going on?" he asked with his gaze fixed on hers. And for the moment, his stare wasn't of the boyhood crush variety, but of the interrogation "Don't screw with me" variety.

Lindsay took a moment before she got started. It didn't appear she was working to jerk him around; she was trying to find the right place to start. "Remember I said there was intelligence chatter with the Jameson name on it?"

Mark confirmed as much with a nod.

"I guess you don't need any more proof now. Please know you can trust us." Lindsay paused.

He actually found comfort in the way she said "us." He repeated, "Us? So are you finally going to tell me what agency you're with?"

"I'll get to that in a minute," she answered.

Mark smirked. Her hesitation led him to believe he'd guessed right on the airplane on Sunday morning. She had to be CIA.

She continued, "We have researched you and your family, and we think we may have found something that on the edges connects you to the Honeycutt Petroleum Company, but we're still not sure what makes you a target." Lindsay stopped and sipped what looked like a Mocha she'd brought with her.

He was trying to figure out where she would have gotten one in this tiny town. He'd ask later.

She continued after taking a second. "It seems there is a connection with your current case. Joshua Knight."

The supposed connection surprised him. Joshua Knight's disappearance case had seemed strange all along - certainly not one that would get the attention of the country's intelligence apparatus, and it certainly didn't seem to be something that would connect his family to a big oil company?

"Knight and the Jameson Family..." he said quizzically.

Lindsay nodded.

"What would an oil company care about my family?" He was afraid he was looking quite inept, but the dots were not connecting all that well.

"I'm getting to that..." Something in her voice gave him the sense that what she had to say would surprise him. "The case you're on.... let's just say it is probably the biggest FBI case of all time, and you're at the core of it."

He was trying to figure out what Lindsay could be alluding to. There wasn't anything that even remotely would have him believe that some guy dying 800-miles from where he had purportedly perished would be anything more than a twisted murder case. But again, practicing full disclosure, he had only just begun to dig into who Joshua Knight was. Mark had to concede the case had some strange circumstances throughout – Joshua Knight and where he'd been found, Myles Honeycutt committing suicide, and Clay Tanis and Rico Sanchez being executed on the Seattle Waterfront. The connection on that level to Honeycutt Petroleum made sense, but he didn't see how his family name fit in with that.

"We've been doing some digging, and there is one more thing I'm guessing you've not come across yet. There is a woman in the mix. Her parents died in 1971." Lindsay paused for a second. She'd placed a great deal of emphasis on the year 1971 and clearly knowing that would raise some alarm bells. Her tone left no doubt another shoe was going to drop. "Her parents were on your grandmother's plane."

"Who's the woman?"

"Her name is Olivia Black."

Mark's mind rewound itself eight months. During the encounter with his father in Paxson the prior November, he'd had a woman with him. She looked to be about Mark's age. Maybe that woman was Olivia Black?

Nenana, Alaska

<u>Monday May 6, 2002</u>

Lindsay and Mark discussed Olivia Black and this interesting piece of information for another good ten minutes or so. She filled him in on who Olivia was as a child. According to Lindsay's research, Olivia was born on in April 1965 to Phillip and Miranda Black in the town of Sitka, Alaska. Her father paid his dues and eventually became a high-ranking member of a tribal organization Mark had barely heard of. Both parents were aboard Alaska Airlines 1866 when it slammed into a mountain outside of Juneau, heading home because one of her mother's uncles had died suddenly.

His mind was now focused on the Day-timer. Olivia Black's father Phillip Black needed to be added to the list.

Somewhere along the line, the conversation shifted to something less pertinent than national security, but nevertheless very pertinent to what had transpired over the last few days. "I was hoping I'd see you again." The words just came out, and he could see the same feeling in her eyes.

He tried not to, but he just had to admire the voluptuous, womanly figure she'd been blessed with. When she'd entered the coach cabin and sat next to him on Monday on the flight from Seattle to Anchorage, he had been struck by her curvaceous silhouette. Guys were so darn one-dimensional and sadly so damn predictable.

"Sorry," he said, realizing he had stared a little longer than he should have. He was waiting for the "my eyes are up here" chastisement; he had never had it said to him, but there's a first for everything.

The weather was warm, and Lindsay was wearing a pair of white slacks, a yellow chemise, and a light blue jacket that to some degree concealed her figure.

"Please don't apologize." She removed her jacket, and the curve of her figure was now definitely on display. He had no doubt it was on purpose. She even took a deep breath – just to tease him.

Suddenly realizing he was still in boxers, he attempted to excuse myself, but she said with a flirtatious smile, "You don't need to cover up on my account."

The two had only known each other for a few days and had only met twice in person, so he had no idea where this little dance was going. She didn't take long to answer his unspoken question. "Did you feel what I felt when we talked on the telephone that first time?"

"I sure did. And when you sat next to me on the airplane… I hope you don't mind if I tell you, I couldn't get over how beautiful you are." Mark said, almost shyly.

She acknowledged the sincere compliment with her own surprisingly shy smile. She had to know she was a stunning woman, but what he found even more appealing was the modesty with which she carried herself. It seemed her confidence was a quality derived from intelligence, experience, and her career; at least as far as he could tell, it was not a result of her physical attributes.

"I've never felt what I'm feeling. I hope this doesn't sound…I don't know… silly." She paused. "Do you believe in love at first sight?"

She said what Mark had felt the first time they talked not even three days earlier. And the veneer of the intelligence operative momentarily disappeared again.

"I do," he said softly. "Actually, let me correct myself. I do now."

"I've lived a very…how shall I say, unorthodox life. I'm a very direct and to be blunt very dangerous woman but…well, I'm still a woman. I've never fallen for someone, so please believe me this is out of character for me."

As Lindsay shared her feelings, Mark could see the look of opening her heart on her face. She wanted to feel this. He hoped she could see he was feeling the exact same thing.

"You felt all this over a phone call and one little conversation on an airplane?" he asked incredulously, looking actually for affirmation of all he was feeling as well.

"Like I said, I'm not wired that way, but there is something about you and me. I don't know how to describe it," she said.

They were adults, and there was something in the way she said it. He not only believed her, but he felt everything she was describing. If a couple of high school kids can find love at first sight, why not a couple of federal agents in their thirties?

"I know what you're saying. That first day when we talked, there was something in your voice. I was already attracted to you."

"So where does that leave us?" Lindsay said, but before he could answer, she continued, "I hate to bring this back to what else is going on. We don't know who's targeted you, and who knows if they might succeed. It's too complicated."

He took a deep breath and just let whatever he was feeling to escape into their lives. "Whatever this is all about, we'll get on with it, and my guess is pretty soon here. As for you and me, let's just see where fate takes us."

"Then fate it is."

Lindsay's soft, harmonious voice had just changed his life. Whatever this assignment was, he was going to see it through, but now he had hope that fate was going to lead to so much more.

He was still standing there in just a pair of boxers. "Excuse me for a second." A few moments later he was back in the room wearing a pair of khaki shorts and a University of Washington tee shirt.

When he came back into the room, Lindsay had sat down on the couch after helping herself to a soda from the refrigerator. She handed him one as he sat down on the couch. He could smell her perfume. To borrow that line again from "Top Gun," this was going to be complicated.

You put Mark on a basketball court, he was smart-ass as can be and would trash-talk the other guys like crazy; however, around an attractive woman it was like Junior High all over again and he was at a loss for words. Right then, it was one of those moments, and they were at a conversational impasse.

Lindsay sensed it and kindly told him to relax.

As much as he would have loved for this to be about Lindsay at the moment, they needed to get back on track with Olivia Black, Phillip Black, and Joshua Knight, et al.

"What do you think this all about? Why is some guy who died thirty years ago all of a sudden so important?" he asked, referring to the crash of his grandmother's airplane and any possible connection to Joshua Knight.

Lindsay paused before she said anything, another attractive quality. "I could say this is above my pay grade, but I don't think that's a fair answer." Another pause. "I'm the one who intercepted the information that the name Jameson was on a list."

He could see it in her eyes. She felt like she hated what her life had become. There was a fair assumption that what Lindsay did was Black Ops, questionable in legality. A "Black Op" is of a nature that the government running the operation can be given deniability.

"So why me...?"

"That is above my pay grade and actually is still a mystery," Lindsay said. She looked deep into his eyes. "That is actually why you're in Nenana."

"That doesn't sound comforting. And what do you mean, that's why I'm in Nenana?" He responded a little more pointedly than he would have liked, so touched her knee and apologized for how that came across.

That was the first time they had ever touched beyond a shaking of the hands. Mark's pulse raced and for a moment he was the intimidated teenager again. Her face was a little flushed.

"I'm technically here for a little more than surveillance…I'm assigned to ensure you stay alive at all costs. Nice thing to reminisce about on our first date or maybe a bedtime story for our grandkids, don't you think?" Lindsay said with a sincere little laugh. "And I know this doesn't make sense now, but you're also here because someone tells me you have the ability to expose a weak spot with relative ease. Human Intel has become a lost art and from what your file shows, you have an uncanny ability to get information from the unlikeliest places and sources."

For Mark, it was feeling a lot like being recruited against his will. "I guess so. I certainly have never advertised it, though," he said. "I can gather white-collar intelligence, but if you're talking about cultivating terrorists into CIs, wow. To steal one of your lines, that's above my pay grade." In the law enforcement world, a CI is a confidential informant, an individual usually from the criminal element who provides information on his or her fellow colleagues for a fee.

As they talked, the aroma of Lindsay's perfume had held Mark captivated. He changed the subject for a moment. "I hope you don't mind, but I have to know what perfume you wear."

"It's Clinique, I'm glad you like it," she said with a smile.

"I do." He was lost in her blue eyes. As he gazed longer, her life of loneliness and torment were more than evident.

Lindsay didn't say a word for a minute, and he was afraid the gaze had lasted a little too long. She looked vulnerable, and he knew it was not a way anyone would have typically described Lindsay. For some reason, he had been able to help that protective layer dissipate.

"I don't want to make a fool of myself, but I need to tell you," Mark started. She didn't stop him, so he kept going. "You're not like anyone I've ever met."

"I hope that's a good thing?"

He didn't know if he was walking over a cliff or into a relationship. "I guess I'm wondering why a woman who's had the life you've had and as beautiful as you would fall for me? I don't have a self-confidence problem, but to be direct as you say, I'm kind of afraid I'll fall for you and then it will all go away."

"Honestly, I'm feeling the same way. Do you have any idea what a catch you are? You're a great-looking guy, smart, and an FBI Agent to boot." She paused. "I'm not naïve, and please don't think I'm arrogant, I know I'm what a man would find physically..." she motioned her arms across her bosom, "...beautiful. But I'm looking for a man who appreciates me for more than that." She paused again.

Mark was getting a view of what a woman must experience, thanks to the superficial way men tended to admire a woman.

Lindsay continued, "And my profession lends itself to meeting men who lead...well, unorthodox lives."

"And you think the life of an FBI agent is normal?"

"It's all relative...not normal in the nine-to-five sense, but you don't live under a variety of aliases, lie better than you tell the truth, and maybe see your apartment once every two months..." Lindsay expressed more than he would have expected; he was getting a glimpse at the life she was living.

"Before meeting you, I was starting to wonder about my career choice. Then you come along running with that cheesy smirk on your face, and then you check me out when I sat down next to you on the plane...That feeling's grown more," Lindsay said, implying she was starting to take stock of her life working for an-as-yet unnamed government agency, and apparently his boyish charm was growing on her.

Mark was at a loss for words. A woman, an intelligence operative to boot, whom he'd only known for forty-eight hours, had some level of feelings for him and apparently those feelings were part of the reason she was having thoughts of a quasi-normal life.

"Lindsay, I really don't know what to say."

"I'm sorry, I didn't mean to open up quite so much."

"No, I didn't mean that. It has been a long time since I've been close to someone, and I honestly have a feeling about..." He paused, debating how deep to get, but Lindsay had opened up, so she deserved that those true feelings be returned. "About you and what may come next. I'd really like to find out."

"I would like that, Mark Jameson." She answered, and he loved the way she said that.

Unfortunately the conversation needed to return to the ominous environment of their professional lives, but he kept two key questions in check.

First one: "Before we get too far ahead of ourselves, I think it's time you tell me who you work for" Mark said politely but with a hint of enough is enough.

"I was wondering when we'd finally get back to that - I'm CIA."

"You owe me dinner," he said, reminding her of the conversation forty-eight hours earlier in row six between Yakutat and Anchorage. NSA or CIA, those had been his two guesses.

"So now we've got two dates." She had him hooked with her sweet voice and warm smile. She sure didn't seem like a spy, but he guessed that was how it was supposed to work.

"Second question..." He paused, not for effect, but because he was still a little intimidated by what was happening. "You said someone says I'm good at exposing weak spots. Who?"

"Need to know." Her flat tone and directness left no doubt she was definitely a spy.

She got up and walked to a window and gazed out. He knew this was going somewhere with what she said next.

"Mark, this is going to be complicated." She'd just paraphrased one of his favorite lines from "Top Gun."

Chapter Thirty-Three

Anchorage, Alaska
<u>Monday May 6, 2002</u>

The FBI had virtually no jurisdiction in the murder of the cab driver, but because there was ample evidence that an FBI agent may also have been a target, they gained some level of clout. Unbeknownst to Sandra and Mark, on late Sunday evening Agent Dani Westford was told she was going to Anchorage. The case that had brought Mark to Anchorage due to being a potential target now made it FBI jurisdiction. Dani's assignment was anything but simple: follow the same leads Mark and Sandra were tracking and put the thing to bed.

After arriving in Anchorage, her first order of business was to check her FBI e-mail account. She had eleven items in her in-box. Seven were related to the RICO case she was working with Assistant U.S. Attorney Nancy Gault, one was an FBI-wide alert, one was an internal Seattle Field Office item, and the last two were the ones that caught her immediate attention.

The first was something she was aware of. Mark and SA Gonzalez had been dispatched to a town just south of Fairbanks to follow a lead.

The second was from SA Gonzalez, indicating that she was transferring a page of Mark's Day-timer; the page contained notes they thought relevant to the dead cab driver, the missing Anchorage DA, and the case of a guy named Joshua Knight who went missing in 1971.

The Day-timer came through as a PDF. She printed it and carried it downstairs to peruse over a plate of fruit, eggs, turkey bacon, and toast.

Anchorage, Alaska

<u>Monday May 6, 2002</u>

The small sofa Lindsay was sharing with Mark had grown claustrophobic; the mix of information she'd been instructed to hold back from him, along with the physical and emotional chemistry the two shared, bordered on overwhelming. Part of her wanted love to just sweep her away, but the job won out, at least for the moment. "Is it alright if I ask you something?"

"Of course."

"We all have a tale of why we're in this business. I'd love to hear your story."

Lindsay saw the pride in Mark's penetrating brown eyes. But before he could start, his cell phone rang.

Mark shrugged and answered. It was Gonzalez. "Trooper Lynch and I interviewed some people at the café and like I said when we got to town, I think we got sent down a dead-end path. I think the Bureau got played on this one."

"So I guess we're heading back to Anchorage?"

"It looks that way. I'm still at the café. Would you like me to pick us up some lunch?"

"That'd be great. I'd love a turkey sandwich."

"Your partner?" Lindsay asked.

"Yeah, she's on her way back."

"You can tell me why you joined the FBI another time."

All Mark wanted to do was get lost in those intoxicating blue eyes.

"What?"

"I'm sorry," Mark said, his eyes still lost in her eyes. A fan of chick flicks, he realized he would regret it if the moment passed.

He remembered the scene in "My Best Friend's Wedding" with Julia Roberts and Dermot Mulroney, the two taking a river boat cruise along one of the Chicago canals. The scene culminates in Julia's character's silence, allowing the moment to pass and with it her best chance to tell Dermot Mulroney's character how deeply in love with him she is.

Mark sensed something in the awkward silence now, as an intuition that had served him well most of his life was screaming for him to just say what he felt. Mark didn't let the moment pass, though it was in a tiny motel room in the middle of Alaska's Interior.

"Lindsay, I'm afraid of scaring you away but I know that I'll never in my life ever meet anyone else like you. I'd like to tell you that it is because you're absolutely the most gorgeous woman I've ever seen in my life, but really it was the first time we talked. I couldn't get your sweet voice out of my mind." Mark laid it out there, scared to death.

The direct approach Lindsay had on the airplane the day before took over. "Agent Jameson, I have this unbelievable urge to kiss you." She gracefully leaned toward Mark, and their lips softly touched.

Chapter Thirty-Four

Anchorage, Alaska
<u>Monday May 6, 2002</u>

It was around ten-twenty AM on Monday and a group of what appeared to be retirees were seated at wooden tables. The folks were laughing and enjoying coffee and breakfast in the Café' Promenade of the Anchorage Marriott Downtown apparently ready to be delivered on a luxurious tour bus to a Norwegian Cruise Line ship.

Dani watched wistfully as the group spread like children in an elementary school cafeteria around the café. Her privacy was now gone, but her mental faculties were focused, assembling the random pieces of information that Mark and SA Gonzalez had passed her way.

Her eyes methodically passed over each bullet point:

<u>Sunday May 5, 2002 - Written aboard Alaska Airlines Flight 81</u>
- ✓ *May 5, 2002 - SA Jameson assigned via request from ASAC Branson to a case in Anchorage, Alaska.*
- ✓ *Subject: Skeletal remains found in a burned-out building near Dimond Shopping Mall. Remains are those of a man named Joshua Knight.*
- ✓ *Federal jurisdiction rationale: According to NTSB database, Joshua Knight perished aboard Alaska Airlines Flight 1866 in September 1971.*

- ✓ SA Jameson Note: Need to disclose personal connection to this case - see bullet #3 (my grandmother was also aboard that flight).

Added by SA Gonzalez:

Sunday May 5, 2002 - Written at Hotel Captain Cook
- ✓ Joshua Knight – working on ANCSA analysis for Honeycutt Petroleum – mentored by Myles Honeycutt – CEO
- ✓ Myles Honeycutt, died 1972 – apparent suicide but no note???
- ✓ Clay Tanis, murdered 1972 – six witnesses all noted assassin was graying man with glasses. Assistant Security Chief for Honeycutt Petroleum
- ✓ Rico Sanchez, murdered 1972 - Alaska Bush Pilot – more research needed. Murdered along with Clay Tanis. Not sure where to start?
- ✓ Native Alaskan-accented caller ("on his term"s") – what the hell???
- ✓ And me – why I am a threat to somebody? Connect the dots.
- ✓ Ronny the Cabby – who the hell is he and why was he shot?
- ✓ And find out what ANCSA is all about?

She returned to her room around eleven AM and made some notes of her own, though much simpler. Instead of hand-written, she used Microsoft Word.

- 1970's: Knight (Anchorage - perished 1971), Myles H. (Upstate New York - suicide 1972), Clay T. (Seattle – dead 1972), R. Sanchez (Seattle – dead 1972)

- o   Connection: Honeycutt Petroleum
- **2000's:** Ronald Johns (Anchorage – shot/killed 5/5)
  - o   Connection: FBI SA Mark Jameson
- <u>Initial Thoughts:</u> Connected to dead cab driver and all other deaths. Disappeared 1971.
  - o   Look into: Why was he in Anchorage?
  - o   Look into: What was significant on Sept. $4^{th}/5^{th}$, 1971?
  - o   Look into: What has opened a thirty-year old cold case?
  - o   Look into: What was so important to Honeycutt Petroleum in   1971?

She smirked, she essentially had the same questions Mark posed, but every agent has their own way to get comfortable with a case. Three glaring things stood out to her: 1) the year 1971, 2) an oil company, and 3) whatever Joshua Knight was working on. She figured the remainder connected themselves to those facts.

Using Google, Dani typed the phrase "Alaska and September 1971." The result right out of the gate raised the hairs on the back of her neck.

For a good ten minutes, Dani stared at the screen on her Gateway Laptop reading about a significant event she'd not heard of before. She rose from her queen-size bed and walked to the window staring south southeast toward the bluish-green Chugiak Mountain Range. Her eyes were fixed on the mountains with a light dusting of snow; she could almost feel the wheels turning in her mind as she contemplated the Google.

An Alaska Airlines flight had crashed on September, 1971. Correlation number one - Mark's grandmother was aboard the flight. And seemingly just to hook Dani, the hit outlined the flight's routing – it originated in Anchorage, Alaska.

104 passengers and seven crew members were lost on the flight. The National Transportation Safety Board and the resulting federal investigation pointed toward "misleading navigational information."

The bottom right corner of her laptop said it was 3:30pm. Her research on the crash of Alaska Airlines 1866 lasted for more than four hours.

Dani was sure that what she'd found had some significance. In her line of work she'd learned that following one track can lead you further away from the answer, but her instincts told her she was on the right track. She'd missed lunch and realized she needed a break from the plight of Flight 1866. Just as she was going to read the room service menu, her cell phone rang.

"It's Mark. Want to take a trip to Nenana?"

Her first thought was, *"Where the heck is Nenana?"* And she wondered what Mark would think, if he knew she was already in Alaska.

Anchorage, Alaska
<u>Monday May 6, 2002</u>

Fifteen minutes later, Dani had ordered from room service and returned her attention to the Knight case. She had discarded her formal pantsuit in favor of a pair of grey shorts and a Seattle Seahawks night jersey moments after hanging up the cell phone.

She'd looked in the mirror as she changed. Her right shoulder still bore the scar of surgery she'd received at fifteen years old, the result of falling from a tree. She gently tapped at her abdomen, wishing she had more time to work out lately. Almost a decade in the service of her government had thankfully not taken much of a toll on her physical fitness. She was in great shape, the result of four days a week physical training she committed herself to, one day of rock climbing each weekend, and her ritual five mile run each Sunday morning.

She looked at her physique a little closer. She'd just reached thirty-seven years of age, and her figure still seemed attractive, yet she had not had a very active romantic life. She was wondering if maybe it was her looks. Her mix of German-American and Irish background gave her a light complexion, strawberry blond hair, and deep brown eyes wide and captivating, her physique modestly curvaceous, and her confidence strong but not arrogant. But for some reason she was not attracting a lot of dates.

As she departed from the view in the mirror and returned her attention to her Laptop, she realized it was her 24/7 dedication to her job that had chased any relationships away.

She leaned back against two large white pillows and found herself on the Internet again.

The break had given her a little new perspective, so instead of "Alaska September 1971," she typed "1971 and Alaska History" into the Google search bar. The Alaska Native Claims Settlement Act (ANCSA) was the first title shown, and the second the crash of Alaska Airlines 1866. She typed ANCSA into the search bar and began to read the returns, typing notes into a Word file. She didn't know if the two were linked, but it was plausible and worth her attention.

She typed "PROBABILITIES" on the top part of the page; for the first two bullet points she typed "Alaska Flight 1866" and "ANCSA." For the third bullet, she typed the name "Honeycutt Petroleum." Above all three, she typed the name "JOSHUA KNIGHT" in large font and in a text bubble.

She returned her attention to ANCSA. There were immeasurable facts about ANCSA. According to one reputable site, ANCSA had two main purposes.

Alaska and its land for centuries had been occupied by several Indian tribes and after Alaska was purchased in 1867, the aboriginal claims to Alaska's land became a disputed issue. More importantly and probably the more potent impetus for ANSCA was the discovery of oil at Prudhoe Bay by the Atlantic Richfield Company (ARCO) in 1968. Suddenly the aboriginal claims to Alaska's land weren't simply a dispute over hunting and fishing rights.

Dani's attention landed on an analysis provided by a government specialist named Richard S. Jones in 1981. The volume of information was astounding. The work detailed the history of native claims and actual title to Alaska land; court rulings at the appellate and supreme court level of what claims and title Alaska natives actually could place on Alaska land; and finally in 1971 the negotiation of the Alaska Native Claims Settlement Act.

Dani in her search realized ANCSA came down to three core but significant quantifiable rights. The United States would recognize approximately $1/9^{th}$ of Alaska land via legal title to belong to Alaska Natives held in the trust of 12 regional native corporations; the United States would establish these corporations with an infusion of $963 million; and in return the United States would receive rights and access to land.

The oil ARCO discovered in 1968 gave life to the Alaska Pipeline that is approximately 800 miles of 48" pipe between Prudhoe Bay on the Arctic Ocean and Valdez, Alaska, on Prince William Sound.

Several legal actions between 1968 and early 1970 including a waiver of rights by Native Groups directly on the intended path of the Alaska Pipeline had the pipeline in contract and permit status with the encouragement of then Alaska Governor Walter "Wally" Hickel. However, those Alaska native groups sought in federal court an injunction for several reasons, but high on the list was the legal concern of non-preferential hire of Alaska natives on pipeline construction contracts.

On April 1, 1970 a federal judge in Washington, D.C. barred the U.S. Department of Interior from issuing any construction permits, citing possible violations of the National Environmental Policy Act. According to the information Dani was analyzing this injunction was the catalyst toward settlement with the Alaska natives. On December 18, 1971, President Richard M. Nixon signed the Alaska Native Claims Settlement Act. Six years later, the Alaska Pipeline was operational.

Dani had become so engrossed in her analysis she had again not paid attention to the time. The laptop read 5:15 PM. She'd had the television on simply for background noise, but now she looked up and the weather forecast had her attention. According to the weather person, Wednesday was going to be overcast and around 65 degrees, still warmer than normal.

On the desk was the glass of Diet Coke and its ice long-ago melted, and a bottled-water she'd barely touched. She found herself parched. Moments later, the bottle was half empty.

Her mind needed a rest and she realized she'd only gotten about five hours of sleep after arriving from Seattle nearly fourteen hours earlier. She closed the Explorer window on the laptop, packed up a few things, and headed for the airport. She felt well-armed with information for her flight to Fairbanks that was scheduled to fly out in a less than two hours.

Chapter Thirty-Five

Nenana, Alaska

<u>Monday May 6, 2002</u>

After the kiss, Lindsay left Mark alone. He was sort of grateful, as explaining her to Sandra would have been difficult to say the least.

Sandra got to the room about a half hour after Lindsay had left. The turkey sandwich was surprisingly good, so the café had his vote. She indicated she was going to get some shut-eye, and she'd booked them a flight back to Anchorage late the next morning.

<u>Around 6:00pm Monday May 6, 2002</u>

The constant tick-tock of an old-fashioned Howard Miller wall clock, the whistle of a brisk but warm wind, and a Burger King advertisement on the 21-inch Sony Television served as the audio stimulus inside the Nenana Motel room that he was occupying.

It was mid-spring, but for some reason the weather was behaving like mid-summer. It was nearly six in the evening and the temperature outside had to be around 70 degrees. Most who do not reside in Alaska would not know it but summers in the interior of Alaska are remarkable, with lots of sunshine and temperatures that sometimes hover around ninety degrees.

Mark was yearning for a nice jog or a hike along the Tanana River that ran right adjacent to "downtown." Nenana had a population of around 400 souls, so describing its city streets as downtown was a bit of an oxymoron. It was an isolated town on the George Parks Highway approximately 55 miles south of

Fairbanks and around 400 miles northeast of Anchorage. Its greatest claim to fame was the Nenana Ice Classic.

In 1917 a group of railroad surveyors waiting for ice on the Tanana River to break, thereby allowing essential supplies to arrive via boat, found a way to bide their time. The surveyors would bet on the date and time when the ice would break, and so started the Nenana Ice Classic which remained a popular game today with much higher stakes. Purses in the six figures were now routine, and the game was common throughout the State of Alaska.

Nenana's most famous visitor, until Mark showed up in their nice little town, was probably President Warren G. Harding, who in 1923 was on hand to commemorate the Mears Memorial Bridge, a railroad trestle spanning the Tanana River. President Harding had the honor of driving the "Golden Stake" at the north end of the bridge.

On the motel's TV, the Burger King ad was followed by an ad for weight watchers. Isn't the free market great? Mark thought one company wants to fatten you up and the other to rescue you from yourself?

He was now beyond claustrophobic. Nenana was a pleasant little village, and he actually was planning to come back sometime, but during the last eight-plus years in the cities of Denver, Phoenix, and Seattle, all he'd known was bumper to bumper traffic. He was ready to get back to that life with the sunroof wide open, listening to Star 101.5 and their edgy humor, headed to a crowded gym and the clang of weights, and a pint of Mac & Jacks at a nice downtown bar listening to people share the travails of their day.

Restlessness took over and he decided a run was a good answer.

Sandra was still deep in sleep, so he left her a note taped to her closed bedroom door.

Donning a pair of navy blue shorts and a gray tee-shirt, he laced up some running shoes and quietly exited the motel room. He only made it about two hundred yards when he was abducted.

Chapter Thirty-Six

Nenana, Alaska
<u>Monday May 7, 2002</u>

Jacob Honeycutt stirred ice cubes in his glass of Diet Coke. Leaning against the oval plane window, he looked out over the wide expanse of agricultural land of Midwest Canada. The private aircraft had been in the air for about three hours, with another five hours of flight time remaining.

The ambitious CEO had made the decision that what had transpired in Anchorage needed to be handled personally. He and his father's only trusted colleague both realized that the Joshua Knight Affair had the potential to destroy the Honeycutt Petroleum Corporation.

The company's Security Chief Adam Ross sat at the aft of the aircraft, studying security tapes from the burned-out building where Knight's skeletal remains had been unearthed a few weeks earlier. Nothing on the tapes revealed the cause of the fire that had brought Joshua Knight back from the dead. Not a spiritual man, Ross wouldn't have given any credence to the odd feeling that ran through his being, except for the momentary chill that ran down his spine.

It was the same chill he'd felt decades earlier as he and Myles Honeycutt had celebrated the signing of the Alaska Native Claims Settlement Act by then President Richard Nixon. He hadn't pinpointed his concern at the time, but age had made him wiser, more conscious of his mortality, and deeply aware that his life had been a wasted one.

Jacob was the opposite end of the spectrum. Greed and its entrapping qualities were all that drove him.

"Adam, may we talk?"

"Be right there." Adam was the only man allowed to speak to Jacob in such a casual manner. Any other subordinate would have replied with great formality and deference.

Adam sat down on the right side of the aircraft, leaning back in the dark leather chair. "You look worried, Jacob."

"I am, something just doesn't feel right about all of this."

Adam took a moment to look out the window, where few clouds dotted the deep blue sky. As the aircraft traveled west, inevitable dusk was bound to catch them.

"I'm feeling the same," Adam replied, avoiding the temptation to add that he had the feeling they were chasing a ghost. The feeling, however, took hold for the briefest of moments as the chill continued to run down his spine.

"Any luck with the tapes?"

"Nope, the building was quiet."

"Has the fire department released anything at all?"

"Their preliminary findings are a faulty wire at the copy machine."

"Quite a coincidence, don't you think? A fire in the middle of the night. Aren't copy machines usually turned off?"

Ross didn't have an answer that would negate Jacob's concerns, so he just nodded his head in the affirmative.

"You're the Special Ops guy. Where do we start when we get to Anchorage?"

"Taking the cab driver out definitely got the attention of the FBI." Ross paused, and Jacob saw the conspiratorial look in his greenish-hazel eyes. "I think I have a way to capitalize on that."

"Care to share?"

"I've lived a long life. You, on the other hand, have a good long future ahead, so I think you should just let me handle this one."

Jacob looked at the man who'd served with his father in Vietnam and realized Ross was right. The aircraft continued northwest, and the two men closed their eyes, building up a reserve for the mission that awaited them.

Chapter Thirty-Seven

Just Outside of Nenana, Alaska

<u>Monday May 6, 2002</u>

Abducted was a bit of an embellishment. Abducted was probably too strong a word. Coerced? Seduced?

Lindsay had pulled up next to him right after he'd crossed the Mears Bridge and asked if he would like to go for a ride.

So they headed south on the Parks Highway toward no particular destination and didn't say a word for at least ten minutes. It wasn't really an awkward silence, it was more an intimidated silence – at least it was for Mark, and that was the second time today.

They both realized that their connection could simply be the result of the present situation they were a part of. They spent the better part of the two hour drive behaving like it was a first date, although not saying so. For Mark, it was awkward being the passenger in the Toyota Four-Runner.

Lindsay shared that she was born in a little town in Florida, a place called Panacea less than fifty miles south of the Alabama state line. She shared that her favorite color was light blue, not turquoise mind you but light blue. He put that one in the memory bank for somewhere down the road.

She loved to listen to Bon Jovi, Poison, and Def Leppard. When Mark mentioned that he loved Air Supply, she almost kicked him out of the Four-Runner.

As Lindsay shared little tidbits about her life, each one won him over that much more. He was feeling something indescribable, feeling whatever it was for the first time. It wasn't simply the beauty he saw in the way her lips moved when she talked, or the glow in her beautiful blue eyes when she smiled, or if it was the way her voice raised slightly when she talked about her cat Bobby. Whatever it was, Mark Jameson had totally fallen for Lindsay Drummond.

That said, he was not done trying to figure out what the hell was going on. "You intercepted that call I got not too long after we got to Anchorage. I'm impressed but I'm very curious. What do you think has me a part of all this?"

"All we've known is a likely 'who,' but we still don't know the 'why' part of the equation. You're a Fed too, you know how this works...we need the why as well." She paused, then continued, "We're doing this to get the guy who has the hit on you out in the open." He could tell from the matter-of-fact look into his eyes that she was being straight up. "So Lindsay, it sounds like you've got an idea of the Who in this whole thing?" The phrase sounded strange, but funny enough it was perfect.

He was anticipating hesitation, but not even close. "Jacob Honeycutt."

The hesitation happened on Mark's end. He searched the recesses of his mind for a moment, trying to figure out what the current CEO of Honeycutt Petroleum Corporation would have against him. "Now I'm confused:"

A discernible smirk found its way across her face. "Funny, I thought you said you were fine on your own. I can replay the game tape if you'd like. I'm pretty sure you thought we were mall security or something like that."

His first instinct was to apologize for that immature comment, but his gut was screaming loudly to keep it in check. "I thought you rather liked my dim-witted humor."

"Uh-huh. Lucky your first calling isn't comedy."

He had no good comeback. "Anyway, back to Jacob Honeycutt. What does he have to do with any of this?"

"Because of 9/11, our electronic eavesdropping liberties have been loosened up a bit," she said rather facetiously. "Between the NSA, the FBI, us, the DIA, and other agencies, we're monitoring e-mail and telephone calls with enhanced scrutiny, and little things are leading to bigger things. And now a lot of our monitoring is domestic. Well, your name came up in a transcript between Jacob Honeycutt and his Chief of Security."

"I'm keeping up."

"The little thing was truly a little thing but your name was on it." Lindsay's voice was almost apologetic as she continued. "The phrase, 'Agent Jameson may end up getting in the way,' was part of a thirty-page transcript. As you can imagine, you're not the only Agent Jameson out there, but the fact that you're investigating the death of Joshua Knight connected that dot for us."

"So Jacob Honeycutt is the key to the why of all this, right?"

"Exactly."

Lindsay's synopsis of Jacob Honeycutt continued for another five minutes or so, and it wasn't that Mark was bored but there was nothing more he could do about being the potential target of a CEO.

"Back to the envelope you left me at the hotel; were you just showing off?"

"Not exactly," she said like she knew something.

"Let's have it, what'd I miss?"

"We weren't the only ones watching you. When you get back to the motel, look at the photo I took of you again. You still have it, don't you?"

"Of course I do."

"Just checking." Her lovely smile gave life to the vehicle as they cruised through a part of Alaska that is more about gentle green hills populated with trees best described as Spartan, certainly not the jagged mountain peaks and lush green forests that Alaska is noted for.

"Sandra and I thought this was going to be a one-day trip, so I guess I'm stuck here without my CD player," he said.

"I read in your dossier you're a bit frugal, but I think you can splurge and buy one here, though thankfully I don't think you'll be able to find any Air Supply CDs around." She couldn't resist that one. He couldn't blame her.

"Okay, okay, back to the photo," he said.

"Just take a look," Lindsay instructed with an air of flirtation.

As much as he was enjoying her company, not to mention the casual glances at her bosom, thanks to Lindsay's hint he couldn't wait to get back to the photo. She looked over at him, smirked again. She was wearing a light blue chemise and he knew she was enjoying the effect it was having. They continued this little song and dance as they headed back to Nenana. She entered the room with Mark for just a moment, gave him a warm hug, and said good night. There was no doubt he was already in love with this woman.

Nenana, Alaska

<u>Late Evening - Monday May 6, 2002</u>

Mark awoke around eleven pm. The last few days had been very intense and physically taxing, but he was still surprised at how much energy he had. The

TV volume was set very low, but loud enough that he could listen to the late news on Alaska's ABC affiliate.

Lindsay's comment about the photograph she'd left at the hotel finally had his attention. As Lindsay had said, there was more to the photograph than Mark jogging along Tukwila's Strander Boulevard with that "cheesy smirk."

She was right, damn that smirk was cheesy.

Anyway, as she'd said, there was more to the photograph. A car was on the boulevard maybe fifteen yards behind him, and in it were two male figures. The driver was wearing sunglasses, and his skin was dark - probably Hispanic or Arabic. The passenger was also wearing sunglasses, his with mirrored lenses, his skin was pale, and his face surprisingly pudgy.

He wasn't sure why Lindsay had pointed this out. The two men could have been nothing more than a strange coincidence. Then he saw it - it wasn't the men that had been the point of focus. It was the man at the bus stop Mark had just run by. He was muscular, fit, and looked military or former military.

Somehow he'd missed him.

He would learn who he was a few days later, but something more immediate interrupted the thoughts about the surveillance photograph.

A visitor at the motel room door not long after eleven pm was the first of two. The first was expected, the second would be a big part of what this journey had been all about.

Mark opened the door on the second knock, thankfully wearing more than a pair of checkered boxers this time.

"Dani!" His voice exhibited a bit of excited relief, as he waved her in to the room. Giving her a big bear hug, he said, "It's great to see you."

"You too, nice place you got here." She said as she scoped the accommodations.

"I didn't know you were showing up this quick. When we talked earlier today, I still couldn't believe that Branson sent you up here."

"I guess the boss didn't think you could handle things all by yourself." There was the wit he knew so darn well.

"Yeah-yeah, smart aleck." They kept up the little banter for a few more minutes, and then Dani crashed on the couch while he crashed in a small recliner.

Early Tuesday Morning; May 7, 2002

Agent Gonzalez was the first to stir that morning, and got the rest of team going around 7:30am with the enticing aroma of brewing coffee.

And the "Today Show."

Sandra assumed Mark had awoken at the sound of the television. As much as she'd gotten to know about him over the last few days, she couldn't have known that he had a bit of a crush on Katie Couric.

Agent Westford removed herself from her uncomfortable sofa moments later. Unlike Mark, she'd been awake for the last hour or so. She'd been lying there, stirring the recent evidence and research over and over in her mind.

All three FBI agents perched themselves with cups of coffee in the drab motel room. Mark was reminded of the days of his youth, camping in the rustic cabins along the Lost River.

Sandra's voice brought Mark's thoughts back to the present. "You said you got my e-mail, so what've you found so far?"

"Where do I begin?" Dani said and looked directly at Mark. He could almost see the wheels turning in her mind.

"I'm going to go with the abridged version." She continued, "How familiar are you with the Alaska Native Claims Settlement Act?"

"I barely knew anything about it until we got the Knight case," Mark answered.

Dani had a perplexed look on her face as she looked at her partner. "Aren't you an Alaska Native?"

"Yeah, but sorry, I was like four or five years old when it was settled. Sandra and I were looking into the connection with our case, but really didn't see anything."

"From the facts I've gathered, it looks like ANCSA may be what your case is all about."

Dani and Mark were both seated on the sofa and she'd had her laptop powering up as they'd talked. A moment later, she had a file pulled up, and she let him and Sandra take a peak.

"Looks a lot like my Day-timer notes, I knew you'd come up with your own way to look at this case," Mark said. She had a Word file up that had a mini-timeline in place. The 1970's were tied to Knight, Myles Honeycutt, and others; the 2000's spelled out the execution the cab driver. At the top, though, was what really caught Mark's eye. In a AutoShape bubble and in large, bold font she'd typed the words, "ANCSA / Flight 1866."

"Flight 1866 I get, what's ANCSA got to with all of this?" He had to query. By now she had to know that was the flight number of his grandmother's plane. He was getting an awful feeling about where this was going.

"Have you heard of the Alaska Federation of Natives – AFN for short?"

"I heard my dad mention it a few times when I was a kid, but that's it."

"You know, for a guy who loves his heritage so much, I'm surprised you're really not familiar with ANCSA history at all." Chagrined, Mark had to agree with her.

"Anyway," Dani continued, "here's what the notes in your Day-timer uncovered." "The government and the AFN were negotiating a settlement of tribal claims to millions of acres of land back in 1971. Joshua Knight was in Anchorage monitoring those negotiations for Honeycutt Petroleum."

"Mark and I knew that part already. Nothing new there," Sandra interjected. Mark was waiting for the right opening to see what the connection with his grandmother's flight was all about. Dani had apparently connected that flight independent of any information or leads he'd provided.

"The Internet is an amazing thing. Conspiracies abound, from aliens landing on a Siberian Ice Field to JFK being a Russian mole, for Pete's sake..." She shrugged.

"The notes from your Day-Timer had names that have been on the grid for thirty years, and yet not one dot had been connected. That was until yesterday when your cab driver was taken out."

Mark realized that Lindsay was right: Sunday evening when he was back in his condo in Tukwila, she'd said his name on the grid might just be tied to national security.

"So ANCSA is the connection?" he asked. Lindsay and Mark had discussed a lot of things, but ANCSA had never come up.

"It sure is. A guy and his wife were aboard 1866 headed for Sitka. Care to guess what their connection is to all of this?"

"I honestly have no idea."

"Come on, care to take a guess?"

"Let's see." There was only one possibility that came to mind, and he had to admit it wasn't much. "Given that you brought up conspiracy theories, I'd say they owned the building where Knight was found."

"Interesting guess, actually…" It was obvious that he was incorrect, but he could tell Dani was considering his hypothesis. "However, what's more interesting is who the guy was. Have you ever heard the name, Phillip Black?"

Thanks to Lindsay, he had just heard the name the day before. The conversation was confirmation that the CIA was pretty darn good at what they do. And he decided right then to avoid answering his partner's question unless she asked again.

"You've got me intrigued, keep going."

"Phillip Black was on the AFN," Dani said.

Mark shook his head. Apparently Lindsay hadn't gotten that far.

Dani noted something in Mark's avoidance of her question. Directness was always one of her strongest attributes, but she decided against employing that trait to an answer out of her partner.

"The Alaska Federation of Natives, right?" Mark apparently wanted to show he was keeping up.

"Yep, and AFN's crowning achievement was negotiating the settlement of the Alaska Native Claims Settlement Act."

"Nice job, Agent Westford! It seems the notes we sent you sort of opened the flood gates." Gonzalez looked impressed, which Dani found gratifying.

"Thanks, but believe it or not, you two did the hard work. All I did was connect the dots," Dani answered humbly.

Hey, you beat me, as usual," Mark added. Then he raised the most pertinent question of all. "Let's see, we've got Joshua Knight, whose connection to all of this is Honeycutt Petroleum. We've got Myles Honeycutt, Clay Tanis, and Rico Sanchez, also connected to Honeycutt Petroleum, and Phillip Black connected to the AFN. And the common denominator is the Alaska Native Claims Settlement Act." Mark took a drink from a bottle of water. "And then we've got Ronald Johns, our dead cab driver. Where does he fit in all of this?"

"That's an interesting story. Ronald Johns actually was more than just a cab driver." Dani pulled a manila folder from her briefcase. "He's a burgeoning author."

"Doing the math, like Mark said, everyone in this whole thing is dead." Sandra interjected. "I've got two thoughts for us to consider. One, it is very probable our cab driver was writing about ANCSA. And two, someone out there has or had concerns about our newly-deceased cab driver, and it is very probable that those concerns are tied to whatever he may have known about ANCSA."

Chapter Thirty-Eight

Nenana, Alaska

<u>Early Morning - Tuesday May 7, 2002</u>

Mark was staring at Dani, suddenly feeling a bit on edge. Whatever it was, he had a strange feeling where all of this was going. His Tlingit tuition was getting better as the case got deeper.

"Mark..." Dani started, looking at him with concern in her eyes, Branson sent me here because the FBI and the CIA have been investigating a threat against a federal agent named Jameson." Dani was now standing at one of the room's windows, fidgeting as she continued. "Both the FBI and the CIA have information that indicates someone deems you a threat. We think we know the Who that has you targeted, and somehow ANCSA and your grandmother's airplane is what you're in the middle of now and what has you on the grid. We're still sorting out how you fit into it..." Dani was going to continue, but was interrupted by a knock on the door.

As he got up to answer, he pondered her phrase *"We think we know the Who that has you targeted,"* rattling around in his mind. Dani had an idea of the Who, and did it jibe with what Lindsay had told him about Jacob Honeycutt?

He answered the door, and to his total confusion, it was Lindsay.

He was going to make introductions, but Lindsay and Dani said hello to one another by first name.

"Dani, what have you shared so far?" Lindsay asked Mark's FBI partner.

"I was just sharing that your employer and mine had uncovered intelligence that indicated a federal agent by the name of Jameson is a target of some kind. I was just going to share that the chatter started not long after the renewed interest in a guy named Joshua Knight by the FBI, and not coincidentally an FBI agent named Jameson was on the case."

Mark was simultaneously impressed and concerned for his safety and the team.

He was sorting out why his grandmother's plane was connected to the ANCSA case, why he had been assigned the case, and at that very moment why the woman he was so interested in was on a first-name basis relationship with Dani.

There was more than a moment of silence in the room as Lindsay and Dani gave each other looks. Lindsay gestured for Dani to finish.

Her voice, slightly raspy and somewhat sultry, continued, "I know you're curious how we know each other." She looked at Lindsay. "We'll get to that, but let me finish my little summary. Philip Black, as I said, was a member of the Alaska Federation of Natives. More important, he was an essential member of the bargaining team for ANCSA. The AFN has maintained an archive of its negotiation files all of these years with a law firm in Anchorage."

Dani had a smile that was almost mischievous. "Well, after I did my little Google journey today, I made some inquires about the law firm. A few years ago, your dead cab driver became a client of the law firm of Richards, Kramer, and Stein."

Lindsay had that mischievous smile on her face as well. She was about to reveal vital piece of information.

"It took a little digging, but the guy's attorney in the firm was a guy named Jon Brady." He left the firm a few years ago, and rumor has it, he left to write a novel." "And?" Mark was tired of being the one in the dark, which he started to introduce Sandra and Lindsay.

Lindsay made it clear there was no need. "Hi, Sandra, thanks for taking care of our FBI agent here. You and your team did a great job in Anchorage."

Dani saw the peeved and perplexed look all over Mark's face. This situation wasn't fair at all. FBI agents weren't accustomed to operating without an arsenal of information, and yet the last half-hour had been just that for her partner.

"You deserve to know how we're all connected. I'm not going to beat around the bush at all. Lindsay, Sandra, and I are connected by the Murrah Building bombing in '95. Sandra and I were both assigned there by the Bureau." Dani could see that Mark was waiting to see how a CIA agent would be connected to an act of domestic terrorism, referring to the bombing of the Alfred P. Murrah Building in Oklahoma City in April, 1995.

"And?" Mark repeated.

"And Ms. Drummond of the CIA quietly had her liaison with me." Dani took a moment and looked at Lindsay and Sandra to ensure they were alright with the content of this conversation.

"The CIA wanted to make sure the bombing wasn't foreign in nature. Lindsay was there to find out just that."

Mark was watching her, and for the first time, his blank poker face didn't betray his thoughts. "So, this case has brought you all back together, I take it. Why?"

Dani looked at Lindsay and let her take that one.

Lindsay looked at the man who'd become more than a part of an Op, and wondered where to begin. She'd wanted to say something ever since they'd met. Dani was actually the one who'd made some calls and gotten Lindsay involved in the quasi-surveillance of FBI agent Mark Jameson.

Ironically, Lindsay was the one who'd made the call to get Sandra Gonzalez and her FBI team giving Mark a protective detail, as a viable threat against Mark's life existed. Lindsay, however, had no idea that the cab driver would be part of the threat. And the fact that he had been taken out was a mystery to her as well.

But she needed to answer the question of the man she was falling for.

"As Dani said, we think somehow you've uncovered something tied to the Alaska Native Claims Settlement Act. We are still are looking for what that is, but whatever that might be, it appears you've got the second largest oil company in the world on edge."

Lindsay paused for a moment and looked for any feedback her colleagues wanted to add. They remained silent.

"As I told you yesterday, we're tracking Jacob Honeycutt, and our intelligence shows his plane landed in Anchorage a few hours ago. He has made a few inquiries, and they're all tied to your dead cab driver and…to you."

Mark had been surprisingly quiet through these revelations. The silence finally ended.

"The FBI assigned me to this case. Someone high up on the food chain obviously knows something. I'm not afraid of what I'm in the middle of, but I'm curious why I'd be put in harm's way."

Dani was the one with the answer. "Director Archer knew I was coming to see you, Mark. You were specifically requested for this assignment by the Director because of your knowledge of Alaska." Dani paused for a moment. "And because you have a personal connection to the airplane crash in question."

"Isn't that a conflict of interest?" Mark asked rather defensively.

"The Director asked that I give you this," Dani replied, handing Mark a sealed envelope. "Mark Jameson" was handwritten on the note.

"You've got to be kidding me, from the Director?" Mark flipped the envelope over a couple of times and then laid it on the coffee table.

"I'll get to that later. Let's get back to why we're all here now."

Nenana, Alaska
<u>Early Morning - Tuesday May 7, 2002</u>

The conversation went in a direction Mark would have expected. Instincts and intuition, thanks to the activity the last few days, were in high gear. And finally, dots thirty-years old had been connected with the death of Joshua Knight and a cab driver.

Whatever Joshua Knight had uncovered in 1971 still was awakening fears in high places. "Knight knew it all, didn't he?"

"It's looking that way," Lindsay answered.

"It seems apparent that Knight was onto something with ANCSA," Dani stated.

"Are you seeing a pattern here?" Lindsay was serious.

"Let's see, Myles Honeycutt hires Knight to follow ANCSA. He dies. And we've got Phillip Black, who dies the week that ANCSA is settled." Mark looked at the women. "Did I miss anything?"

"I've always liked the way you condense things," Dani said and looked at Lindsay before she continued. It didn't look like she was looking for her approval, but more wondering if Lindsay wanted to drive this conversation. Dani seemed to get an unspoken approval to keep going.

Dani continued her summary of why the Alaska Native Claims Settlement Act was looking to be at the heart of what were now looking to be horrendous criminal acts.

"Let me add one more thing that on the surface might seem like nothing more than a strange coincidence, but now I think is a lot more." Dani took a drink of water. "I'm not sure what this tells us, but I think it is very significant. As we've noted, Myles Honeycutt is on the list. All by itself, Honeycutt committing suicide wouldn't be significant, but what happened a few days earlier lends itself to our little mystery." And like a good attorney in front of a very engaged jury, she paused briefly to let the anticipation rise.

"A week or so before Honeycutt's death, the National Transportation Safety Board had released its report on the crash of your grandmother's plane..." It was the first time she'd made it personal. "The NTSB blamed it on faulty navigation equipment and pilot error. Nothing we've found would on the surface controvert that finding, but there was a name in your Day-timer that might be-very good reason to reopen the NTSB's investigation."

Mark wasn't sure where she was going. He didn't recall anything that seemed remotely related to the investigation of the airplane crash.

Dani didn't leave that one dangling at all. "Rico Sanchez was in your Day-timer notes, interesting guy. The Internet didn't have any information on him but funny enough the NTSB did. Sanchez apparently was the pilot of a bush plane that had lost contact with the Anchorage Air Traffic Control Center on the day your grandmother's plane crashed. In fact, her plane was diverted because of Sanchez's plane. When the NTSB interviewed him, he indicated that his instruments had gone dark not long after he'd taken off from Juneau."

Mark had been detached from the personal impact this case had on his family. Time has a funny way of making something painful less so. Up until this point, listening to the summary Dani and Lindsay were sharing, there was a strange matter-of-fact impact.

Now as he listened to what Dani had just said, he imagined his grandmother seated comfortably in her seat, trusting in the engineering marvel that is a jet aircraft and in a couple of well-qualified pilots. Having flown enough to know that feeling, he wondered what she'd experienced. Just like that, this case had become personal.

Now his anger was growing with each passing second. Someone needed to pay, but at that moment he had a more pressing question. Someone else was playing in the sandbox with them because Ronny the Cabbie was taken out within feet of a team of armed FBI agents.

"So do we think Sanchez lied to the NTSB?" He was going to say more but then like a lightning bolt, the connection hit me. "Holy shit, Sanchez was killed along with the Head of Security for Honeycutt Petroleum!"

Deep in his memory, Mark could hear the sarcasm of one of his uncles, saying *"dumb,"* as he put those pieces together. *He's probably looking down on me now and thinking that all over again. Can't say I'd blame him. Sometimes, I take a little longer than I should.*

Mark missed that uncle deeply, as he missed his grandpa.

A strange calm settled over Mark. He didn't know if Dani, Lindsay, or Sandra felt it, but an otherworldly aura inexplicably filled the air. Closing his eyes for a moment, he felt that his grandmother was right there. Mark's father had taught him about the legend of the Kushtaka, the Land Otter and its ability to take many forms. At that very moment, he was a bit afraid that was the experience he was having.

He tried to open his eyes but the muscles in his eyelids were unresponsive. The ladies in the room must have thought he was having a mental lapse, because he certainly thought that was the case.

The room grew dissonantly silent.

The rise in his heartbeat was the only sensation he understood. An immeasurable period of time lapsed by, when suddenly the sound of jet engines and the hum of flaps deploying filled the air. His eyes were free of the inexplicable stranglehold, and when he panned the surroundings, he realized he was aboard his grandmother's ill-fated aircraft.

He was seated in a window seat on the right of the aircraft. The sky outside was foreboding and black, the rain on the oval window torrential. He had been on the Yakutat to Juneau flight countless times as a child and as a young adult. The feeling of the aircraft's descent was unmistakable, as a slight break in the dark clouds revealed a thick forest, mountainside. They were too low.

A beautiful, warm voice took control of the air. He looked around and wondered if anyone else heard the voice. All of the faces were blank, and their eyes were deathly dark. "It is time, my grandson."

His heart, his soul was filled with fear, but also filled with the sense that his grandmother's soul was not yet at rest. Then he heard his grandmother's scream loudly in the lifeless cabin. "Bobby!" She screamed his father's name.

He was going to scream with her, but as quickly as this vision appeared, it vanished.

Mark's eyes opened, and he found all three women were still in the room just as he'd seen moments before. They had no idea what he had just experienced, as the time that had lapsed must have been mere seconds – or the blink of an eye. Dani was continuing the conversation, confirming what had been said moments earlier about the connection between Bush Pilot Rico Sanchez and Honeycutt Petroleum's Security Chief.

"Now we're all on the same page. ANCSA is the key to this case," Dani said flatly.

Lindsay chimed in. "So now we've got to find out what Honeycutt Petroleum had to with all of this. It seems pretty clear that oil profits were involved."

"And I think we need to get in contact with the attorney our cabbie was working with," Mark added, after clearing his throat, pushing past the disturbing vision. "If he's writing a novel and it relates at all to what we're in the middle of, it seems that he and our deceased Cabbie struck a nerve with Honeycutt Petroleum."

Chapter Thirty-Nine

Nenana, Alaska
<u>Mid-Morning - Tuesday May 7, 2002</u>

The conversation had been very involved, the array of facts the most interesting Mark had ever encountered as an FBI agent, and knowing that somewhere in the myriad of conjecture, concrete evidence, et al was information on what had taken his grandmother was strangely poetic.

For all of the chatter, it came down to just a few simple things he had stated to his fellow agents, at least as far as he could tell:

Joshua Knight found something about the ANCSA negotiations and was killed passing that information along to Phillip Black. Based upon circumstantial evidence, it appeared that Honeycutt Petroleum, more specifically Myles Honeycutt and a few of his security team, were behind the crash of his grandmother's airplane, and somehow Mark been roped into the case. And finally, an attorney named Jon Brady had information that solidified the implication of Honeycutt Petroleum's involvement.

"So, what are our next steps?"

"I guess we have a road trip in mind? And just when I was getting used to Nenana." Mark's tone was actually more cheerful than sarcastic.

"Sandra, may we talk for a bit?" Dani asked Sandra, reacting to a nonverbal cue Lindsay had just shot her way.

With Dani and Gonzalez leaving the room, Lindsay and Mark were alone again. The modest motel room was occupied by the one woman on the planet who could leave him speechless and behaving more like a teenager than, in his humble opinion, the thoroughly competent and damn good FBI agent.

"Sounds like we're probably heading to Juneau soon, so as much as I know..." Lindsay paused.

"Know what...?" He prompted, echoing her flirtatious tone.

"As much as I know how cliché it might sound..." She blinked those gorgeous blue eyes. "I hope this is what I think it is," she finished, sitting down on the sofa next to him.

"Lindsay..." He paused. "I'm falling for you."

She met his gaze, her legs brushing against his. Mark felt the heart palpitation that comes along maybe two or three times in life. This beautiful woman was right next to him, and she felt for him everything he was feeling for her.

They didn't say another word. She leaned in and her lips softly touched his. It was sensual and so much more. She put her hand in his, and he'd never felt anything quite like that before. The bond between them was undeniable. They shared the gentle kiss for a few more moments and still held each other's hand as they emerged from the kiss and simply gazed at one another.

Lindsay spoke first. "When this is all said and done, please make sure we keep alive what you and I have started."

"There's nothing, Lindsay, I want now more than that." He had always been a hopeless romantic growing up and somehow at almost 37 years old he had finally met the love of his life.

"I was hoping you'd say that, but I hate to say it, right now the job comes first, and we've got a bit of a drive ahead." Lindsay squeezed his hand and left to round up the troops.

Mark put on a Seattle Seahawks sweatshirt and a pair of sunglasses. A half hour later, after packing up their belongings, the team headed out into the warm Alaska air. There was an egg-white GMC Yukon parked not more than fifteen feet from the room.

Sandra had decided to head south for Anchorage to work with the Bureau brass on what their research had uncovered so far. And the FBI had approved the decision to head to Juneau to interview Jon Brady. The only caveat given was that no non-FBI personnel be present. Someone obviously knew that Lindsay and the CIA were now intertwined in this.

As they got in, Dani was in the driver's seat, and she glanced over at the sheepish grin Mark was trying to stifle. Again he wished he were a better poker player.

The Suburban was silent for a moment, and then Dani just couldn't resist. "Mark, I always knew you liked the busty ones."

"That's not true, there was...there was the girl from the golf club," he defended himself.

"You just liked having a sexy girl in the cart with you! Nice try, Romeo," She teased.

"How about the pilot with American Airlines?" He was digging a deeper hole.

"She was drop dead gorgeous, and you love airplanes. Doesn't count, next?" Dani needled like a little sister.

That was how he'd always felt about Dani. She'd been assigned to the Seattle FBI Field Office three years ago, about six months before he'd been transferred to Seattle from the Phoenix office. She was a very good agent, but more than that she was one of the most loyal, driven people he knew. If you were her friend, it was for life.

"So let's talk about that last guy you dated," Mark began.

They departed Nenana Tuesday around 2:45pm or so. From that moment forward, Mark's life would never be the same.

Interior, Alaska

<u>Late Afternoon - Tuesday May 7, 2002</u>

Mark started documenting on his laptop what had been going on since Sunday morning when he had had the dream of flying from Washington, D.C., to Seattle with his dad and then woke up wanting to pummel some bully back on that elementary playground. That one he should let go, but he was afraid to.

Afraid he'd lose that edge that ironically he had gained because of the abuse on that playground. Regardless, he would love the chance to kick that bully's fat ass.

He grabbed the CD player and plopped in Def Leppard. Lindsay had loaned it to him, since his collection embarrassingly didn't include that one. "Rock of Ages" played as he continued to document the last four or five days. It was actually kind of refreshing to have time to just sit still and think about how he had gotten there.

He liked to say that he'd wanted to be an FBI agent from the moment he could walk, but he took a long route around to get there. He spent his early twenties commercial fishing because he'd fallen in love with it while working with his grandfather. His grandfather's work ethic was second to none, and Mark had learned so much from that.

He loved to sit in the skiff and watch him methodically and with ease remove salmon entangled in the net. Years and years of repetition were evident. Mark learned it, and he thought he was pretty good, but not even close to his grandfather's level. But what Mark really missed about him was a Tlingit prayer. He had no clue what the prayer was in his native language, a language in which he could only count to ten and say a few choice things, but it was beautiful, and even now twenty years later he could hear him start it. He hoped God was blessing him in heaven with his grandma.

Not too long before he turned 23 years of age, his grandfather passed on. That was tough beyond anything Mark could express. He fished for another year or so, and at nearly 25 years of age he decided it was time to pursue his dream.

Enrolled at Western Washington University as a mid-twenties freshman, Mark was a walk-on football player and ended up a four-year letterman although his playing time dwindled as he entered his senior year and almost 28 years of age. He was definitely out of his league on some days, but he enjoyed the time, and the guys treated him as an equal.

He played free safety, and in his junior year had a memorable game, intercepting a pass at his team's five yard line and returning it 95 yards for the winning score. It was one of those moments he thanked God every day for.

Mark graduated with a 3.40 grade-point average. Not great, but good enough combined with a minor in Spanish to get him accepted to the FBI Academy. The winter of 1995, he graduated after four intense months at Quantico, Virginia, and was given the credential of FBI Special Agent. His father and mother long-since divorced and amicable, along with his stepmother took him to dinner and toasted what they knew all along he would become. Another memory he thanked God for every day.

That journey somehow had led to the back roads of Alaska's Interior in early May, 2002. And what had started this whole thing a few hours ahead. It was time to get back in the saddle.

Chapter Forty

Juneau, Alaska

<u>Mid Afternoon - Thursday May 9, 2002</u>

Shadows ranged up and down the Gastineau Channel between Juneau City proper and mountainous Douglas Island to the west. The sky was a hue that can only be found in Southeast Alaska - pure, beautiful, and crystal clear blue.

The whisper of the twin engines of a Lear Jet on approach strangely accentuated the magic of the morning. A mix of man's artistic, mechanical creativity and God's paintbrush came together as the whisper of the twin engines of a Lear jet on approach into Juneau International Airport, its silhouette cast against the deep green of a thick forest surrounding the entire valley as it cascaded toward the brackish-green waters of Gastineau Channel.

To the east, the rocky peaks of the Alaska Coast Range and Mendenhall Glacier held Jacob Honeycutt's attention as his aircraft gracefully descended over marshy wetlands from the north. A slight headwind from the south suspended the flight momentarily in air, seemingly begging to stay afloat for just another moment. Surrendering to the law of gravity, the Lear jet touched down on the grey runway.

It taxied to a small terminal at the northern end of Juneau International Airport, where an ordinary black Ford Escape awaited the five gentlemen who exited the aircraft.

Each man wore a casual polo shirt and khaki pants. Beneath sport jackets, each man was armed with a pistol that they'd grown comfortable with. All except

Jacob Honeycutt; he was here strictly because Jameson had made this very personal, but he was going to keep himself at a distance as things went down.

One of his men reminded him, "Sir, as far as the flight manifest goes, you deplaned in Anchorage a few hours ago and you're on a plane headed for the Katmai Peninsula."

Chapter Forty-One

Juneau, Alaska

<u>Late Evening - Thursday May 9, 2002</u>

"911, what is your emergency?" A Nine-One-One operator stated authoritatively as the call was connected. Her white-on-green digital display indicated the call was originating from 3699 Hayes Way.

"Ma'am, I think there've been gunshots next door." A man's voice, clearly but not quite calmly stated.

"May I have your address, sir?" The 911 operator asked, following protocol and confirming the address the system had indicated was genuine.

"I'm at 3699 Hayes Way?" The man answered still quite concise but the fear was evident in his voice. With the address confirmed the address, the 911 operator followed ingrained procedure and dispatched multiple police units to the scene.

"What is your name, sir?"

"My name is Jared Crabtree." His voice diminutive and with a hint of a New England accent.

"Jared, do you still hear shooting?"

"No ma'am, nothing."

"Jared, I am going to stay with you on the line until police officers arrive. Are you at a safe place in your house?"

"I'm upstairs in my bathroom. I can see the house next door from here."

"Can you see anything going on next door?" 911 asked. As she did this, another call from Jared's neighborhood had come into the 911 call center.

Another 911 operator managed the call, its content indicating a shooting had just occurred on Hayes Way.

"Just a bunch of lights coming on…" Jared's answer was indicative of other neighbors reacting to the gunshots. Jared's right hand was shaking as he held the wireless telephone to his ear.

Wired-rimmed glasses served to accentuate the wide-eyed fear in his pale blue eyes. In his 46-years of life, he'd not ever felt the real possibility that he might be in grave danger.

In the middle of a bowl of popcorn while catching Sandra Bullock's Miss Congeniality, the distinct pop of gunfire couldn't be mistaken, he had no doubt that gunshots had gone off at his neighbor's home.

It had taken him no more than a few seconds to decide to make the 911 call. No more shots were ringing out and he found solace in the silence that now enveloped the neighborhood but the unknown of what had happened next door was unsettling.

The telephone in his hand with a 911 operator on the other end was a welcome friend at the moment.

"Jared, have you seen any movement in the home next door?"

"Nothing…and there are no lights on in the house at all."

"Do you know your neighbor's name?"

"Jon Brady." Jared replied having lived in this neighborhood for the last fourteen years and had gotten to know Jon Brady well. A couple of barbeques during the summer, countless times helping each other dig out of their driveways after a heavy snow, and all of those anonymous moments a neighbor shares.

"Does he live alone?"

"No, his wife's name is Molly." Jared provided his response. "They don't have any kids." He added.

"Did you hear any fighting before the shots?" The question was posed by the 911 operator to determine if the shooting was tied to a domestic dispute.

"No ma'am."

"Have Jon and Molly fought in the past?" The inquiry continued along the domestic disturbance tract.

"No ma'am. Not that I am aware of."

"Has Jon ever shown any signs of violence? Do you know if he owns a gun?"

"No ma'am, he is a quiet guy."

"How about Molly? Any signs of violence? Does she own a gun?" The inquiry switched the conversation to the other possible subject in the house.

"Ma'am, no to both questions...In fact, I think she's out of town. We had a barbeque over the weekend and she said she was going to Minnesota to see her family." Jared's response painted a picture of a tight-knit neighborhood.

The inquiry returned to the situation next door. "Do you see any movement?"

"Not a thing, there are still no lights at all."

Each inquiry from the 911 operator was met with concise responses from Jared for the next few minutes until Jared heard sirens entering the neighborhood.

Jared watched as a police cruiser entered the street from the west.

"The police should be there now. Can you see them?"

"Yes ma'am, they're here."

"I'll stay with you until you see an officer at your door."

Moments later Jared opened the door to two imposing figures standing at his door wearing police uniforms emblazoned with the symbol for the city of Juneau, Alaska. "The police are at my door."

"Take care, Jared." The 911 operator stated and the call ended moments later.

The police officers quickly gathered general facts about Jon Brady and the residence next door. The two officers remained at the door as two more Juneau police cruisers and two Alaska State Troopers arrived on the scene.

Just as a multitude of officers proceeded to exit their vehicles; a figure slowly emerged via the front door of the Brady's home.

The man was bleeding profusely and he was moving at less than a crawl onto the lawn.

"We have an injured subject." An officer communicated into the microphone on his shoulder collar. "We need EMS here now!" He realized Emergency Medical Services was already dispatched but seeing the injured man exiting the house heightened that urgency.

There were now eight police officers on scene. Like all police departments, procedure and protocol exists when shootings are involved or the possibility of domestic violence. The officers began to follow protocol but you can ask any police officer, when the moment presents itself instinct simply kicks in.

Officer Jason Montoya sprinted to the man crawling on to the lush green well-manicured lawn. Montoya's partner, Officer Caleb "Mac" Macintyre sprinted to the injured man as well. The remaining officers trained their guns on the home providing cover for Officers Montoya and Macintyre.

The man muttered something and his muffled utterance gave Montoya an idea of who was on scene – "I...I'm FB...FBI."

The man stammered once more but was much more audible to Montoya and to Macintyre – "scene...is...sec...secure..." With that, the man stopped out of breath.

Montoya saw the FBI badge on his right hip, clipped to a pair of Levi's blue jeans. The federal shield was all he needed to see.

"Get in there, federal agent down!"

Montoya and Macintyre continued to remain huddled over the injured man as the other six officers using well-honed training, entered the home with weapons drawn.

The continued cadence of "clear" reverberated loudly as the officers moved from room to room. As two officers entered the basement, "we have a subject in the basement" was heard to each other officer loud and clear.

"He's dead." One of the officers stated. It was painfully obvious to the officer as he observed the subject's body lying on the bottom of the stairwell with a small bullet hole in his forehead and two bullet wounds in his chest.

"We have two other subjects, male and female...both unconscious." Officer Michele Mathis stated. The officer looked around the carpeted basement. She saw blood splatters all around the basement and saw the evidence that a very violent confrontation had occurred.

On the lawn, the officers were administering first aid to the bleeding subject. The blare of ambulance sirens were growing closer with each passing moment. The officer's assessment of the subject's injuries were that they were life threatening. It appeared he had been shot in the chest and there was a hole the size of a quarter through his left bicep.

"Agent, can you hear me?" Montoya stated to the man lying on the ground and then repeated the question.

"Da...Dan...Dani..." In continuous distress, the injured man muttered a female's name.

"I need help here!" Montoya yelled. Jared came over and offered what little assistance he could render. As he kneeled down next to the bloody individual he was taken aback. The only bullet wounds he'd ever seen were those on TV and those on a Sitka Black Tail Deer his father had taken down with a 22-caliber rifle when he was a teenager.

The man's wounds were not nearly as tidy and the blood seeping out of the victim's chest, Jared actually found quite nauseating. An emergency response vehicle from a nearby fire station arrived and EMS personnel within a few short moments began to administer first aid.

A second EMS team was downstairs in the basement administering first aid to the man and woman who'd been hit.

No more than twelve minutes after Officer Montoya and his colleagues had arrived on-scene; two men and a woman – all three with severe injuries were on gurneys and being prepped for transport to a local hospital.

Montoya assisted the EMS team load the injured male who'd crawled onto the lawn into an ambulance. The man muttered something to Montoya as they lifted him onto the gurney. Montoya squeezed the injured man's hand. "I've got it. Just hang on."

As he watched the ambulances depart with sirens blaring, Officer Montoya pressed the mike on his right shoulder. "We have two federal agents and a civilian en route to Bartlett." Montoya stated, referring to Bartlett Regional Hospital approximately four miles away.

Two of the Juneau Police Officers in separate vehicles provided an armed escort for the ambulances as each departed the normally rather quiet neighborhood. Montoya then instructed the remaining officers to secure the crime scene.

Montoya removed a cell phone from his right hip phone holster and dialed the Chief of Police. "Ma'am, we're out on Hayes Way near the airport. We have two FBI agents and a civilian who have been gunned down; they're all in bad shape..." Montoya continued and with that statement; Juneau, Alaska would soon become the center of the federal universe.

Montoya sprinted down the stairs into the basement. Reaching his right hand to the top of the ball collection pouch at one end of a pool table, he found a latch and a manila envelope fell through. The envelope was there just as the injured agent had mustered the strength to say it would be.

Reasonable logic and the bloodbath in the basement all told Montoya the envelope he held in his right hand was a vital piece of evidence in a federal investigation. Little did he know he'd just played a brief but essential role in unearthing a thirty-year old tragedy for the conspiratorial truth it really was.

Montoya's training got the best of him. Though the envelope remained closed – the Juneau Police Officer's seasoned peripheral vision catalogued the words hand-written on the thick manila envelope – "ANCSA – the Real Truth."

Chapter Forty-Two

Northern Virginia

Late Thursday May 9, 2002

FBI Director Terrell Archer smelled the sensual, sweet aroma of Estee Lauder as his wife of thirty-one years gracefully placed her curvaceous torso on their loveseat.

It was just after eleven in the evening and he was enjoying the quiet time the two were sharing together. He'd returned from a trip just two days earlier.

He'd been briefed by Assistant Special-Agent-in-Charge (ASAC) Walter Branson on the status of an investigation Special Agent Westford and Special Agent Jameson were conducting searching for the person who had put the name Jameson on the intelligence grid and whomever had caused the disappearance of a man named Joshua Knight in 1971.

The Director had learned the agents were en route to Juneau to follow up on a lead. He had requested an update by no later than Friday morning, but was hoping the call from his team would wait just a bit.

He turned to his wife and smiled. She had recovered well from a one-year battle with ovarian cancer and was nearing her fifth year cancer free. She was fully enjoying life again, and one of her most treasured routines was just sharing a quiet moment on the loveseat with her husband.

It was late enough in the evening that the work day had been disconnected. It was just the two of them.

Sylvia's cancer battle had strengthened an already strong marriage.

They were both in their late fifties, but their marriage had found a second wind. The "I Love You" moments were more plentiful, more weekends were spent in bed just holding each other, and their intimacy had gotten that youthful intensity back.

Terry had quietly given his notice to the President six months earlier of his intent to retire. His last day on the job was scheduled to be November 12, 2002, Sylvia's five-year anniversary as cancer free.

He was already beginning to feel the freedom as the weight of his highly political office began to drift from his shoulders. The years he'd lost in the job were coming back and he was becoming a husband all over again. Now he held his wife tight and let his hands roam over her body. They embraced and let the moment capture them, let their love for one another take them away.

An hour later, as the two sat at their kitchen breakfast bar sharing a glass of merlot, Terry looked at his wife and thanked her for the moment they'd shared.

"Honey..." Terry started.

"You okay?" Sylvia asked.

"I...I love you so much." He looked at her with a glossy hue in his eyes. "I'm so sorry you ever got sick. I was...I was so afraid I was going to lose you."

Sylvia looked at him and didn't say a word. The strength of their marriage spoke volumes. She reached over and squeezed his hand.

The moment, sadly true-to-form, was interrupted by the ring of the private line dedicated to FBI business.

"Son of a bitch!" Director Archer couldn't hold back his frustration. "Just a few more months," he said in an exhausted tone. From the moment he'd tendered his resignation, he had a laser-like focus on November 12, 2002.

Sylvia looked sympathetically at her husband. She knew her husband's world involved things that were not often seen by the general public, but in the end were what kept them safe. Moments like this, she knew what toll the job had taken.

Director Archer answered the phone. "Director, you have a call from Seattle's ASAC Branson." It was one of his agents who worked the security detail.

After being patched through, Branson wasted no time with small talk. "Director, we have two agents down in Juneau, Alaska."

Director Archer tried to remain calm, but his first words betrayed his demeanor. "Shit! Who...?"

"Agents Mark Jameson and Dani Westford."

The two briefly discussed logistics and hung up. Director Archer would be on an FBI Citation Lear Jet and airborne by 1:00am eastern time.

Sylvia sensed the heartache her husband was feeling when he'd hung up the telephone. "Two of our agents have been shot."

The two were silent. The only sound in the room was the quiet hum of the refrigerator and the sound of a sprinkler out on the lawn.

Terry was deep in thought. He had another call to make, but decided to wait until he knew a little bit more.

On Board the FBI Director's Jet

Early Morning Friday May 10, 2002

"Director, you have a call." An agent aboard the aircraft handed Archer a secure telephone. "It's ASAC Branson."

"Walt, what's the status?" Archer asked as he accepted the telephone.

"Director, both agents are still in surgery," Branson stated "What are their conditions?"

"SA Jameson has a bullet wound to the chest. SA Westford has two bullet wounds to the chest. They don't...they don't think she's going to pull through." Branson continued the verbal briefing, choking up as he spoke of the condition of two of his agents.

"Walt, where are you?" Archer asked.

"I'm at Elmendorf Air Force Base; we'll be catching a military transport down in the next twenty minutes or so."

"Good, I'd guess we're at least five hours out. I've got another call to make. Check in with me when you get to Juneau," Archer ordered.

"Yes, sir."

Archer hung up and then dialed a cell number he knew all too well.

"It's been a long time," the man answered the call from Director Archer.

"Too long my friend."

Silence took hold for a moment. It was 45-degrees or so on the rocky beach on Orcas Island's northern coast, and what he was hearing compounded the bone-chilling feeling that was taking over.

"Something's happened," Director Archer started, and shared his disconcerting news about the shot agents. Both men were well-versed in the dangers that went with the job, but even those in the business could hope against hope that good luck would prevail.

"Where?" The man asked.

A short time later, an FBI agent arrived at his secluded cabin.

Ten minutes later, still en-route Director Archer received another telephone call.

It was ASAC Branson again. "Sir, I received a call from RSA Wiley of the Juneau FBI satellite office. It appears another individual had entered the home and started the firefight."

Archer was quiet for a few moments. "No one interviews our agents until I arrive, are we clear?"

"Yes, sir," Branson said.

"Nice work, Walt. I'll see you in a few hours."

"Thank you, sir." Branson answered as he walked up metallic steps, boarding a dark gray military DC-9.

Chapter Forty-Three

Orcas Island, Washington State

<u>Early Friday Morning May 10, 2002</u>

It had been thirty-one years; the deaths of Myles Honeycutt, Clay Tanis, Rico Sanchez, and others were designed to clear the slate. For a myriad of reasons, many lives had been destroyed, but in the end, like everything else, the cause was sadly very simple. Conflict is usually about money, love, power, or ego. In the case of the Alaska Native Claims Settlement Act, it was money and power – an almost gaudy, incalculable stockpile of it.

The conflict ventured from lawsuits, to board room bickering, to shareholder dissent. And for a few souls, it was life and death.

The last known living soul connected to the deaths of Myles Honeycutt, Clay Tanis, and Rick Sanchez stood on a rocky beach, drinking in the cool Saturday morning sunrise. The man was distinguished and handsome with salt and pepper hair and dark skin, youthfully belying his nearly sixty years of life

He was on the northern coast of Orcas Island in the northwest corner of Washington State because his occupation dictated it. "Tough life," he kept telling himself as he savored the aroma of a freshly-brewed cup of coffee and watched a flock of seagulls ride a gentle breeze a few feet offshore.

The late evening before, he'd pounded away at the laptop keyboard until his eyes could no longer focus. The wireless connection was turned off, and a jamming device was on the mahogany desk, securing the discreet nature of the man's laborious, marathon-intense project.

He had finally fallen asleep around two in the morning, but sensing something was out of synch. He couldn't place the sensation, but deep down the feeling seemed to border on life-altering.

He awoke and the world inside his mind was strangely unsettled, a wrenching feeling in his gut that felt almost mystical. His heart felt it too; the feeling was of two worlds colliding.

As he stood on the beach, the feeling had only grown stronger and stronger.

The sound of pebbles and stones shuffling beneath the man's Timberland boots was interrupted by the ring of his cell phone. On the other end was the Director of the FBI, an old friend.

Within fifteen minutes, with the escort of an armed FBI agent, earlier the man was departing the scenic Orcas Island beach, driving a few miles toward the town of Eastsound's Airport. Through tinted windows, the calm and glassy surface of Puget Sound gave way as the rented Chevrolet Cavalier headed south on North Beach Road. Beneath 70-foot alders and red cedars with trunks sometimes 10 feet in diameter, stood mobile homes and three-bedroom ramblers.

As North Beach Road approached its intersection with the Mount Baker Road, the two men trained their eyes in all directions, searching for any signs of vehicular threats. The men scanned the dirt-track walking-trail that ran parallel to Mount Baker Road for any signs of suspicious activity. Seeing none, the Chevrolet turned right and headed west just a couple of hundred yards.

The man's intense gaze found a momentary escape beyond the vehicle. A woman tossed a ratty old tennis ball for the entertainment of an energetic golden retriever. The dog sprinted a good thirty-five or forty yards toward the dog park fence. It retrieved the ball in the time it took for the Suburban to pass. The man was trying to recall the last time he'd had a dog. Too damn long, he decided.

With a rattle of metallic deer spikes, the vehicle turned to the north toward the rural, single-runway airport. On the tarmac was an orange San Juan Airlines' Cessna 207, which the airline's regular passengers affectionately called "the pumpkin plane."

The clock on the dashboard read 6:45am. He was booked on an Alaska Airlines flight out of Seattle-Tacoma International leaving at 8:25am for Juneau, Alaska. It would be at least four hours before he would allow himself to feel anything other than the hidden fear building with each passing moment.

Chapter Forty-Four

Juneau, Alaska

<u>Late Evening, Thursday May 10, 2002</u>

"Where am I?" Mark asked the nurse. She and another nurse were pushing him down the lit hallway. "Can you hear me?" He screamed at the nurse on the right, but she didn't answer.

He could feel the dull ache in his chest and the sting in the left arm, but seemingly he felt almost euphoric as light after light passed by on the ceiling. They seemed unusually bright.

He could hear the nurse screaming, "His pulse is weak and thready...BP 60 over 40!" They entered a room that smelled a lot like Lysol or maybe Pine Sol and he felt some hands touching his legs, his torso, the back of his head. The hands lifted him and laid him on a cold steel table. "That's cold!" He yelled. Again they didn't hear him.

The nurse was still right there. She had dark brown eyes and she looked awfully familiar. Where had he seen her face before?

The pain was gone. Mark was dizzy but at the same time he felt like he was flying. Again, he saw the nurse's beautiful brown eyes, and he began to cry.

"Grandson, I have waited so long to see you. You have grown into such a fine young man. You have made us so proud," Wilma Jameson said, her voice a loving soft tone that he had never experienced before; it was like a peaceful, warm wind you feel when you walk along the beach.

He tried to reach out to her. She spoke this time in Tlingit, and he understood every word she was saying. "Grandson, hold my hand. We are here to take care of you." He couldn't hold back the tears as her beautiful face filled his eyes.

"Hello, Grandson." His grandfather put his strong hand over Mark's, and his soul began to experience a spiritual dimension he had never known.

"Grandpa, I've missed you so much," he said, a torrent of joyful tears streaming down his cheeks. The pain in his chest and left arm were gone. He should have been scared, but all he could feel was elation.

"Grandson, take my hand," his grandmother said. He felt the air beneath, and as he looked down, they were floating away into the Alaska sky.

The ascent was swift. He closed his eyes and felt the wind breathing all around. The peace was invigorating and overpowering, almost a shock to his system that there were no worries whatsoever.

His grandparents released their grip and let him take to the air on his own. Opening his eyes, he saw something before him he'd not known in far too long. It was his family's fishing grounds. The warmth in his grandfather's heart he could feel in his own, this wondrous place where their bond had grown into a most treasured memory.

Everything around them was all so familiar, but all so new. Strangely the air had no smell and no sound, but all the same Mark knew the scent of the pine needles on the trees and the song of the seagull as it sailed the breeze. The sky seemingly had no color, but the hue of a deep blue had enveloped the Lost River Plateau he'd known so long ago.

The tales he'd known as a little boy had come to life. Wing to wing, soaring with his grandparents up and down along the gentle winds over the *winding slow-moving Tawah Creek with its lush plumes of tall Dune Grass reaching into the sky.*

Lumbering through the dune grass was a brown bear, his shoulders muscular and almost a good foot above the grass. With each breath the bear took, vapor trails filled the clean, crisp Alaska air.

Farther downstream they flew until they were at the confluence of a creek known as the Tawah and the Lost River. Another brown bear, much bigger and a little darker in color, had just snagged a plump Coho. The Lost River was boiling with Coho Salmon as they soared west toward the river's mouth.

The river was only 50 feet wide at many points, with spotty sections of sandy beach leading up rises to patches of dune grass and sporadic Sitka Spruce trees lining the river.

"Grandson, welcome home," his grandmother said as they gently soared into an old cabin facing the crashing waves of the Pacific Ocean.

Entering, he felt a gust of wind, and a great man adorned in a reddish-black cape entered the room. Mark had never seen him before, but as his grandparents kneeled before the man, Mark did as well.

"Anwhakxleet," he said. It was a name only his father had used. He'd called once when Mark was passing through Minneapolis-St. Paul's Airport, and somehow the conversation came around to Mark's Tlingit name. His father shared that Anwhakxleet meant "the one who clears a path through the snow."

The man's face held; a look that legends are made of. "Anwhakxleet," he said. All of his words were Tlingit, and Mark understood each one. In his adopted language, the words came through.

"Anxwhaklxeet. Time for you it is not. There is more for you to do." The black fabric of his seemingly endless sleeves gracefully swayed as he pointed south over Mount Fairweather reaching high into the pure blue sky. Mark looked at his grandmother and grandfather as they knelt beside him.

Reaching out to touch his grandmother's face, Mark loved the feeling of her cheeks so soft and angelic.

"My grandson, right you must do. Hate you must not." Mark's soul felt every word.

"Chosen you are, my grandson; right you must do, hate you must not." His soul felt every word his grandfather repeated.

And a great wind swept the room. Wing to wing again, the family was soaring out over the Pacific Ocean. Mark rode the wind with the eagle and the raven.

His grandfather guided him toward the majesty that is Mt. St. Elias, 18,008 feet of bluish-white ice and snow. Their flight swooped over mountain goats as they hopped along narrow ridges of granite rock. His grandmother held his hand as the three lowered over Yakutat Bay. A humpback whale leaped with great force from the greenish calm water and Mark could feel the spray on his face.

His grandmother looked his way, and the smile across her face was full of light. Mark wanted to stay right there, but as if she could feel that thought, she said, "Grandson, go you must."

Mark looked at his grandfather. "My grandson, it is not your time." His face was just as Mark had remembered it. Each wrinkle had its story to tell, and as Mark thought this, he said, "Someday, Grandson, many tales I will tell you."

As they descended over fishing vessels docked in the boat harbor, they squeezed Mark's hands tightly. The warmth of their touch was something he didn't have the words to describe, and he couldn't wait to feel it again.

They descended on a rustic old white home nestled on the rocky beach in the Village. The aroma of burning alders in the woodstove and the smell of percolating coffee took hold of Mark.

His memories had never been here before, but his soul knew this place well. He could sense the bouquet of his mother's perfume and the tang of his father's pipe.

They were no longer soaring, but still floating from room to room. There were the old quilts and the old rocking chair that had followed the family from Yakutat to Juneau to Vienna, Virginia. A crib in the corner was seemingly our destination; they hovered over a tiny infant slumbering peacefully and innocently.

Mark watched the rise and fall of the infant's tiny chest with each breath. As his grandparents gently caressed the baby's soft cherub cheeks, he could feel all of the love, pride, and joy they had always had for him.

Again a powerful gust of wind enveloped the room. "Anxwhaklxeet, chosen you are," the great man spoke. "Go you must."

The serenity in their touch was still there even as their hold gracefully drifted away. As their soft silhouettes faded into the deep blue sky softened by a blanket of pillow-white clouds, Mark could feel the warmth and tenderness still there protecting him.

The sky became blinding and bright, and the wind they had been soaring was fading away. The voices of his grandparents were drifting farther and farther. He was desperate to hold onto their world, but a deafening silence was taking hold.

Chapter Forty-Five

Juneau, Alaska
<u>Early Morning Friday May 10, 2002</u>

It was early Friday morning when Director Archer's G-5 Gulf Stream touched down at Juneau International Airport.

The buzz in the control tower began not long after a call had come in that a VIP government jet was en route. It didn't take long for the rumors to start. One of them stuck.

One of the controllers had heard over the police band that two federal agents had been shot and nearly killed. The controller had even heard that one of the agents had killed some guy who might or might not be a terrorist.

Confirming this, a grey military McDonnell Douglas DC-9 had landed a couple of hours earlier and had parked away from the main terminal. It was still light when the aircraft had arrived, and according to one rumor, many of the men and women getting off of the flight were dressed in dark suits. Not exactly army issue.

The Citation Lear Jet pulled alongside the Military DC-9, and the rumor mill was rampant. This was exactly the way the world now worked. A seemingly benign arrival, and only a slight breather before ABC, NBC, and so on showed up. The area was sealed off as five well-dressed and formidable men departed the G-5 painted a striking creamy white and adorned with the United States Flag prominent on the tail.

Security assessed the tarmac for any signs of a threat. Resident Special Agent Gregory Wiley and eight agents were awaiting the Director's arrival and had done the same. If anyone wanted to bring harm to Director Archer, they'd be neutralized with swift and effective ease.

Seattle ASAC Walt Branson walked up to Director Terrell Archer, and the two shook hands. ASAC Branson led Director Archer to an SUV, and moments later an entourage of FBI vehicles was headed toward Juneau's Bartlett Regional Hospital.

Director Archer made a telephone call after he'd gotten into the SUV. ASAC Branson looked to his left at a large department store named Fred Meyer's that was well lit and had at least twenty cars in its parking lot. He looked at his old-fashioned watch, the hands pointing toward 1:00 in the morning.

Archer finished his telephone call and gave his full attention to ASAC Branson. "We're a long ways from our days in Miami, aren't we?" He stated. "I hate to say it, things seemed much simpler then."

"I'd agree, Sir." Branson said with a heavy sigh.

"Walt, please, it's Terry. So what's the status?"

"SA Westford was flown to Harborview in Seattle an hour ago. We haven't had an update, but she's in critical condition. SA Jameson is in intensive care. The doctor who treated him says he should be dead." ASAC Branson briefed Director Archer as the two rode in a black FBI SUV southbound from Juneau International Airport along Egan Drive on the north shore of Gastineau Channel.

"She says he has three broken ribs, significant blood loss, and a quarter-inch hole in his left arm. The bullet went all the way through," Branson continued, shaking his head with a twinge of anger. Dani and Mark were his agents.

"They're both fighters, I take it?" Archer said with a prideful, almost fatherly smile on his face.

"That they are, sir." Branson smiled back then looked out the window over the quarter mile-wide channel at Douglas Island and its forests deep and green. He'd never been here before, but the purpose of his trip had poisoned the spectacular scenery for him.

They discussed the status of both FBI agents for a few more moments, and then Archer switched gears. Not to slight their injuries, but the bigger picture still played a role. "Has the media gotten wind of this yet?"

"Somewhat. We couldn't control the rumor mill after they found our agents. The Juneau police reported in one of its transmissions that two federal agents were on the way to the hospital. Thankfully the media didn't put two and two together until our plane landed," Branson summarized. "We've cordoned off the hospital entrance area to emergency vehicles only. You won't be getting hit with questions for the time being." Branson watched as the FBI vehicles that had taken the lead just ahead of their own made a left-hand turn onto the Glacier Highway.

A minute or two later Bartlett Regional Hospital had become essentially the safest place a person could be in all of Alaska. There were armed FBI agents, U.S. Marshals, Alaska State Troopers, and Juneau Police Officers seemingly everywhere.

"Walt, before we head in I have a favor to ask," Archer said. He continued in a low voice.

"I'll take care of it," Branson said with a wry smile.

"Thanks." Archer patted Branson on the shoulder.

"Let's go check on Jameson. And as soon as possible, I want to get to Seattle to check on Ms. Westford."

Chapter Forty-Six

Juneau, Alaska
<u>Thursday May 9, 2002</u>

The team- Mark, Dani, Sandra, and Lindsay- had arrived in Juneau on a little Cessna 207. The pilot had to be on the Company payroll. He was good. Mark recalled his name as Craig or Greg.

What was memorable was that the route navigated through some very mountainous terrain and then into Juneau, passing over the Juneau Ice Field. In all of Mark's years, he'd never had the privilege of seeing Alaska in a bush plane. The ice-blue glaciers seemed to reach up to them, the mountains like extensions of the wingtips.

It seemed quite definitive that the Honeycutt Petroleum Corporation was indeed behind the downing of Mark's grandmother's airplane. But it was frustrating because the people responsible were all dead. It's hard to exact revenge on a dead man. The vengeful feelings Mark had were brewing with every mile between Alaska's interior and Whitehorse. By the time the Cessna landed in Juneau, he was ready to piss on Myles Honeycutt's grave.

When they landed, he realized they still needed to figure out who had them painted as targets. He'd tried getting hold of his father, but his cell phone had no coverage. He must have been holed up somewhere.

On the drive to Whitehorse, Lindsay showed Mark a photograph of Jacob Honeycutt. With nothing against people who are attracted to those of the same sex and not wired that way, Mark had to admit that Jacob Honeycutt was a good-looking guy. He also had a bit of empathy for Jacob; the guy's father had committed suicide. But if he was indeed behind all of this, then Mark was hoping he could help Jacob join his father in the great beyond.

Chapter Forty-Seven

Juneau, Alaska
<u>Evening Thursday May 9, 2002</u>

Dani and Mark arrived at Jon Brady's home sometime around seven on Thursday evening. Mark surmised that Jon at one time was a pretty good lawyer and obviously had done pretty well. The home was nice and Mark was a bit envious of the guy. But more important, he wasn't home yet. They didn't have a key and needed to find another way in.

Anyhow, they weren't exactly going in the front door, every once in a while, it is a little more interesting to enter through a window or other means. They voted to enter through the basement door.

Lindsay had arranged for three of her people in Whitehorse to board an Air North flight to Vancouver. All three loosely were similar to Dani, Lindsay, and Mark in appearance, in the event that somehow Jacob Honeycutt or whoever was after them had gotten on their trail. So Whitehorse did have a role.

Jon Brady's home was in a quiet Juneau neighborhood, the property's backyard heavily-wooded and very secluded. Lindsay had researched the guy, and learned there was no security system to worry about, but as they entered via an alternate door they encountered a state of the art security system.

As they entered the home, a couple of menacing-looking four-legged creatures approached. The communication from the CIA had been weak. Apparently Lindsay knew this little piece of knowledge, but decided Dani and Mark didn't have clearance for this fact.

As it turned out, the four-legged creatures were not even close to vicious, just a silver tabby cat and an orange tabby that greeted them with the sweetest little meows. Mark had a fondness for cats, so when the silver tabby rubbed its soft fur against his finger he didn't think Lindsay would ever see him as a tough guy again. Come to think of it, he didn't think she really ever had. Admitting to liking Air Supply doesn't ever do a man good.

Lindsay had arrived fifteen minutes ahead of Dani and Mark, sort of a quasi-advance team of one to ensure no threat existed.

Dani and Mark both knew the basement would be clear, at least they thought it would be. They were wrong, finding Lindsay and Jon in the basement. She'd gotten in by knocking on the door as a government agent. Mark was sure she scared the shit out of the guy, lawyer or not.

Lindsay and Jon were seated on a couch, with two wine glasses on the coffee table.

The look on Lindsay's face was priceless as they entered. Typical FBI playbook, breaking and entering: Mark was sure that was the endearing thought going through her mind.

Before them was a dark, handsome man in his late fifties or early sixties with graying hair and black eyes that at the moment were a bit wide with anxiety. Mark couldn't blame the guy; he had two FBI agents break into his basement while he was having a nice social moment with a gorgeous woman who'd said only that she was a government agent.

After some awkward introductions, the situation got down to business. Lindsay caught the two FBI agents up.

"Mr. Brady here is indeed writing a novel about the Alaska Native Claims Settlement Act." Lindsay looked at the Feds for a moment; the three exchanged an unspoken moment of justification. "It seems he learned quite a bit about ANCSA while working at the Anchorage law firm you'd been researching." Lindsay looked directly at Dani.

"So, Mr. Brady, I'm not sure that you get it, but you have awoken a sleeping giant," Mark stated with a hint of admiration and annoyance. The guy had to be good to have the attention of Honeycutt Petroleum - again, assuming they were the other player in the sandbox.

Brady hesitated in his reply. It was hard to tell if it was the intimidation of three federal agents invading his quiet residential life, or if there was purpose and measure he was searching for. The way his hand shook as he held a glass of red wine led Mark to believe it was the former.

"Agent, the book was purely fiction. Ronald Johns came to me with some story of a guy handing him a manila envelope at the Anchorage Airport back in the early 70's, and the guy was scared for his life. Ronnie found me at the firm a few years back. He'd been researching what firm held the AFN's negotiation records, and lucky me, I was the Associate in charge of those records."

His comments confirmed just how good Dani was at her job. She'd done research and made telephone contacts that reflected what he'd just shared.

"Hold on a second," Mark said, and Dani clicked the stop button on the tape recorder. "Before we go any further, may I have a moment with Ms. Drummond?"

Lindsay and Mark headed up the stairs into the orderly kitchen. "Lindsay, I would hate to have to testify before a Grand Jury and indicate that the FBI had a

CIA agent present during our questioning of a material witness. I think it best that you head back to the hotel. Dani and I will interview Mr. Brady here, and I'll catch you up afterward."

Lindsay seemed a little surprised at how easily he had transitioned to assertive FBI agent from the slightly goofy guy she'd disarmingly turned him into with her womanly wiles.

"I hate to say it, but I agree. You better keep me in the loop when you and Dani get back." She was a professional and knew the rules. But there was a connection in her eyes that wasn't waning at all.

She gently touched Mark's hand, her blue eyes holding a warm smile. She didn't say a word and she didn't need to. She leaned in gently and kissed him. The soft caress of her lips on his was by far the most wonderful feeling he had ever known. He held her hands as they kissed and let this moment that God had given take hold.

She squeezed his hands tight. "See you at the hotel," she whispered seductively.

"Wow." That was all he could come up with as she walked out of the kitchen to the front door.

Just like that, Mark went from the together FBI agent back to the goofy guy who was captured by a woman's wiles. All he could do was watch as her hips swung out the door.

Thankfully, as Mark walked back down the stairs into the basement, he had found his way back to being an FBI agent. And for once, his poker face was successful. Dani didn't have any clue how badly he wanted to be driving away with Lindsay rather than trying to solve this freaking case. Hell, all of the bad guys were already dead anyway.

"Mr. Brady, you were telling us that you'd met a guy named Ronald Johns," Mark continued.

Like any good attorney, Brady took his time contemplating his thoughts. He wanted to formulate an articulate, but more important, defensible answer. "First things first; I assume you want to tape this conversation?" He asked.

Dani answered, "I'd like to, Sir, with your permission."

Brady nodded his approval.

She removed a tape recorder from her right jacket pocket and placed it on the coffee table in the middle of the room, rendering the *Time Magazine* and the television remote all of a sudden insignificant.

"Second thing: please confirm that you are investigating the death of Joshua Knight and any relationship that death may have to do with Honeycutt Petroleum Corporation."

Lindsay nodded again the affirmative. He asked that Dani verbalize as such.

"Sir, are you taping this conversation?" Dani and Mark both asked almost in unison.

"I'd prefer we keep this off the record." He was playing a cat and mouse game, just like lawyers love to do.

"Off the record, Sir, this is an official FBI inquiry, and if deposed I'd be forced to disclose what you tell us," Dani answered.

"On the record, I would like to disclose something. The novel we're speaking of is..." For some reason he leaned forward and stated quietly, "...is above the ball return of the pool table."

Dani couldn't figure out why he would make that a matter of record, but so be it. Dani and Mark both looked at the pool table. Thirty-year-old secrets were just ten feet away, but the agents had to find out what else he knew first.

"Duly noted, so are we agreed that everything else you tell us will be on the record?" Dani was professionally relentless.

"Very well..." He made direct eye contact with both agents as he spoke. "As I said, the novel was based upon Ronald's story that honestly I thought was his imagination on overdrive."

Dani waved him on to continue. Sometimes silence is the best interview technique.

"Ronald sat in my office and spoke with the great clarity of the day he'd driven a man named Joshua Knight to the Anchorage Airport. He repeated on a couple of occasions that it was September 4, 1971. He said he would never forget that day because a few hours later a flight that had originated in Anchorage crashed."

Dani continued to stare directly at the man. "Continue, Sir." She handed him the glass of red wine he'd had sitting on a coaster on the coffee table.

"He was sure the guy had died on that airplane that Joshua indicated he was going to Juneau." Brady paused and sipped the merlot. "Ronald said that Joshua told him he was oil economist in Anchorage following the ANCSA negotiations."

Brady stopped for a moment and looked first at Dani and then at Mark. The look in his eyes was priceless; it was evident they'd appreciate what came next. And Mark was impressed with his recollection of the conversations he'd had with Ronald. The facts he was recalling were seemingly verbatim and crystal clear.

"Ronald indicated that Knight said his company had been spying on the negotiations."

"Sir, your recollection of conversations with Mr. Johns is very strong. You must have been a very good lawyer," Mark replied.

"I was able to hold my own, but I'll tell you I don't miss it one bit."

There was something behind the way he'd answered. Resentment seemed like the obvious answer, but it was something else.

Dani caught on and didn't let it go. "Sounds like you've got a bit of a beef with your former profession?" It was part question, part observation.

Like a good lawyer again, Brady hesitated. "I spent a good twenty years suing people, defending those who probably deserved to be sued. Then Ronald comes along with his wild-eyed story. I looked into the facts he'd intimated, and they were spot-on."

"So you leave the firm to write a book?" Dani sensed something and wasn't letting it go.

Brady was smart enough to sense Dani's skepticism. "I'm nearing sixty years of age, and my wife and I have saved our money very well. It was now or never." There was something in his answer that on one hand sounded plausible, but on the other manufactured.

"So you decided to retire a few years early and spend the time writing that novel you always wanted to?" Now it was Mark's turn to reply with skepticism.

"Not exactly; like I said, Ronnie's facts were spot-on. I saw this as an economic opportunity as well. And the fact that the FBI is in my home asking me questions about a book I'm writing has me wondering how much truth Ronnie was actually alluding to. Have you interviewed him about the book?" Brady's question was genuine. He had no clue what had happened to Ronnie.

"Not yet," Dani answered, keeping the knowledge that Ronnie was deceased under wraps. "Besides Ronnie, what other research have you tapped into?"

"I've made some calls to members of the AFN, researched the public records that are available - including a trip to the Library of Congress last year - and I've made some inquiries to Honeycutt Petroleum. I'm sure you've learned that Myles Honeycutt committed suicide and one of his security chiefs died within a week of each other?" Brady corroborated a fact the FBI was well aware of.

"I hate to tell you, Mr. Brady, but somewhere along the line your novel and its research became more than fiction. As you said, here the FBI sits in your living room." Dani looked at Mark and then at Jon Brady as she replied.

It was funny, after thirty years Mark was expecting a climactic moment but was reduced to sitting in an attorney's basement, staring at an ordinary coffee table; drinking bottled water, and listening to a rather drab oration of a guy going through a meltdown.

Brady took a moment to drink a glass of water and grab a handful of cashews from the coffee table. Mark looked at him and almost felt that he had some strange secret he had stored in his mind, dying to come out.

"Agents, I'd like to continue, but I'd like a moment to take a breath, when I return I'll tell you everything." He paused and reached for a sheet of paper he had in the breast pocket of a white dress shirt he was wearing. The shirt still had the look of being neatly pressed. Mark was trying to figure out how he'd stayed looking so sharp this late in the day? After two hours, Mark's tie was loose and his sleeves rolled up.

The basement had a full-size restroom Brady momentarily escaped to.

Dani and Mark had done a perfunctory casing when they had first walked into the home, but Brady's momentary absence provided them with an opportunity to assess the surroundings. The two agent's eyes panned the room, getting a lay of the land.

Walking around the room, Mark was impressed with its amenities. The basement was well groomed, with a dark, thick-shag carpet, a 55-inch Panasonic TV, a hide-a-bed couch, two recliners, and the now very intriguing pool table.

Chapter Forty-Eight

Juneau, Alaska
Friday May 10, 2002

Dani offered to go upstairs and get them something besides water. Mark asked for a soda of some kind, and she headed up the stairs, leaving him alone in the basement while Brady relieved himself.

From the dossier Mark had read, Brady had arisen to the level of junior partner at the age of 47 and now the time he'd put in he was reaping the rewards; his portfolio was in the millions. That explained the comfy, well-equipped basement. The 55" TV would be nice during March Madness. Mark was an NCAA Basketball fan, enough said.

The basement, despite the nice furnishings, was making Mark nervous. It wasn't just the Tlingit thing, but FBI intuition as well. He did his best to assess where advantages and disadvantages existed in the layout.

Brady came out of the restroom and saw Mark admiring the TV. Mark mentioned March Madness and learned that Brady's wife Molly was as much of a sports fanatic as he was, and so the two had agreed to the indulgence of a very choice television.

As the two awaited Dani's return, they walked to the far wall of the basement where a group of photographs were orchestrated along the wall, featuring the Brady couple taken throughout Southeast Alaska. The best shot as of a whale breaching within feet of their boat. With great pride, Brady described Molly's passion for capturing spontaneous, unscripted photographs of nature at its wildest.

Dani came down the stairs with drink bottles and joined them in admiring the photographs. The agents were enjoying this brief escape from the case.

When they had arrived, Mark had a strange feeling about the home, and had attributed it to Brady and whatever secret he was going to divulge. After he'd indicated there was a draft of a novel tied to ANCSA in the ball return of the pool table, Mark couldn't wait to get it into FBI hands.

He was wrong for the second time in less than five days.

Out of nowhere, that sixth sense that Mark attributed to his Tlingit heritage had the hairs on the back of his neck on edge. The room had an aura that he would have had difficulty describing.

Have you ever stood in line at the grocery store and just felt that presence from behind that someone is watching you? You turn around and sure enough it's an old friend or worse, someone you were doing your utmost to avoid. And then you ask sometime later, how did you know someone was there?

Mark was having that strange sensation. Except as he panned the room, Dani and Brady were the only people in his line of sight and definitely not the source of any angst. Mark's mistake – he didn't sense something was awry until it was too late.

He saw a shadow descending the stairs, so he whispered to Dani and directed her attention to the stairs. "We have company."

Almost simultaneously, Mark turned to Brady and motioned for him to get behind him. Brady ducked down on the ground behind Mark as the shadow morphed into a human being on the stairs.

"Brady, you have company. What an unfortunate turn of events," a man's voice facetiously stated from the edge of the carpeted stairs a good fifteen to eighteen feet away.

Mark's Glock .22 was out of its holster, and he didn't hesitate. He had purposely positioned himself facing the stairs.

"Dani, down!" Mark yelled and raised the pistol with no clue whether the guy was a threat or not. Within a millisecond, it was painfully obvious.

The lighting in the basement left something to be desired, but it was enough that Mark could see the man's face. He was blond and lean, late fifties, with an actor's look. His demeanor held an arrogance Mark wanted to blow away, literally.

Dani was just kneeling beside the couch to the left when the first shot rang out.

Mark felt his left arm explode. He'd blown a knee in college playing football and had thought that burning sensation was the worst he'd ever known. This topped that a hundred times over. He did get lucky, if you can call getting shot in the left arm lucky, only because he was right-handed.

The report of another shot reverberated around the room and immediately he heard a heartbreaking grunt. "Dani!" He yelled, turned, and saw she had been hit in the chest. Then a third report filled the room, and the bullet sailed right past his head.

Then a fourth shot rang out, and he heard the guttural grunt that no one wants to hear. He didn't know where she'd been hit but Dani was hit again!

Mark's heart was beating at a rate that a cardiac surgeon would find unsafe, but surely the doc would think a flurry of bullets flying by was probably not ideal for his health either.

He swore and dropped to the ground - not the graceful, athletic somersaults you see in the movies, but a hard thud onto the ground. There was fear, and he would not be ashamed to admit it. But he wanted to kill this motherfucker.

It occurred to Mark that because the shots weren't volleying out with a constant rat-tat-tat, this guy had a revolver. At least it wasn't an automatic weapon. Mark's pistol had an eight-round clip, so he had seven to go.

The guy had fired four times, so Mark was hoping against hope that he had a conventional six-round clip.

The stairs were a good distance from where Brady, Dani, and Mark were located. Thankfully, a clean shot is much harder to come by in a firefight than a shot lying in wait, so the guy had not immediately fired the fifth round. He was assessing the situation too.

This piece of shit in the sandbox had obviously anticipated only Brady being in the house. Because Dani and Mark had sneaked onto the property, any reconnaissance the guy had done wouldn't have had them noted, and Lindsay departing out the front door would have done a great job of giving him the impression Brady was alone. And because they were in the basement, any heat signature equipment he'd be using would have registered an empty house.

Brady, Dani, and Mark had been talking quietly and calmly. Hindsight is 20/20, but Mark was thankful they had had the sense to talk in the basement.

The graceful drop to the ground left Mark right next to Brady, who had also been hit. He could see Dani was in bad shape. There was an entry wound in the middle of her chest and a lot of blood seeping from her hip.

He couldn't reach Dani even though she was only five feet away. The fear that she was going to die was quickly replaced by the most basic of human emotions - they were boxed in, so it became very simple very fast. Kill the guy or be killed.

His left arm was burning like crazy and it was making him a bit lightheaded. But the adrenaline was keeping the pain somewhat at bay. Brady was unconscious, but breathing. He'd been hit in the abdomen, the entry wound was actually relatively small, but the amount of blood was not.

Caring for Brady's wound would need to wait.

The asshole had a gun, and Mark had one. He momentarily thought it irrelevant to identify himself to the man hell-bent on killing him, but there a competitive cockiness had taken hold. Mark wanted the guy to know who was going to shoot him. This fucker was going down.

"FBI, you're under arrest, you piece of shit!" Mark yelled, realizing the comment was just a taunt. It was obvious this wasn't going to end peacefully.

The silence was highly revealing. Mark didn't think the guy had any idea that he would have encountered a well-armed basement.

"Who the fuck, are you?" the man asked, breaking the silence.

"FBI, you fuck!" Mark couldn't resist. "If you were a better shot, I'd be dead by now." He added, doing his best to distract him with a little mocking.

The distraction didn't last long enough, as the guy recovered very quickly. "Well, asshole, in a moment...you will be!" The guy answered with a conviction that at any other time Mark might have actually found impressive.

At that moment, though, Mark would have been more impressed if he realized this was a no-win situation, dropped his weapon, and surrendered.

"Drop your weapon," Mark said calmly. They couldn't really see one another, but it was worth a try.

"You first, asshole," the guy said with a mocking laugh.

At least Mark could testify under oath, if need be, that he'd given it the old college try to make this end peacefully.

The pool table provided pretty good cover. The shooter couldn't see them, but as a result they couldn't see him. Mark crawled to the pool table at the end with the ball-return. Grabbing a stripe and a solid, Mark decided they might provide a distraction. He tossed one ball against the interior wall and tossed the other one at one of the sliding glass door windows. The one against the wall hit with a thud, and the other shattered the sliding glass door.

The distraction worked just enough. As Mark rose from behind the pool table, the shooter just for a second looked at the shattered sliding glass door. Mark thought he would have done the same. Poor guy, now that Mark had the advantage he raised the Glock.

At Quantico, as mentioned earlier, one of the training sites is a mock town known as Hogan's Alley. Agents and candidates train over and over, encountering situations that hone their ability to assess a situation, make a quick but rational judgment, and neutralize a threat.

Hogan's Alley was paying dividends right then and there. More important, and Mark didn't know how she had done it, but Dani had gotten him an opportunity to visit The Farm once in late 1999.

The Farm is the CIA's main training facility, known as Camp Peary in Williamsburg, Virginia, and also as the Armed Forces Experimental Training Activity for the United States Military.

That day in late 1999 Mark met a former Navy Seal who had become an instructor at The Farm. Nick Van Pelt and he hit it off. Any chance he had after that, when Mark was in D.C. on Bureau business, the two would get in a good run.

On one of those runs, Nick was explaining to Mark a close-combat technique he'd been taught and practiced to perfection. A version of it was taught at Quantico, but hearing it from a Seal who had no doubt used the technique on more than a shooting range target gave it credibility.

The technique was simple: two shots straight at the chest and then raise to the head. The rationale was sound as the head is a smaller target than the torso.

Mark saw the guy's torso and fired two shots right at his chest. Without hesitation, he raised the weapon and fired the next one right at his head. All three shots met their mark. *Thanks, Nick,* Mark murmured to himself.

Unfortunately, the left arm wasn't the only place Mark was hit. The asshole died right there but his last involuntary movement, before taking his one-way trip to hell, was to pull the trigger on his Ruger. The bullet nailed Mark just below the right lung, breaking three ribs and putting a serious damper on the moment. The asshole could be crossed off of Mark's to-kill list, but he wasn't in the best condition to enjoy it.

Chapter Forty-Nine

Between Seattle, Washington & Juneau, Alaska
<u>Friday May 11, 2002</u>

After a 35-minute flight aboard the pumpkin-colored Cessna to Seattle's Boeing Field and a twenty-minute drive to SeaTac, the Orcas Island man was at a gate in the D-concourse awaiting the boarding announcement. He heard the distinct squeak of a microphone come through the overhead speakers. Instinctively, he reached for his briefcase.

A woman's voice over the gate areas speaker system took any momentum away. "We have been informed our aircraft has experienced a mechanical difficulty. We are being told it is likely at least a five-hour delay before a new aircraft will be available."

With that, the four-hour journey he had anticipated would turn into nearly a full day. With a feeling of urgency, he boarded an Anchorage-bound flight and hoped he'd get a connection there that would get him to Juneau at a halfway decent time. The connection in Anchorage was seamless, and now several hours later he was near the end of that journey, finally on an Alaska Airlines jet within two hundred miles of his destination. He was prepared to face the past, but with each passing mile beneath him, the past was now the present.

He remembered a phrase his father had said over and over again as he was growing up: "Believing a lie doesn't make the lie the truth; it simply makes the lie a truth waiting to be found."

As the flight continued its ascent into the clear blue, South Central Alaska sky, he reached into the pouch of the seatback in front of him and grabbed the novel *The Bannerman Solution* by John Maxim. Bannerman had "retired" from the intelligence business but kept getting pulled back into the game. Life sometimes imitates art, and right now he wished it didn't. It had been more than almost three decades he'd been playing this role, and he wondered for a moment if he'd ever get the opportunity to end the charade.

He finally ventured from the book after consuming seventy-five pages, as outside the window Lituya Bay passed beneath the aircraft. Even from 30,000 feet above, he could see the historic impact of the earth's geology below. In 1964, Lituya Bay had experienced an earthquake and landslide-driven tsunami that was still evident on the sides of the mountains. The tree line abruptly changed from rocky face to lush green forest.

He was well aware of the history that had transpired along the rocky coast, but the history he was pursuing was one hundred miles ahead. His attention returned to the book as he followed John Bannerman's journey of revenge, until the flight made its descent into Juneau, Alaska. This time of year, mid-spring, southeast Alaska's daylight was nearly round-the-clock, resulting in a beautiful view of heavily forested islands, calm seas, and snow-capped mountains. He stared down at a lush rainforest as the aircraft banked gently into a southwesterly turn; this journey was tied to the crash of an Alaska Airlines aircraft in the very forest below three decades ago.

The crash of the Alaska Airlines plane was the impetus for a trail of lives lost and lives destroyed nearly thirty years later.

The next chapter in the legacy of Alaska Airlines 1866 had gone into motion six months earlier when an FBI Agent had by more than mere happenstance begun to connect the dots in the 1972 murders of oil CEO Myles

Honeycutt in Upstate New York with the execution of two men on the Seattle waterfront.

He knew the consequences, and he was the only one. The name Jameson was on the grid; that a threat was imminent against an agent named Jameson. Only a handful of people knew why Mark Jameson had been targeted, and his father was one of them.

He realized his mistake. It had happened so many, many years earlier. He'd been angry, cocky, and hell-bent on letting the criminal know before he died who his executioner really was.

He'd learned from a corporate security chief by the name of Adam Ross that Myles Honeycutt was the evil behind the killing of 111 people in Alaska. Ross said under no circumstances would he confess to this fact, but he did offer the names of all men involved – including his own.

The day that Myles Honeycutt had formulated the plan to bring down an airplane filled with innocent people, the trajectory of this government operative's life drastically changed, and now with it so had FBI Special Agent Mark Jameson's.

His father's words just couldn't escape his thoughts. "My son, believing a lie doesn't make the lie the truth; it simply makes the lie a truth waiting to be found.

As he stared out the window across the beauty of Alaska, he realized his father was right. The truth was on the verge being found.

Chapter Fifty

Juneau, Alaska
Early Evening Friday May 10, 2002

Juneau, Alaska is not only one of the most picturesque cities in the United States, but probably in the world. The city and its borough of approximately 30,000 people are nestled in the lush Tongass National Forest.

Mount Juneau at 3,576 feet towers over Alaska's State Capital and is an annual threat for an avalanche, though none has been recorded in modern times. Words simply cannot do justice to the beauty Mount Juneau and its sibling peaks give to this temperate region; no matter the time of the year the mountains provide a splendor unsurpassed in its pure and miraculous beauty.

Just south of Mount Juneau is 3,819 foot Mount Roberts. Connected to downtown Juneau, an enclosed tram takes tourists to the 1,800-foot level of the mountain; where they have the opportunity to enjoy views of the Gastineau Channel, Tlingit art, the occasional black bear, and a bald eagle display.

Among state capitals, Juneau is unique in that it is not accessible by road. Tourists arrive in Juneau by airliner, cruise ship, Alaska State Ferry, or private air or water transport. When the weather is foggy and stormy, the city can be cut off from the rest of the world.

Probably the most notable and famous natural phenomenon in the Juneau area is Mendenhall Glacier. On most days (rain or shine), Mendenhall Glacier is visible to the east when an aircraft is landing from the north. The glacier is nestled in a canyon about 12 miles north of downtown Juneau and coincidentally is 12 miles long. Its source is the Juneau Ice field and surges west until it meets

Mendenhall Lake. On clear days, at the Mendenhall Glacier Visitor Center tourists and locals alike can view mountain goats traversing the narrowest of ledges, bald eagles soaring among invisible wind currents, and every once in a while a bear cruising the lake shore.

Today, as the aircraft descended below one thousand five hundred feet, the operative saw Mendenhall Glacier in the distance. He was observing God's artistry on an exponential scale. The mountains, the glacier, and the beauty that is Alaska were right outside his window, as the aircraft was below 1,000 feet on its final approach into Juneau International Airport north of downtown Juneau.

A feeling of dense irony struck him as he watched the marshy green lowlands bordering the airport's northern boundary. The beauty and innocence of Alaska's lush green mountains, the work of God's hand, and held dark secrets of the work of mankind's deviant nature. A part of his soul had left him back because of what had happened in this part of the world back in 1971, and as hard as he tried, he couldn't escape it.

His thoughts were on a host of issues. There was the telephone call from FBI Director, Terrell Archer, the reason he was coming to Juneau, after an FBI agent had picked him up on Orcas Island earlier that day.

Thirty years earlier, he'd killed all of the men involved, and yet ANCSA and its tentacles of mortal greed were reaching and snuffing out lives in its path.

So, if all of the players were dead, who was the new player in the sandbox?

Somewhere between Anchorage and Juneau, seated in 2A with the John Maxim espionage novel in his hand, the realization struck him of what had opened the ANCSA floodgates again – Jacob Honeycutt.

His mind returned to October 16, 1972. Hatred and revenge in its most primeval form: it had driven a rational decision but a very irrational and unprofessional approach. "Never talk to your mark, and just take the damn shot," he'd been told over and over.

The man, first and foremost an intelligence operative, knew what steps needed to be taken. He had come to Juneau to end a man's thirty-one year old charade. As the flight touched down, his heart began to ache; he was actually fearful of what would come next.

October 1972 flooded his memories often. He'd had specific targets then: There was the pilot who'd flown a Piper Apache out of Juneau, Alaska, on September 4, 1971, and caused Alaska Airlines 1866 to be diverted from its original flight path. The Piper's pilot had been paid a very handsome sum for four hours of work, paid in cash, the cash source – Myles Honeycutt, Chairman of the Honeycutt Petroleum Corporation? That diversion had led Alaska Airlines 1866 into the path of an electronic jamming device in the Chilkat Mountains. The device planted by Clay Tanis a day earlier.

Over thirty-years, he'd solved the "who" and the "how" behind the downing of the Alaska Airlines 1866, and ironically he was now here because of the "why."

FBI Agent Mark Jameson had accidentally uncovered the "why."

Chapter Fifty-One

Juneau, Alaska
<u>Late Friday Evening; May 10, 2002</u>

Mark felt the familiar warmth against his right hand; it was one those feelings he had always hoped for. Even buried deep in an anesthesia-induced state of semi-consciousness, his heart was filling with a new and affectionate exultation.

"Mark, please come back to me." It was a familiar, soft voice he was hearing, and for the briefest of moments his heart was lost. The void of leaving his grandparents and returning to the present was overwhelming.

His eyes fluttered, struggling to come back to the moment. It was not his first, but the vision with his grandparents was the most vivid he had ever known, and one he hoped to know again somewhere down the road.

That sweet soft voice continued to bring him back. Over and over again, the pleas danced in his dreams, beckoning him back. Lindsay's words raced to his soul. "Mark, I love you so much," she said, his clouded eyes stared into her ocean of blue.

Tears were streaming down her cheek and landing on his. Tears were also cascading from Mark's eyes, landing on the sterile white pillow case. Lindsay gently hugged him. His entire being and entire soul wanted nothing more than to hold her tight. As badly as he begged his body to cooperate, his voice couldn't reciprocate Lindsay's words. As Mark's eyes found Lindsay's, he could sense his grandparents watching over them.

And through the murky haze, the sense of another presence in the room.

Lindsay held his hand tight as his body and mind tried to exit the cloud-cover. The surgery had been Friday evening, to remove the bullet from his sternum and to repair to some extent the damage to his ribs.

From what the doctors had told him, in the fog, the broken ribs simply needed time and antibiotics to stave off the possibility of infection. After they removed the larger threat, they needed to assess the damage his left arm had suffered when the bullet had literally passed right through.

It seemed the bicep muscle suffered some harm but no nerve damage. He had dodged a bullet there– well almost.

Lindsay was gazing at Mark with the haven of her blue eyes, but the strange sense of disorientation had complete hold of him.

He had been out for nearly a day and was barely exiting unconsciousness. And the last thing he saw at Brady's home was the first thing that he thought of as he momentarily escaped the fog.

"Dani, is she alright?" It was the first thing that came to mind. The image of Dani lying on Brady's floor, bloody and unconscious, had him frightened of the truth.

Lindsay had a heartbroken look on her face. She didn't say anything for a few moments. Tears were streaming down his cheeks as Lindsay squeezed his hand.

"Lindsay, tell me." Mark swallowed hard, awaiting her answer.

"She is in bad shape. She crashed twice on the way to the hospital, and she is on life support at Harborview in Seattle." Lindsay was soft in the tone of her voice, but the words were direct, just as he would have expected. He knew Harborview is a top-notch trauma hospital in downtown Seattle.

Dani's energetic enthusiasm for life was contagious, and the news that her heart had stopped twice was more than hard to hear. Mark had a lost feeling inside that he hoped he would never ever experience again. It was easy to get lost in the emotions, but Lindsay saw that look and brought him back to the harsh reality. "It's up to Dani to fight for her life." She didn't sugarcoat it.

He wasn't sure if she was being brutally honest or motivating him to finish whatever else might be tied to this awful mess that they were in the middle of. Mark was thinking the latter. He saw the kick-ass look in those gorgeous eyes.

So they moved on. Discussing Dani any longer wouldn't provide any level of comfort, and more likely would introduce more fear and unnecessary noise into the equation.

Lindsay didn't wait for another question. "One of the Juneau Police Officers has checked on you a few times. He said you'd know what he meant – the ball return." Her comment trigged a memory from the night he'd been shot.

Mark remembered a police officer squeezing his hand and telling him to hang on.

While he was lying on a cold steel gurney being transferred to an ambulance, Mark had motioned for the cop to lean close and had told him to look at the pool table.

Mark fell back into a deep sleep with that very thought.

Chapter Fifty-Two

Juneau, Alaska

Early Saturday Morning; May 11, 2002

FBI Director Terrell Archer and operative Robert Jameson sat in a quiet room at Juneau's Bartlett Regional Hospital. The room had been thoroughly swept for bugs, but the men were still cautious and quiet as they spoke.

It had been two days since the shooting at Jon Brady's home. Even though Mark Jameson was out of the proverbial woods, Director Archer felt a deep sense of guilt.

"Jon Brady has said he owes his life to Mark," Archer stated. "He says he and Mark connected somehow," he added in a complimentary tone.

"That kid has always been able to strike up a conversation with anybody," his father answered with pride.

"Honestly, that's one of the reasons Mark is such a good agent. He sees the good in everybody and connects with that side of their character. I've been briefed on his interview tactics, and we've actually thought about bringing him to Quantico, but you can't teach that," Archer stated with a hint of envy. "And it seems he's good with a pistol, too. He took the shooter down with three well-placed shots."

"Poor bastard..." Robert said facetiously, borrowing a line he'd heard in the movie "The Rock" some years earlier.

The two men smiled.

"We've been tracking something for the last six months, and with Mark being caught in the shootout, it seems the threat was real. Maybe you can help us with it. For all of our resources, we can't figure out why Mark is on someone's threat list," Director Archer stated.

Robert contemplated briefly what to say. He'd spent the last thirty years living a complicated life, and thankfully that chapter was about to close.

"It's not about Mark, it's me." With that statement Robert Jameson began the first steps to end a thirty-year charade, a career in the shadows.

Juneau, Alaska

Early Morning Saturday May 11, 2002

"Say what?" It was all Director Archer could muster after Jameson's comment from out of the blue.

Robert Jameson had known this moment would one day come. It had started at the Washington National Monument on a cold afternoon in October 1972.

"Terry, this conversation never happened. Thankfully, I'm truly going to retire," Jameson said with a relieved smile on his face. Actually there was something cooking behind the smile, and Archer saw it.

"Our government is damn good at what it does. I don't think the average citizen knows how hard people like you have worked to keep us safe. Then Bin Laden sends his nut job pieces of shit into the World Trade Center, and all of a sudden the FBI and CIA are a bunch of dumb-ass bureaucrats," Jameson continued.

Archer knew this was going somewhere very interesting and into a world that even in his role he'd probably only read about in briefings, so he wasn't about to interrupt.

"As I said, this conversation never happened," Jameson repeated. "I am an author, that is the truth, but I am also CIA, and only Director Wickford and a few CIA agents know who I really am."

Director Archer had seen a lot over the years as an agent and then as the FBI Director, but he knew this conversation was historic even if it never happened.

"A very big part of my assignment in the end has been a simple one. I have a contact inside of Mossad. I feed information to Mossad, and most of the time we let Mossad do their thing." Jameson looked at Archer with a smirk. "Nice little arrangement. We find the dirt, and then our hands are clean when certain things happen."

Mossad is Israel's version of the CIA, but probably better. What Agent Jameson appreciated about Mossad is that Israel doesn't mind being visible when they settle the score. Back in the early 1970's at the Olympic Games, terrorists brutally executed several Israeli competitors. Israel returned the violence with violence and executed the terrorists in cold blood. "Hoo Rah," as the Marines would say.

Mossad has also shown unmatched success at protecting their agency from internal leaks or moles. Our Aldrich Ames sits in prison. If they've ever had an Aldrich Ames, the consequences for that individual are far less civilized.

"Do you remember the crash that Yasser Arafat was in back in the early nineties? That was Mossad, but it was our Intel that prompted that op," Jameson said absent of pride or shame.

Director Archer nodded slowly. Almost anyone in U.S. intelligence or law enforcement knew of a moment like Yasser Arafat's miraculous survival of a plane crash in the Libyan Desert.

"Our target wasn't Arafat. It wasn't in the papers and no one ever knew, but one of his lieutenants was ready to take over the PLO. Arafat was a known entity. His Lieutenant, on the other hand, had been cultivating a relationship with an up-and-coming terror network...Al Qaeda." Jameson dropped the first bomb. "My book, *The Meeting*, read it and you'll never believe in fiction again."

"Arafat was in on the op. He knew he would probably die, but he kept saying he had more to do," he added. "The guy was a crazed fanatic, but his passion and belief were genuine. And there are others and you're probably wondering why I'm telling you any of this?"

Director Archer was momentarily silent. Jameson was describing what he'd always wanted to do, to play outside the lines. "I am."

"I'm telling you because, well, one of my ops was very personal. It's why my son was shot," Jameson answered, his brown eyes staring at the carpeted floor. "We've known each other for a long while now, but I can't tell you what I'm about to tell you." He waited for an assurance from Director Archer that the conversation they were having was not only off-the-record but lost in a vacuum.

"I don't know how familiar you are with the case that Mark and a few of your agents have been investigating. I've been following their investigation, and I had sincerely hoped they would hit a brick wall." He paused and looked around the room. He trusted Archer, but being in the sterile room surrounded by four walls and no view of the outside world had him feeling a bit claustrophobic.

Archer replied that he had actually gained quite a bit of familiarity with the case, given that the agents had made inquiries regarding Jacob Honeycutt, CEO of the second largest oil company in the United States.

"Then you're aware the agents were looking into the connection of two murders in Seattle to the death of Myles Honeycutt back in 1972?" Jameson asked, and the Director nodded.

"I'm not one to beat around the bush. They've found the connection..." He took a deep breath. "A connection that leads back to..." Jameson pointed at himself

Archer chose to stop the conversation. "Bob, I think this is a conversation you need to have with the agent who's handling the case."

Chapter Fifty-Three

Juneau, Alaska
<u>Early Morning Saturday May 11, 2002</u>

Warm rays of sunshine penetrated the windows. A nurse had come through not too long after Mark had regained a modicum of consciousness and opened the blinds. Warmth radiating through the white sheets had a soothing effect on his body that had been subjected to multiple traumas, still compounding on one another like interest on a thirty-year mortgage.

The analogy was fitting. Mark hated writing that $1,400 check every month for about 1,200 square feet of space that he only saw when going to bed and on the weekends – when he had a weekend. The FBI, believe it or not, is not really what you'd call nine-to-five, more like seven to seven.

Or on-duty on a Saturday morning in a hospital room in Juneau, Alaska, a few days after having a couple of bullets breaking ribs and a hole through the left bicep...

Which led to finally learning what this entire journey was all about, starting with the guy who'd just walked into Mark's hospital room.

Have you ever woken up downstairs when you thought you were upstairs? Or worse, you've woken up thinking you'd slept for an hour and found it was more like ten? Or worse, you've woken up not knowing exactly where you're at?

Lucky Mark, he got doors one, two, and three.

The sun was shining through the blinds half-drawn. He vaguely recalled Lindsay holding his hand the night before and her alluding to something about a

Juneau Police Officer stopping by the room a couple of times. The soft feel of Lindsay's warm hands wrapped around his was a feeling he never wanted to escape.

And, vividly, the journey with his grandmother and grandfather to the family's fishing grounds was somewhere deep inside his soul.

The fog he'd been buried in for the last couple of days was slowly dissipating. A part of Mark wanted to stay lost in the strange safety of the haze, but reality was calling and he knew it. The escape was painful. Ribs were burning up, his left arm was wholly immobile, and he had little clue to why he was in so much pain. Somewhere in the recesses of his mind, he realized that he'd been shot. His head was aching and starting to get a full sense of all that had happened. The image of Dani lying on the floor in Jon Brady's basement repeated itself.

Looking around the room in a haze, he saw a dark figure seated formidably in a green institutional chair, watching him awake from the unwanted rest. Mark's body was not moving well, and he was pretty weak but not weak enough to keep his mouth shut. "Where the fuck am I?"

"Hi, Mark," the dark figure replied. The voice was one Mark had known his entire life.

"Dad!" he said incredulously, still not able to move and now freaking out even more.

Mark couldn't believe he was sitting there talking to his dad in the middle of "who the hell knows where," which prompted a repeat of the first question, minus the F-bomb. "Where the hell am I?"

"Juneau's Bartlett Hospital." His dad paused. "Son, do you know what happened to you?"

That was the sixty-four thousand dollar question. And Mark was drawing blanks. "Tell me."

"Mark, you were in a shootout." His father filled in the blanks the traumatic events had blocked. The conversation with Lindsay was coming back to him, too. Dani had been shot and she was in bad shape.

Mark had lived a lifetime in one week. He'd met a woman who had stolen his heart, he'd watched a man die, his grandmother's plane crash was no accident, and he'd been shot, and now he was learning that his dad was a spook with a body count.

His eyes met his father's in intensity. He wanted to know how Jacob Honeycutt had figured out who had killed his father.

His dad obliged, taking Mark on the journey his life had followed to intersect in this hospital room.

He asked Mark to close his eyes. He'd done this when Mark was a kid; he had a natural ability to transform words into pictures. The request strangely fit in with the week Mark had experienced. As he listened, indeed the journey came alive vividly in Mark's mind.

I was seated in a restaurant, drinking a glass of wine and watching a sailboat tacking in a light wind. There was an aroma of baking bread in the air, overpowering the salty smells of Puget Sound. The waiter brought me a bowl of steamer clams. Not quite as good as your grandmother's, but the buttery taste was still very enjoyable. A few random rays of sunshine cast themselves across the table, giving the glass of Merlot a haunting shadow.

As I lifted the glass of wine, my heart began to race and I began to sweat. The room seemed to be spinning. I was afraid my time had come.

There were people all around me, and yet I was so alone. Then the room stopped, and it grew deathly quiet. Everything seemed to be going black, and then the strangest thing happened. My mother, your grandmother screamed my name.

An hour or so later, the phone rang on my nightstand and the words on the other end broke my heart. Your grandmother's plane had gone down. It took me a long time to believe she was gone. Actually, I don't think I've ever fully believed it. Until yesterday, I hadn't realized why. Her soul is not at rest.

The Tlingit way of life is a very spiritual one. Everything we do in life leaves a footprint and every footprint we leave finds its way back.

The picture his dad painted was both spiritual and real. He'd had an existential, horrific loss of self at the very moment Mark's grandmother had passed. Yet she had not fully passed. Her son's life was haunted by the things he'd done in her name; and her soul yearned for peace to find his father. Now Mark knew why.

"I killed two guys, Clay Tanis and Rico Sanchez. They were operatives for Honeycutt Petroleum, and killed your grandmother." Mark's dad said the names of the dead men who'd become an integral part of the ANCSA Case. He paused briefly, letting that fact sink in, but Mark could tell he wasn't finished.

Mystery solved, well not quite.

"Dad...I get the distinct impression Jacob Honeycutt thinks you took out his dad, too..." The question wasn't meant to be accusatory, but Mark felt the tone came across as such. "Did you?"

The look in his father's eyes as he replied was one of the coldest, Mark had ever seen, one he hoped he would one day master.

The silence continued and probably would have prevailed for a little while longer, were it not for an imposing figure entering the hospital room. He looked vaguely familiar but Mark couldn't place where he had seen him.

"Agent Jameson, you look a little better than the last time we met." The guy's voice was deep, almost baritone. He was tall – NCAA College Basketball tall, but muscular, more like an NFL linebacker. Seeing his biceps in the dark polo he was wearing had Mark wanting to get back in the gym. He was afraid Lindsay might get a crush on a Juneau Police Officer, and that would be all she wrote.

Despite the guy's obvious ability to employ a vise-grip, his handshake was merely firm. "Jason Montoya. I doubt you'd remember, but we met the other night." The Juneau Police Officer, who'd been the first on-scene after Mark had been shot, introduced himself.

"Mark Jameson. I guess I owe you owe you more than I can say. Lindsay tells me you handled things quickly and probably saved my life..." Mark wanted to continue, but Montoya waved away the thanks.

"Just doing my job, Agent Jameson," Montoya answered in that genuine manner that true public servants typically reply. What he'd done was heroic, but he brushed it off.

"It's Mark. This is my dad, Robert."

"Jason."

With that, there really wasn't a lot of small talk. Montoya lifted a brown manila envelope in his left hand.

Brady's home was a crime scene, especially the basement where Mark had killed the yet-to-be-identified shooter. Having that manila envelope in his custody was actually a violation of law.

After the cadre of officers had ensured that Dani, Brady, and Mark were safe, Montoya's primary responsibility had been to secure the crime scene. By removing the manila envelope, he'd technically obstructed justice. That was a secret that would be forever kept.

Montoya was not an advocate, nor in the habit, of breaking the law, but according to Jon Brady, the manila envelope held something the government would definitely be interested in.

"Agent Jameson..." Montoya ignored Mark's request to use his first name, walking over to look out the window. He turned back. "...I think you've earned the right to have this." Montoya had an expressive look on his naturally-tanned face as he laid the envelope on a golf magazine on the nightstand.

He nodded at Mark and his dad, and left without another word.

Chapter Fifty-Four

Juneau, Alaska

<u>Late Monday Afternoon May 13, 2002</u>

After Robert Jameson's little revelation, the FBI Director decided it best that Mark be moved to a more private facility, not solely for their sake. In fact, Mark thought the safety of folks in and around Juneau's Bartlett Hospital were the Director's primary concern.

Mark's recovery was going better than anticipated, so he was moved late Sunday to an undisclosed location – at least to the media and the outside world. Scottsdale, Arizona, has a very private airport with traffic that is, to say the least, elite. The Jameson family was not what you would say fit the definition of elite, but they needed to arrive somewhere discreet.

As the aircraft touched down sometime around 5:30 Monday morning, dawn had already broken. The mountains of the desert southwest were a stark contrast to the sprawling mountains of Southeast Alaska, but Mark felt right at home. Having been assigned to the Phoenix FBI Field Office for a year or so back in the late 90's, he recognized the familiar sensation of Scottsdale's warm dry air, in stark contrast to the temperate, crisp fresh air left behind in Juneau.

Mark was a little abashed, but the United States Government was taking very good care of him. Two doctors and a very effective team of nurses were ensuring that he was receiving top-notch medical attention.

The broken ribs had definitely put on hold any chance of a run for the next few weeks. In fact, he was out of breath walking from the nice queen-size bed to the bathroom. Mark blinked at the Jacuzzi tub, porcelain sinks, granite tiles, and an impressive skylight.

Mark had to say it was pretty cool.

In the early evening after he'd enjoyed a nice dinner of salad, grilled chicken, rice pilaf, and a glass of Pinot Grigio, his dad stopped by. They talked about a myriad of subjects, ranging from the Seattle Mariners and Seahawks to the stock market to Mark's stepmom he had come to love as much as his biological mother to golf games and finally to their professions. Well, Mark's for the time-being. As always, his dad would share his side of things in due time.

A nurse came in to let his dad know they were going to give Mark a sedative soon, and given that the evening was being cut short, his dad didn't seem prepared to follow up on the conversation they were having in back in Juneau. That was just fine with Mark; he just wanted to watch a little TV and read a newspaper. But the conversation wasn't quite done.

His dad wanted to hear about Mark's first arrest. Qualifying that a bit, he wanted to know about the first time Mark had drawn a weapon on a suspect. He'd been on several arrests and raids, and there is a rush that goes with each one. But the first time it was just Mark and the other guy was exhilarating.

Putting on the blue windbreaker with the highly-visible FBI Logo gets the adrenaline going. But for a sense of comfort, the feeling of the pistol on his right hip and the one carried in his shoulder harness can't be beat.

Mark's dad munched on an apple while Mark sipped on his glass of wine. It was funny, he had been an agent for eight years, and for some reason this was the first time Mark had discussed his career.

That first time he got the chance to raise his weapon and yell, "FBI, hands up now!" That was a moment he would never forget. Right up there with the first time he held a girl's hand, the first time he scored a touchdown, and the first time he – well, let your imagination fill in the blanks.

So Mark did his best to give an idea of what that first arrest was like. And oddly enough, it was the arrest he'd dreamed about recently.

"You sure you want to hear this?" Mark wanted to make sure his dad wasn't simply looking for a story that would put him to sleep. "It was at a bank robbery in downtown Denver where I was first assigned. A young Caucasian guy had just held up a Bank of America, two blocks from our office. My senior partner Mike Hollis and I had just stopped by a Starbuck's and we were heading back to the office. Dad, our timing was impeccable." Mark paused. Just to give you an idea, Hollis is definitely one of the coolest customers on the planet. He doesn't always play quite by the book, but Mark wouldn't hesitate to have him as a partner in a fight.

"Hollis saw a female customer running from the bank as I was sipping on my Mocha. He said something like, some kind of Fed you are, and he pointed at the bank." Mark smiled at that particular part of the memory. "He said, 'Shit's going down and you're all hoity-toity with your girly mocha. I don't drink Mochas anymore."

"I dropped the mocha and we were sprinting for the bank entrance. Hollis at the time had to be around 43. He was moving at a good clip, I was duly impressed. I did pass him, though."

His dad laughed at that one. "Always the competitive one, aren't you?"

"You want me to finish this or what?" Mark shot back.

"Anyway, passing him was worth a good ribbing over a beer later. The woman was running in our direction. Hollis stopped her and confirmed that a robbery was in progress. She told us that the assailant was acting alone. He was young, was what she'd remembered, and he was very nervous."

Mark paused. "We were on the entrance in no time at all. Hollis told me to hold back, we needed to wait for backup but be prepared to breach if we heard any shots at all."

"A breach never became an option. The guy came walking out with two money-filled bags. Poor guy had no idea the federal building was just a couple of blocks away."

"I was nearest the door on the right side as we faced the bank entrance. The guy thought he had more time then he saw me in the nice blue jacket. I guess it gave me away, or maybe it was the shit-eating grin he saw in my eyes." He paused again.

"Always the cocky one, aren't you?" His dad couldn't resist another interjection.

Mark gave a shrug of the shoulders that pretty much said, "I guess I am." He continued, "Whatever it was, he knew I was a Fed. At that moment, it totally hit me that I was an FBI agent. Those four months at Quantico kicked in like muscle memory."

His dad smiled, and Mark knew he liked the golf analogy. Repetition is impressed upon students by golf instructors until their body reacts the same way with each swing, a concept known as muscle memory.

"I had my gun out and pointed at the poor kid." Mark stopped for a moment, almost feeling the sensation of the warm Colorado sunshine and light wind that was in the air that day. 'FBI, drop the bags and don't move a muscle!' I yelled. That was April 1994 but I remember it like it was yesterday."

"Was the rush everything you expected?" his dad asked, and Mark could sense he was wondering about the psychological aspect, not the physical.

"I'm not sure what you mean." Mark said.

"Was it because you're a cop, or was it the guy thing...the adrenaline rush?"

There was a bit of awkward silence in the room as Mark contemplated what it had meant. He hadn't really thought about. He'd spent his whole life wanting to know that moment. "Both, I'd have to say."

His dad smiled and didn't need to say it. He appreciated the honesty. Guys who become cops can pretend all they want, that it is solely about doing what is right, but there is a rush that goes with carrying a gun and catching the bad guy.

Then his dad verbalized something that caught Mark off guard. "In case I haven't said it in a while, I'm very proud of you. Not because you're an FBI agent, but because you've always been true to yourself. Not to mention damn handsome – just a chip off of the old block." The last sentence was coupled with a grin.

The Next Morning – Tuesday May 14, 2002

The sedative the medical team gave Mark was a strong one; he slept until 9:30 or so the next morning. Usually up around 5:30am to get in a three to five mile run, Mark had to admit the four extra hours felt very good.

His dad was there when he woke up, and so was Lindsay. Unlike the prior night's conversation, the conversation went directly to the ANCSA case.

And another government employee had joined in.

Agent Sandra Gonzalez had arrived in Scottsdale the prior evening, after spending the last few days following up on the leads Dani had put together. Dani had done a great job putting a connection together between Clay Tanis, Rico Sanchez, and Myles Honeycutt. Mark recently learned that his father had dealt rather handily with those players, which left two compelling questions - the first of which had started this whole freaking thing.

Question One: How did Joshua Knight perish in Anchorage when he was supposed to have been found aboard an aircraft that went down?

Question Two: After thirty years, Knight's remains are unearthed and a cab driver named Ronald Johns ends up dying because he's given life to a novel about one brief meeting with the guy. Who connected that dot? Was it Jacob Honeycutt or someone else?

After some time catching up on Dani's condition and Mark's, the team got down to business. Sandra indicated she'd located some information that they would appreciate.

"So, what's the good news?" Robert asked.

"I've found a link between the AFN and Honeycutt Petroleum."

Robert jumped in with a direct response tempered with professional respect. "Phillip Black, right? He was on the airplane that went down that Knight was supposed to have been on."

"Sir, there's a deeper connection that we've turned up."

Mark couldn't wait to hear what would be more compelling than a connection between the deceased oil economist Joshua Knight and Phillip Black. Gonzalez didn't disappoint.

Lindsay looked at Mark. They had been on this journey for a relatively short period of time, but it didn't feel that way at all. He was hoping against hope that Gonzalez would connect a dot that could put this thing to rest.

She didn't disappoint.

And two pieces of the puzzle connected in an instant. Lindsay had mentioned Olivia Black a day or two before he was shot but thanks in part to the rather heightened pace with which things were happening, that fact had moved to back-burner this very moment.

Chapter Fifty-Five

Syracuse, New York
Late Tuesday - May 14, 2002

Jacob Honeycutt sat in the large home his father had called their "little getaway." Long since removed were the trophy stuffed animals that his father had so treasured. Jacob had done his best to remove any remnants of his father's memory.

Myles' death had been the defining moment in Jacob's life. Every decision he had made was to honor his father's legacy, and in conjunction to find the man who'd stood on that very property and directed his father to take his own life.

The crack of the pistol had sent Jacob into a state of shock that lasted for a good two weeks. Jacob had insisted to the police officers that a man wearing a mask had been on the property, but the police laid little to no credence to the young boy's assertions.

In the end, nothing would bring back his father, and he wanted to kill the masked man himself anyhow.

It had taken nearly thirty years to learn the man's identity. It was an anonymous call from a man who had a deep voice. Little did Jacob know that the man with the deep voice was a Native Alaskan who'd made a different call to an FBI agent by the name of Mark Jameson.

Jacob Honeycutt had the name Robert Jameson in his cross-hairs, and he had been so close in Juneau. The man with the deep voice had informed him that a retired attorney, Jon Brady, was writing a novel about the fraudulent settlement of the Alaska Native Claims Settlement Act. The man said he'd seen the draft and indicated it would be mortally detrimental to the survival of Honeycutt Petroleum.

He'd gotten the call a few hours before he jumped on his private aircraft. Between Syracuse and Anchorage, a plan was formulated to have Adam Ross infiltrate Jon Brady's home, destroy anything associated with the novel the man was writing, and silence Brady permanently.

In Juneau, Ross would do the dirty work while Jacob stayed in Anchorage. The two would reconnect in Syracuse. But something happened in Brady's home, and Ross was killed by an FBI agent. The government would not disclose the man's name, but he'd learned that the agent was Mark Jameson.

Adam Ross dying in the home of the man writing a novel about Honeycutt Petroleum's clandestine role in the settlement of ANCSA was immensely frightening. Jacob was not easily frightened, but the agent's last name gave him the awful feeling that he and his family's vast world-wide oil conglomerate had just been wrapped into a tightly-wound, neatly-wrapped act of revenge.

Jacob sat on the couch and stared at the slow-swirling ceiling fan. An Associated Press reporter based in Juneau had already written an article indicating the FBI had identified the deceased man as Adam Ross, Chief of Security for Honeycutt Petroleum. Within the article, a connection was being made with the death of Joshua Knight as an oil economist who'd been employed by Honeycutt Petroleum. It mentioned that Jon Brady was a retired attorney with a law firm who'd maintained the negotiation records for the AFN and ANCSA, and finally that there were indications the FBI was opening an investigation into the crash of an Alaska Airlines plane back in 1971 because it had been discovered that Joshua

Knight was a passenger aboard that aircraft along with an AFN negotiator, Phillip Black.

Competitive to the core, Jacob had never experienced defeat. He'd lost a few battles, but never the war. Staring intently at the ceiling fan, swirling beneath the dark timbers of the large log home, Jacob realized everything his family had built was going to crumble. If the reporter's assertions had been untrue, he would have found a way to win, but any attempt now to refute the facts would only dig a deeper grave.

On the very spot where his father had taken his own life, ordered by a man he now knew was Robert Jameson, Jacob now stood with tears streaming down his handsome face - he raised a pistol to the right side of his blond mane and pulled the trigger.

Chapter Fifty-Six

Scottsdale, Arizona
<u>Late Tuesday - May 14, 2002</u>

The federal agents were discussing the ANCSA case when a U.S. Marshal on the premises indicated they definitely wanted to turn on the TV.

"This is Natasha Burbidge with WSYR. I'm on a rural road a few miles north of Syracuse. We're monitoring a situation unfolding on the estate of Jacob Honeycutt, CEO of Honeycutt Petroleum Corporation, the world's second largest oil conglomerate." The reporter was tall, a freckled redhead, her blue eyes a font of energy. Behind her, it was evident that a wide variety of law enforcement agencies were onsite.

"The authorities are not providing any information whatsoever, but we have observed the coroner arriving on the scene. The history of the Honeycutt family has been a tragic one. Myles Honeycutt committed suicide here thirty years ago, and his wife took her own life some years later. Our research department has learned that Myles' parents tragically perished in an automobile accident in the late 1950's." Natasha's report was tempered with the appropriate amount of empathy but it was obvious that she was well aware of what the exposure of this report would do for her dreams of landing a network assignment.

Robert looked at the TV and politely asked Agent Gonzalez to see if she could find an office to get in contact with the FBI Director Archer's office and see what facts she could get. Sandra's absence left Robert, Lindsay, and Mark to continue to sort out the puzzle pieces. Her absence also presented the opportunity for Mark to divulge something to his father. Knowing he was a spook, it probably would make him proud that Mark had decided to play outside the lines.

Dani and Mark had been shot because they were on the trail of a key piece of evidence in the disappearance of Joshua Knight, the novel draft. Lindsay and Mark now had it in their possession the entire time. No other person knew they had the file, except Jon Brady and Officer Jason Montoya.

The two guests left in Mark's room lived by a different set of rules; consequently, it seemed appropriate to reveal the questionably-obtained evidence that he had in his possession.

Mark had been anxious to open the file in the hospital room back in Juneau; however, the presence of the FBI, U.S. Marshals, not to mention FBI Director Archer himself, had left Mark hesitant to do anything but file the envelope away. He had no idea it would be in the presence of his dad that they would take a look at the draft.

And Lindsay had done some homework without checking with him. Freaking CIA and beautiful women, they play by a different set of rules.

Lindsay had left for a couple of hours back in Juneau, not long after Officer Montoya had left the file. At the time, he hadn't a clue why, but now it was clear. She'd had the file converted to PDFs.

"Dad, Jon Brady is an asset?" Mark asked.

Lindsay took the cue and removed the manila folder from the laptop case, but rather than remove the document from the folder, she powered up her laptop.

"So have you reviewed the files?" Mark just had to ask.

"Nope, I just wanted to make sure that the files that got you and your partner shot would never disappear," Lindsay said with a disarming smile.

She double-clicked an icon on her laptop, and just like that history was on display on the twelve-inch screen. Lindsay's screen backdrop was a beautiful white Alaskan malamute – another glimpse into her likes and dislikes.

It was kind of funny watching the PDF come to life. This file was evidently very dangerous, and only five people knew it existed; and yet with the click of a few buttons this file could easily be sent via e-mail anywhere in the world.

Mark's father looked at Lindsay. His dad had killed the Who (Myles, Clay, Rico) for the *what* (my grandmother's airplane crash). The file on Lindsay's laptop held the *why* and Mark sensed his father knew that.

The PDF was well over six thousand pages. It was pulled up, and Mark's dad looked at both Lindsay and Mark with an almost sad look.

"Lindsay, is that the only copy you have?" Mark's dad asked barely above an audible whisper.

"Sir?" Lindsay queried and then answered, "It is."

"Close the file." His eyes closed momentarily as he directed Lindsay.

There was an awkward pause in the room. The sunshine outside almost seemed hazy, as a strange sense of chaos had suddenly enveloped Mark's mind.

"Mark, Lindsay...Let it go. Sometimes we need to let sleeping dogs lie." His father's tone was resigned.

"There is a key piece of evidence I need to share with you, and then, please let it go."

"Cloak and dagger is maddening, Dad. What is it?"

"Your investigation and its assumptions have been spot-on, all but one."

The comment felt heavy on Mark's shoulders. He took great pride on being meticulous, so missing something was unacceptable.

Mark's dad wasted no time in laying the cards on the table. He looked directly at his son. Lindsay either knew what he was about to say or more likely, this was meant to be a lesson for his FBI agent son.

"Son, you're good at what you do, and I know you've heard this before, but all is not always as it seems." His dad paused, his stare piercing. It wasn't disappointment; actually, Mark was not sure how to describe exactly what it felt like.

"Agent Gonzalez brought up the name Phillip Black. He was allegedly killed because he wanted to hold up the ANCSA negotiations. It was precisely the opposite..." The room's aura almost felt haunted.

"Mark, Phillip Black is the reason this all started. He was leaking information from the ANCSA negotiations to Honeycutt Petroleum."

"What? Nothing we've found indicated that Phillip Black wanted to delay the negotiations. We had nothing to corroborate that, but given that he was killed, we gave it high plausibility." Even as Mark answered, doubt had seeped in. "How do you know he was leaking information the other way?"

"The Shadow Squad, son - do you remember the woman you and Agent Gonzalez picked up in Paxson last fall.?."

The comment was a shock. Months earlier, he and Agent Gonzalez had made a purported arrest in front of some patrons at a Paxson, Alaska restaurant. The intent was to get a woman into protective custody.

At the time, running into his father in Paxson didn't make sense. Now, months later, it all fit together.

His father continued, "Well, I've got a cassette tape that to this day no one else has ever heard."

Lindsay's eyes squinted ever so slightly. She had an appreciation for what Mark's father had done.

It is funny. People can be told a secret, but to keep it can be wholly excruciating. Mark's father had been carrying a secret around for a very long time, and not the run of the mill "did you know your neighbor is sleeping with her boss" kind of secret, but the kind that can destroy a multi-billion conglomerate of an oil company.

"Your investigation brought this back to life. Or more precisely, unbeknownst to you, a ghost dragged you into this. Lindsay, please play this." He handed her a CD to put into the laptop.

A couple of double-clicks later, they were listening to the voices of men who were now ghosts.

"We're getting very close to a settlement. The government is offering around one billion dollars, and we're starting to talk about a tentative agreement. It plays right into our plans." It was the voice of Phillip Black.

"We've got a problem. Joshua Knight has become a complication. He's found the deal actually could be a lot richer. He's calculated the Prudhoe oil field will be operating at a minimum for at least the next seventy to eighty years and will yield trillions of dollars in oil," Adam Ross responded.

"Has he shared the news with anyone other than you or Myles?"

"We've had him under surveillance ever since he got to Anchorage. He hasn't passed this information to anyone."

"Then let's let him believe that he has passed the information. We need a ruse. We need Knight to believe we're not comfortable with the offer. Does he know who your source is?"

"Knight has seen transcripts, but we've had the names redacted. He has no idea you're our source."

"We need him to get in contact with me."

"What for?"

"We're going to let him believe I'm one of the good guys. We need him to trust me – I'm going to tell him that I'm going to be a dissenting AFN member who doesn't think the government's offer is satisfactory."

"How do we get him in contact with you?"

"Miranda and I have to fly back for a family funeral the day after tomorrow. Let's come up with a contingency plan – some way to get rid of Knight once and for all. He's served his purpose."

A prolonged silence.

"You've got something in mind, I can tell, Phillip Black added.

"That I do, my friend."

"Will you pause this for a second?" Mark's dad said before the next recorded sentence was uttered. "The rest stays along that track. I know you don't have any way of knowing if Phillip Black is really the voice on the recording, except for one thing. I'll get to that in a second."

He removed the CD and handed Lindsay another one.

A guttural grunt came first, then what sounded like the thud of a fist against human flesh, the sound of bones breaking. "This is not going to go well for you, Mr. Black." It was the voice of Robert Jameson.

"Please...please don't!" Phillip Black pleaded.

A reverberation of breaking glass. A dreadful, imploring wail took over.

This scenario repeated itself for another two or three minutes: torture and pleas, pleas and torture. Then finally some substance took hold.

"You've sold your soul and taken some lives with it. And sadly for you, my mother was one of the people you killed," Robert Jameson said.

A palpable silence created a ten to fifteen second void as the CD continued to move forward. The violence seemed to have stopped, or maybe it was enough to convince Phillip Black that Mark's father meant business.

"I...I don't know what...what you're talking ah...ah...about."

"I've got all the time in the world, Mr. Black. I have no qualms continuing this little conversation, but the longer it takes, the more you're going to want to simply die."

"I...I...I really..."

"Enough! Mr. Black, answer my fucking question!"

An almost expected bone-crushing thud comes next, followed by the whimpering of a defeated man.

Okay...okay Phillip Black's voice was barely audible, then more silence.

A tug of empathy took hold of Mark as he listened to the sobbing and whimpering of a tortured human being.

"Mr. Black, this is not a game, so I hope you're not just toying with me."

"I'm...I'm ready to tell...tell you." The voice was now resigned. *"Fifty million dollars...and fifty...fifty-thousand shares of Honeycutt Petroleum. That...that's what I asked for."*

Then came the sound of Phillip Black drinking something. Jameson had probably given him a pain-killer to keep the conversation lucid.

"So did you approach them, or vice-versa?"

"It...It was me."

"Why?"

A very long pause resonated, but Mark's dad held his abuse in check. At least as far as the CD indicated.

"At...at first, it was all...about revenge." Black's voice was shaky.

"Enough of the mumbling. Speak like a fucking man, you piece of shit. Any more stuttering and I take off your fingernails one at a fucking time. What kind of revenge?"

There was a momentary pause, then more drinking sounds. And it seems that his father's command had done the trick.

"Come now." Black said his voice now composed. *"You must have a clue as to the answer by now if you've found me."* He was speaking as if he had the upper hand.

Mark looked at his dad as the CD continued. Whatever Phillip Black had just said on the CD clearly still pulsed its way through his father's being. The anger and the thirst for the death of Phillip Black ran deep.

"Your daughter, why kill so many and sell out your own people for Olivia?" Jameson's voice again.

"Wow, I've given you way too much credit," Phillip Black stated with surprising condescension.

Just to maintain a level playing field, the sound of what had to be a breaking bone. Black screamed, and Mark had to admit it was a little difficult to take.

After a few minutes, Black recovered enough to have a lucid conversation. His father must have given him something to dull the pain, because there was no notable stammering as Black continued with the coerced but nevertheless creditable confession.

"Olivia is not my daughter. My wife was nothing more than a fucking slut. Olivia's true father is an Inuit Tribal leader, but I didn't know that until my wife told me just a few months before the ANCSA negotiations were closing down."

He continued, "Wouldn't you know it, the Inuit and I both ended up on the AFN, and then ANCSA comes around. What a wonderful confluence for me, spending every day in a room with the guy who'd fucked my wife." Black coughed.

"May I have another drink?"

After a few moments, the conversation resumed. And Mark couldn't believe how calm his father was. He didn't believe the anger was gone but his father was suppressing it.

"So, Mr. Black, why crash an airplane full of innocent people? You said earlier that initially it was all about revenge. What did you mean by that?"

The CD was virtually silent. Mark couldn't hear any discernible movement, no breathing, nothing. The silence lasted for at least a half minute. Mark was beginning to wonder if Phillip Black had checked out.

"I wanted my wife dead. I'm not going to deny that at all. And yes, I wanted to kill the little Inuit piece of shit who'd had his way with my wife but the idea was all Ross. He said he'd take care of my problem and in the process take care of Joshua Knight."

"Are we going back down that road? Let's skip the bullshit. You've had a lot of time to make peace with who you are. Be a man for once in your useless life!"

The comment caught Mark off-guard. "A lot of time" didn't compute. He gave his dad a quizzical look and hoped the query would be answered as the recording moved along. Mark wasn't disappointed.

"Come on, who do you think made the anonymous call that led the FBI to the Paxson Lodge where Olivia and you were staying?" Black answered.

Even Mark's father had a moment of silence; it was almost certain that wasn't the answer he was expecting. But he didn't take long to re-engage.

"Did you have an epiphany, or better yet, are you dying? I can oblige you soon here and put you out of your misery."

Mark had no doubt his dad meant every word. He was just a little envious he wasn't the one who'd get to pull the trigger, but his father doing so would serve as poetic justice. What came next was a surprise, but not as much to Mark as it would be to Lindsay. It was a world she wouldn't understand, but one Mark been engaged in very recently.

"May I call you Bob?" Black asked.

"If you must," Robert Jameson answered with annoyance."

"Bob, as much as I know you'll hate to admit it, we come from the same people.

"Something runs through our veins that we can't escape, and I know you know what I'm talking about. It's why you and I are in this moment. I took your mother from you, and now it's my turn. Revenge runs deep in our blood."

Mark's dad was unusually calm and quiet, both on the CD and here in the present. He obviously knew what was coming, and he allowed Lindsay and Mark to fully immerse in the encounter. Phillip's voice was almost reduced to a whisper as he continued. Mark's dad must have known the transition was coming as he redirected the laptop's mouse and nearly doubled the volume.

"I deserve to die for what I've done, but I need you to know something first. I'm in no position to make demands, but I am going to anyhow, and then you can get on with your business."

Mark's dad obviously had the upper hand in the situation, so the need to terminate Phillip Black didn't have great urgency. Mark could almost picture his father rotating his pistol in the air for the tortured man to continue the conversation.

"First, I have well over seven hundred fifty million locked away in five Switzerland accounts under separate aliases. I want four of the accounts liquidated and spread back equitably to each ANCSA Regional Corporation and their subsidiaries." A cough.

"Second, there is an account I'm holding in the Cayman Islands. I've left it there precisely for a moment like this. That money is meant solely for my daughter. I've seen to it that she has been taken care of her entire life – she had

five thousand shares of Honeycutt Petroleum Stock that she has divested well, but the Cayman Account is priceless. "Another pause.

"And last - ."

Mark's dad abruptly stopped the CD with Phillip Black in mid-sentence. Lindsay and Mark both looked at his dad and assumed the remainder would be the last moments of Phillip Black's life.

"So what is this all about?" Lindsay showed no hesitation, her tone interrogatory.

"ANCSA was the impetus for the Shadow Squad. My boss was its founding member, and I was its first recruit. The first op was obviously personal, but we were played right from the start. Phillip Black didn't die aboard your grandmother's plane," he said, looking right at Mark, and then continued, "We truly believed he'd been killed. We wouldn't have known that Phillip Black was a conspirator, and our research showed Black had died on your grandmother's plane."

"What benefit did Honeycutt Petroleum gain from the settlement of ANCSA, and what was the great urgency?" It was Mark's turn to jump into the conversation.

"It was rather simple. Agent Gonzalez surmised something she mentioned to me earlier – insider trading." His dad's comment lacked finality.

Like listening to a joke and waiting for the punch line, his father's pause left Mark and Lindsay on pins and needles.

"Myles Honeycutt and Adam Ross were both operatives of the United States in Vietnam. Adam Ross was never quite the nut job that Myles turned out to be, and he finally made a choice to do what was right. I think he's the one who sent me the first cassette, because he knew that my mother was on the plane they'd brought down." Mark's dad stopped and looked down at his feet. It was amazing: Mark could almost see the past intersecting with the present in his father's mind.

Phillip Black wanted to kill the guy who'd been doing his wife, and his thirst for revenge played right into things. Life is full of missed opportunities and sometimes awful coincidences; well, this was one of the latter. Phillip Black was on the AFN side of negotiations, and Honeycutt was looking for someone who was willing to corrupt the bargaining process.

"The novel you surreptitiously got your hands on from Jon Brady's basement intimates that the AFN was close to settlement and that Phillip Black was its strongest negotiator. When he purportedly perishes in the airplane crash, the strength of AFN goes with it and a few months later ANCSA is settled out. What no one knows is that Phillip Black had purchased 50,000 shares of Honeycutt Petroleum stock under an alias, and after his death Honeycutt Petroleum gifted another 50,000 shares of stock to Olivia in 'honor of her father's service to his people.' How are you two doing keeping up so far?" he briefly queried.

Mark and Lindsay both nodded for him to keep going.

"Sadly, the crash was all part of the plan. Kill Phillip's wife, take his power out of the bargaining process, and finally kill Joshua Knight who'd figured out the AFN should be holding out for more money – lots of it." His dad rubbed a couple of fingers together to formulate the image.

"We figured out the value of Phillip Black's holdings are somewhere just south of one billion dollars, and that isn't all of it. There is more to divulge, a much larger trail to a bank account in Zurich, Switzerland. Phillip Black demanded that Honeycutt Petroleum transfer $25 million in cash annually each September 4th to the Zurich Bank Account. The account paid just two and a half percent interest – any residual interest the bank retained as its fee. Ironically, he'd requested the account be named Black Olive."

Mark didn't get it for a moment.

"Olivia Black - Black Olive, geez are you sure you're a Fed?"

"How much cash is sitting in that account?" Lindsay jumped in faster than Mark – no big surprise there.

"About one point six billion as far as we can tell...and Olivia Black allegedly has never known of its existence. But annually she's taken a vacation to the Caribbean, and according to sources down there, she has a numbered account with holdings of approximately thirty million dollars. The remainder of the money still sits in Switzerland, but from the trail we've reconstructed, one million dollars has been transferred annually from Zurich to her numbered account since 1972. She has only tapped into the account for untraceable activities...well, untraceable to our official sources," Mark's dad said with a sly smirk on his face.

Lindsay jumped in. "We have traced withdrawals over the years totaling eight million dollars; all of the signatures are Olivia's."

"What has she used that much money for? She's just a regular citizen, that's gotta show up somewhere." Mark put in.

"We're not sure."

Mark could almost sense his dad hinting for Lindsay and him to read between the lines, but for what?

"And for clarification's sake – that interrogation you just listened to was two days ago," his dad added, though Lindsay and Mark had already figured this was very recent thanks to Phillip's directives in regard to Swiss bank accounts.

"I have two questions," Lindsay said. "If Phillip Black is still alive, did he kill Joshua Knight? And if Jacob Honeycutt has killed himself, what happens to Honeycutt Petroleum?" She was nothing if not direct.

Chapter Fifty-Seven

<u>Tuesday June 18, 2002</u>

A month had passed since Mark's dad had shared the CD recording of his rather one-sided rendezvous with Phillip Black, and the diversified group of facts tied to the ANCSA operation. As an FBI agent, Mark had been taught to see things through from beginning to end, but the ANCSA case and the way it had seemed to end had left a bitter taste in his mouth.

Were it anyone else, the FBI probably have followed up with a full-court press and interrogated his Dad until they found out what Phillip Black's final moments were like, but for two things: 1) it was his Dad, and 2) his Dad would never cave. Well, a third thing: Mark didn't think he would have gotten away with waterboarding his dad. Not because it is against the law, but because he'd kick his ass.

But his father did volunteer some things, in fact, significant and material things that cleared up some burning questions.

Law enforcement and intelligence officers are sent down wrong paths more often than they would care to admit. This case had Agent Gonzalez and Mark chasing a wild goose to Nenana that panned out to nothing, gave them belief that Ronny the Cabbie might solve the whole damn case, and last and certainly not least, this case got Mark inaugurated into the Shadow Squad. The Squad's role was actually very simple – some things stay hidden beneath the shadow of the public eye and some things end up getting front page press. ANCSA and its impact was definitely one that stayed buried, and Mark wasn't even given the entire truth.

Top of the List - *The Alaska Native Claims Settlement Act (ANCSA) and its settlement for $962.50 million was truly a bargain for all involved, for all except Mark's own people. It seems his father's little torture of Phillip Black revealed that Black had personally determined that the Alaska Federation of Natives (AFN) should be asking for much more – the impetus for Phillip Black and a clandestine contact with the late Myles Honeycutt.*

According to Phillip Black, Myles Honeycutt really didn't care who prevailed with the settlement of ANCSA; only that back in 1971 it would settle in the next year or so. That one would have been perplexing, were it not for the nice executive summary his dad had provided regarding the dollar value Phillip Black had placed on selling his soul.

One thing Mark and Lindsay couldn't pin down was how Joshua Knight had gotten off of his grandmother's airplane somewhere between Anchorage and Juneau, hence, surviving only to die elsewhere. At whose hand?

Robert Jameson's interrogation of Phillip Black answered that question.

Joshua Knight had gotten in contact with Phillip Black aboard Mark's grandmother's flight and had handed Black a single page from a yellow legal pad. That piece of paper Mark was intimately familiar with, as it was the impetus for Jon Brady's novel draft. Brady had seen the copy that Ronnie the Cabbie had somehow attained.

Ronnie had spent thirty years quietly investigating the crash of Alaska Airlines 1866. The deaths of Myles Honeycutt, Clay Tanis, and Rico Sanchez all landed on his radar screen, and the dots began to connect. All were men who'd worked with Phillip Black. Either Phillip Black himself had died, or he was the one who'd played a great game of cat and mouse and taken each man out.

Mark would love to have interviewed Ronnie, because he sounded like he was not only bright but immensely loyal and lived life wholly based on integrity. Like a lot of details in this case, Mark's dad had some information on that.

Ronnie wasn't really shot – it was all a ruse. Phillip Black, as of six weeks ago, was alive and kicking and needed to believe that the only other link to the ANCSA novel draft had died. It seems Phillip was greedy right to the end, wanting sole authorship over a novel he'd titled *ANCSA - the Real Truth*. Mark found it quite impressive – given the level of sophistication, coordination, and cooperation it took to set up an FBI showdown in the middle of an Anchorage street with buy-in of the Anchorage Police Department.

Olivia Black did not know that her father was alive and had not died aboard his grandmother's flight. Mark had wondered what had sent Agent Gonzalez and him to Nenana. It came down to the simple human trait of survival. It seems the government needed whoever was after Ronnie to believe he'd died, including Mark.

Why Mark? To protect him. Great job the CIA did, wouldn't you say? The only two truly injured in this whole thing weren't CIA at all, but two FBI agents, Dani and Mark. Well, and the guy that Mark had shot in Jon Brady's basement.

Dani thankfully, was doing well. She was released from Harborview in early June, about three weeks after being shot. Director Archer asked that she take a three-month leave of absence to let the wounds (both physical and mental) heal and dissipate with time.

And why were Dani and Mark shot? They say never completely trust anyone. Well, whoever the hell "they" are sadly are quite right. Somehow, it was a setup, and the guy Mark had shot was actually an operative for one of the wealthiest men on the planet – Jacob Honeycutt.

How did he get there? Phillip Black was the guy with the Native-Alaskan accent who'd called Mark when he arrived at the Anchorage hotel and said it had all started with him. Black made a very similar call to Jacob Honeycutt right after he hung up with Mark.

Mark was not sure what had happened to budding author Jon Brady. He'd not seen him since the shootout in Brady's basement, and all he had been told is that he was in witness protection.

There were many other truths that had been learned along the way.

Lindsay Drummond was the woman Mark had spent his life hoping beyond hope he would fall for. He realized how he had a weakness for blond hair, blue eyes, and curves, but the connection went much deeper.

His father was a spy extraordinaire. He'd orchestrated and shaped historic events for our country, as well as others that Mark had actually read about. He was sworn to secrecy, not only as his son but as a federal agent, from ever revealing the private conversations the two had shared. The look in his handsome, dark brown eyes left no doubt that he was a patriot through and through, and he had no regrets whatsoever for the life he'd led.

As for Mark, he learned that life has twists and turns that you cannot predict nor prepare for; you must simply assess and react. If you've ever driven in rush-hour traffic, that is exactly what he means. The asshole ahead of you hits his breaks without warning – what do you do? If you're following too close, brake hard and swerve into the lane with the least amount of risk and then flip the piece of shit off.

And more important, you have to be someone others will trust and then reciprocate that trust, which sort of sets the plate for the ending of this journey.

Chapter Fifty-Eight

Outside of Lake Tahoe in Northern California
Tuesday June 18, 2002

"That's me," Lindsay bellowed as her intimidating blue eyes watched the carabineer exhibit the distinct return of vertical tension. Mark was pulling the one hundred fifty feet of speckled-green rope up the face of a rock formation affectionately known by climbers as Knapsack Crack.

In climbing circles, Knapsack Crack actually is pretty tame, but Mark was finding the climb exhilarating. Lindsay and Mark had spent the first week of their lives together being federal agents, and after Mark was released from the hospital in the latter weeks of May, Lindsay had given him an ultimatum. If their relationship was to become about more than physical attraction and the chemistry they had developed rowing down the dead end that is ANCSA, she wanted something that was a "we moment" but nothing to do with their careers or how they had met.

So they found themselves two hundred thirty-five feet or so up a cliff and Mark couldn't think of a truer test of faith in another human being. Lindsay and he were attached by only a rope designed solely for the purpose of keeping each other alive.

As his foot gently hugged a vertical ledge no wider than six inches, he heard Lindsay yell loudly "on belay" and he confirmed "belay is on." Within a few seconds, Lindsay followed with "climbing" and he gave her the go ahead with the simple words "climb on."

The tension that he was experiencing being in the lead position one hundred feet above Lindsay was familiar, but having the climber on the other be that one someone in his life made the moment all the more surreal.

Lindsay had never climbed before, but she was one of the most driven people Mark had ever met, and so it was at her suggestion that they take a trip together and do something exhilarating, spontaneous, and wholly new for her. Mark suggested a golf trip to Cabo San Lucas and she almost broke up with him right then.

She said she wanted to do something memorable and adventurous. Mark had climbed all over the country, from the Red Rocks outside of Las Vegas to the Bat Caves outside of Bellingham to the spot he decided would be most appropriate to share a climb with Lindsay.

Lover's Leap is a confluence of vertical and near-vertical granite-rock faces that reach into the Northern California sky about twenty miles west of the southern shores of Lake Tahoe. Climbers from all over the world come to this well-hidden treasure to capture a primal connection with nature.

It was around ten or so in the morning, and even though it was mid-June and the sun was already shining bright and high above, there was a crisp, cold bite in the air. There was no wind to speak of, and not a single cloud could be seen.

In Mark's opinion, it was a perfect morning for a climb.

Here they were, forty-five minutes or so into the 325-foot ascent having ascended the first 125 feet or so to a tree that served as the first pitch. (Simple definition: picture a rock wall with points A, B, C, D and so on – Point A is solid flat ground, and point B is 125 feet almost straight up. The climb to Point B is pitch one, where both climbers will need to ascend and then start a second ascent to point C that is 110-feet of climbing – pitch two. Mark had covered essential instructions with Lindsay, such as 1) feed rope up as he ascends but be very conscious not to create a large amount of slack, 2) the right hand will be her brake hand designed to arrest a fall should he have one; 3) breath in and out normally to offset any anxiety she might encounter as she climbs up, and 4) several other safety measures.

Mark was now at point C of the ascent, 235 feet above where they had started, and Lindsay was climbing to him. It was obvious her climbing skills needed some technical honing, but her athletic ability compensated for the technical aspects. She was maybe twenty-five feet below Mark, and he told her to stop for just a moment.

"Lindsay, I'm going to take away any slack, okay." She was near enough that he didn't need to yell, so it was pretty conversational at this point.

"Is everything alright?" she asked.

"Totally, I just want you to drink in this moment. Keep your right hand on that large outcropping to your right and raise your right foot just a bit and let it rest in the crack."

Her blue eyes were hidden beneath a dark pair of mirrored sunglasses, her voluptuous body disguised beneath a gray sweatshirt and black climbing nylon pants, but as Lindsay stared up at him at that moment he found her more beautiful than at any other time he had known so far.

Lindsay's right hand and foot were placed just as he hoped. "Okay, slowly twist around and take a look."

Gazing down, Mark was trying to imagine what Lindsay would be feeling. Fear, nausea, exhilaration, hope this moment would soon be over? Those were all things he'd experienced the first time he'd made this ascent five years earlier.

"Holy shit! I'm scared to death." Lindsay nearly screamed, "But this is awesome!" She followed moments later. She turned around and Mark didn't think he had ever seen anyone climb the next twenty-five feet with such expediency.

He secured her to a belay held by three roped cams. They were seventy-five feet from the top of the three-pitch ascent, and at that moment his mind was on keeping them both safe, but something happened as he started to provide her instruction on the last part of the ascent.

"Mark, I am so in love with you." Lindsay's words took him by total surprise. She reached her hand out and held his. They couldn't see each other's eyes beneath the sunglasses, but there was a tear or two in Mark's eyes and he could see one falling down her cheek.

"Lindsay...I love you so much." He knew at that very moment that he wanted to spend the rest of his life with her.

Chapter Fifty-Nine

Just North of Juneau, Alaska

<u>Tuesday June 18, 2002</u>

The man read the National Transportation Safety Board report with sorrow and amazement.

The NTSB report had been released decades earlier. Its finding had found that the crash of Alaska Airlines 1866 on Saturday September 4, 1971, was accidental, tied to faulty navigation equipment and pilot error.

So many years earlier, the man had deplaned Alaska Airlines Flight 1866 in Yakutat, Alaska, just a few hours before the ill-fated plane would collide with a mountain just north of Juneau. As he read the NTSB report, he ran his large hands through his tousled brown and graying hair and truly regretted all that he had become.

So many years earlier, his world had been simple, horribly so, but still quite simple. He'd shot, stabbed, and blown up Viet Cong soldiers in a jungle in Southeast Asia. Initially, he'd found the war senseless and futile, but as time went on it had become sadly nothing more than a matter of survival.

Watching fellow U.S. soldiers being loaded on helicopter transports in those atrocious green body bags had taken its toll. He'd grown to hate the Viet Cong so vehemently that taking their lives had begun to provide a sense of purpose and satisfaction.

On the second page of the NTSB report, his eyes were haunted by nine words: "All 104 passengers and seven crewmembers were injured fatally." They crashed into his cerebral cortex to his very core.

"Who had he become?" He realized just how powerful and damning words could be. It was one thing to kill soldiers in battle; it was quite another to orchestrate the downing of an aircraft filled with innocent passengers, one who was the mother of someone he'd spent his life loving as if she were truly his daughter.

But he'd done it. "For revenge...and for money," his mind chided him.

In-Country, in Vietnam, he'd been a member of a Battalion Marine Regiment since early 1963. On a wet, rainy day in late 1965 in a thick, chest-deep rice field outside of what is now Hanoi, the man's life changed dramatically.

Two fellow Marines, Myles Honeycutt and Adam Ross, had seen the disjointed look in the man's brown eyes. Within a few months the men were killing political figures, Viet Cong, and others in cold blood.

Honeycutt and Ross taught him the dark world of black ops and the art of becoming invisible. Honeycutt and Ross cultivated the man into an effective and dangerous intelligence asset. In-County, the man had become known as "The Silent Sword." He quietly killed.

The Vietnam War was so unpopular with the American public that the honor that goes with wearing the uniform adorned with the American flag was not only absent, but the man came home on May 21, 1970, to taunts that only reinforced his hate. For whom and what, he didn't know.

But even more painful, he'd come home and learned his wife had strayed and had an affair. She was pregnant with a child that was not his.

By late summer 1970, thanks to a confluence of events, the opportunity presented itself and he'd approached Honeycutt with an offer that would make the men rich – gaudily rich. Myles Honeycutt and his family were majority shareholders of an up-and-coming oil company already worth nearly four billion dollars. In the early 1970's, that was sheer wealth. But Myles wanted more.

The man's approach was simple: employ the skills he'd learned in Vietnam and take out the enemy. He had the blood of Viet Cong soldiers on his hands, the pleading cries of Vietnamese military officers in his head, and the arrogant and misguided musings of a traitorous American soldier somewhere in the recesses of his mind. Those had not whatsoever haunted him, most especially the traitorous American he'd shut up with one bullet.

In Vietnam, he'd killed to stay alive and because killing was all he knew. But September 4, 1971, was different.

He had told Honeycutt only part of why the Alaska Airlines flight needed to be brought down, only that the Alaska Native Claims Settlement Act and its ratification depended on it. Now, thirty-one years later, as he ascended a rocky peak, his thoughts settled on that fateful decision. He felt remorse, but also strange aura of calm. Even at sixty-six years of age, at six-foot one and 185 pounds, the man was solid muscle; the twenty-pound backpack had not presented any challenge as he'd trekked through the Chilkat Mountain Range just northwest of Juneau.

The blood of 111 (well 110) people was squarely on his hands. He'd spent his entire life with that truth buried deep in his memory, and he knew that he'd gotten away with it, until a month earlier when Robert Jameson's interrogation had induced a long-awaited confession. Jameson and he were cut of the same cloth, and he had reminded Jameson throughout the interrogation of that very fact. He made no excuses for the evil man that he'd become, but he'd begged Jameson for three things.

In a couple of hours, one billion dollars would be transferred from equity accounts held in Zurich to an account in the Cayman Islands. The funds would be transferred to the United States government on one condition; the government would first provide $750 million to the Alaska Native Tribes to provide some modicum of fairness to the original Alaska Native Claims Settlement Act.

And the person who held the password to the Cayman account that would drive the transfer was now Robert Jameson.

Black's second request was very personal – he begged Jameson to keep the truth of who he was and what he had done buried from Olivia Black. But as he knew, nothing was for free so he offered Jameson $250 million, which he quickly refused. Jameson did want something in return – not money, but something more personal.

Even before Jameson's violent interrogation, he'd known his life was an awful lie, and he knew his God knew it. He also knew his time was short.

His world had imploded. Myles Honeycutt, Adam Ross, and he had become evil men. He'd made a deal with the devil, and the deal he'd orchestrated with Honeycutt could not be undone. The man had sold his soul, and he knew it. He only hoped his God would hear the confession he was about to make.

He paused, and the first time in a long time he took a deep breath and embraced life and nature. To the east, his vision was filled with gentle mountain vistas reaching toward heaven. Lush green forests and rocky peaks abounded. As he gazed down 2,500-feet, the brackish-green of the Favorite Channel waterway took hold.

He continued to feel that strange sense of calm. A gentle breeze wove its way up and down the steep slope. The climb had been strenuous but relatively safe. He'd brought cams, crampons, pitons, and carabineers but only had to employ them for a couple of moderate climbs in certain spots, and for each much less than a pitch.

He stood now in the epicenter of the crash of Alaska Airlines 1866. He was responsible for all the lives that had ended on this very spot.

Tears began to fill his eyes. The gentle breeze calmly passed over his face and he felt at peace with what the decision he'd made. With confidence and moral conviction, he began to speak his confession to his God.

"Dear God, I know you know who I am. But I myself had forgotten for a very, very long time the man that I used to be. My real name is Phillip Black, though no one has known me by that name since September 4, 1971. I'm the only son of William and Emily Black. As you know, they both passed on while I was serving one of my five tours of duty In-Country." He paused briefly and stared at the clear blue sky above. "Lord, I'm here because I've lived a life I wholly despise."

Phillip's voice wavered as he continued, "God...God... please forgive me for...for all that I have done."

He dropped to his knees and closed his eyes. The wind was warm and calm, long shadows cascading across the ridge as the late afternoon sun slowly began its ritual descent in the eastern sky, and the only sound that filled the canyon was the occasional cry of an eagle as it soared gracefully across invisible currents of wind.

"My Lord, you know what I've done, but my culture believes I need to cleanse my soul in the wind." His voice was soft as he whispered his prayer.

"My Lord, the blood of every one who passed here...I am so sorry..." A lump filled his throat. "It is my fault."

The sun peeked from behind a cloud and illuminated his being as a lull in the wind gave him pause.

"My life has been nothing more than a lie. My wife died here, and my life died here. I have a daughter who doesn't know who I really am. She's seen me hundreds of times and doesn't know that by blood I am not her father. My Lord, please let her live a good life, and I beg you to let her never know the truth. She knows me as Jon Brady, her attorney. I've spent every moment of that existence protecting her from an awful truth. That her father...not her biological father, but me... that I killed her mother and sold my soul for so many wrong things."

The confession continued. Then, without ceremony, Phillip Black aka Jon Brady buried a hand-written note from Robert Jameson in a small wooden box beneath a white cross. The name on the cross read "Wilma Jameson."

Black knelt at the makeshift gravesite and wept.

"Your son is a good and decent human being, and what I've done has tormented him his entire life. He spared my life so I could come here on his behalf. He's felt your spirit weeping night after night, and he wants you to be set free. He knows that is what you have been waiting for." Phillip Black was weeping as he spoke, the tears freely flowing down his dark cheeks.

"Your son Bobby misses you, but he wants you to go home to your lord." Phillip actually felt the souls of those he'd taken surrounding him. Their spirits weren't filled with hate – they were filled with an unbelievable sense of forgiveness.

Black was a God-fearing man and had been taught never to take the easy way out, but his soul was at peace with this decision. An eye for an eye, he'd always been taught.

After he buried his climbing gear and the only evidence of how he had gotten here were a few footprints that would dissipate with the next rain storm, he prayed one last prayer.

"My Lord, please forgive me, for I have sinned. I entrust to your will my humble soul."

He stood at the precipice of a steep ledge and stared down at the rocky drop. His right finger pressed gently on the trigger, and the crackling report of the Ruger Pistol filled the canyon as all went black.

CPSIA information can be obtained at www.ICGtesting.com
Printed in the USA
LVOW03s0150070214

372617LV00003B/78/P